THE
ELEMENTAL

BOOK 1 OF THE FIRE TRILOGY

LISA VELDKAMP

Dragon Moon Press
Alberta, Canada 2016

Cover Design by Rhianna Davies
Edited by Marisa Chenery

Previously published by Booktrope Publishing as *The Elemental*, 2015

This is a work of fiction. Names, characters, places, brands, media, and incidents are either the product of the author's imagination or are used fictitiously. Any resemblance to similarly named places or to persons living or deceased is unintentional.

ISBN 13: 978-1-988256-49-8
Library of Congress Control Number: 2015916861

The dedication of this book is split by the power of three.

First, to my family, partner, and friends for supporting and believing in me, even when I did not. A special thanks to Mariska, for test reading The Elemental and putting up with all my crap. To my entire Booktrope team. Elizabeth Flynn, my book manager, always there when I need you, thank you so much. Marisa Chenery, my editor. I promise to keep the head-hopping to a minimum from now on. You are amazing! To Rhianna Davies, your artwork rocks, girl! And to Lisa Gilliam, my trusty proof reader. Last, but certainly not least, to Karin de Haas, my editor in Holland, for all your hours of hard work. You saved me from total embarrassment.

Second, to Barista Café in my hometown, Alphen aan den Rijn. You provided a home away from home, spoiling me with yummy goodness, and most of my book was written at this wonderful place. You guys are the greatest! Save me a spot for books two and three!

Third, to Placebo, who were the source of inspiration for writing this book. Your music and lyrics bring me earth, air, water, and above all, fire. I wish you many more years of creating magic together.

PROLOGUE

JUST BEYOND the outskirts of Shoreditch, into Hackney, lies London Fields. It's a beautiful park with a bit of a bad rep due to the incidents of a few years back, but on a sunny day, skaters practise their latest moves, children play, people enjoy a picnic, or some guy plays his guitar. Today it seemed deserted, except it wasn't. Just around the corner, behind the trees, there was movement. Twelve women stood in a circle, chanting and looking up to the sky. One of them looked frantically around as though she waited for something, someone.

It was quiet on the streets of Shoreditch, London. Way too quiet. And dark. No working street lights. No red buses, no taxi drivers honking their horns, and stores all seemed to be closed. Lots of people were inside one specific house, watching television. Candlelight provided light inside the house, and a generator could be heard humming in the backyard.

A man came round the corner. He talked into some sort of old-fashioned device. "I'm almost home, honey, I'm almost home. Just keep the door locked and the windows closed." He sounded frightened.

Two teenagers, a boy and a girl, ran toward each other, and the girl called out to him. "I want to be with you when it happens!" He wrapped his arms around her as soon as she reached him and then they hastily disappeared into an apartment building.

The ground vibrated beneath Leah's and the other women's feet. They raised too much energy. "I don't know how much longer we can hold the circle!" Leah shouted toward the woman opposite her.

She looked toward the sky and saw nothing but black and some stars. She knew very well, however, that beyond the blackness there was an asteroid the size of several London Fields on a path to destroy them all, unless they could connect to it first and save this bloody planet. Where the hell was Kate?

Ten seconds. Their lives depended on ten seconds. They wouldn't be able to see it until it hit the atmosphere and then they'd have ten seconds to connect to it before it hit the ground, maybe even less. Leah looked over her shoulder once more. This was starting to look a lot like a suicide mission. In the distance, something moved toward them. It was a woman. She was running.

A WEEK EARLIER

"KATE! KATE, are you coming? I'm starving here!" Leah leaned over the railing and moved her weight to the left.

She was tall for a woman, with long legs, currently balancing on Chanel boots. As it would seem, they were lovely to wear, but not very practical when it came to standing still for several minutes. Being so tall and striking, carrying her height with gusto, Leah could intimidate the crap out of an entire room full of people. It was something she still didn't realise herself. Though she did notice everybody automatically shut up when she walked into a room just to see if she had anything to say.

From inside the apartment, Kate yelled to her friend that she'd only be a moment.

Leah, or Lee as Kate liked to call her, had been her best friend for as long as Kate could remember, and she could remember quite a lot. They'd grown up together in Amsterdam, and had spent hours and hours in each other's rooms or outside. Kate used to lie on the ground while Leah would read her the latest musings of her mind. Kate was probably her worst critic, as she simply adored everything, but she'd been a driving force in Leah's life to pursue a career in writing. That had taken flight after she'd written *Frozen*, a historical novel with a dark twist, while staying in New York. It became a bestseller almost overnight, and an international one within a month. Leah hadn't known what hit her. For months, her life had been dominated by press conferences, signing sessions, interviews and what not. Having a publisher in New York, who went by the name of Violet and who also became a dear friend to her, Leah had decided to settle down in that city. Though Kate knew her friend always had a soft spot for the Big Apple, she was sad to have her dear friend move so far away from her. They flew across the ocean on a regular basis, but it just wasn't the same as dropping by for coffee or a nice chardonnay.

When Leah published *When Autumn Comes* and it became another bestseller, her income increased so much she indulged herself in buying a London apartment, much to the delight of Kate. They'd visited several apartments together, and when they finally stood in a very nice one on Charing Cross Road, Kate had said, "I think you should buy this one. It's perfect for you, because this is where the books live."

Leah had laughed at that, but did indeed buy the apartment. So for the last four years, she spent about six months on this side of the pond and six months in the Big Apple where Kate and Deborah were regular visitors during Leah's stay there.

It was Saturday, and Leah had just flown in from New York where she'd had a brief meeting with her publisher. She looked quite excited, apparently eager to talk to her best friend. Kate, however, seemed to be taking her time.

A woman in her mid-thirties appeared in the hallway. "Sorry to keep you waiting, darling. I know it's dangerous to deny you breakfast," she said, laughing.

Leah smiled. "You know me too well."

Kate pressed the button on the lift and then pushed some of her hair out of her face. It was starting to get impractically long. On the plus side, she was getting rather creative with different types of braiding.

The lift doors opened, and they stepped inside. "Albion, I presume?" Kate asked.

"Yes, I think I can just manage two blocks on these boots, which are definitely not made for walking." Leah flashed a wicked grin. "Albion it is!"

Once they stepped out of the lift, a man entered the building. "Could you please hold it for me?" He held two boxes and what appeared to be an orchid clutched under his arm.

Kate thought he looked rather tall and impressive, but then again, most people seemed tall to her. Even wearing high heels she couldn't reach Leah's height. "Sure," she said, smiling. "Moving in?"

"Yes," he replied, putting down the boxes to block and hold the lift from going up. He held out his hand to Kate. "Tristan Visconti. Nice to meet you."

"Catherine van Dyk," Kate replied while shaking his hand. Tristan frowned slightly while letting go of her hand. She looked at him, feeling a bit confused. Was there something wrong with her hand? She pulled out of his grasp. "Well, welcome to the building. Are you moving into apartment 3B?"

"Yes," he said with a glance at Leah.

"Oh, I'm sorry." Kate looked at her friend. "This is my very good friend, Leah Winter. Leah, say hello to Tristan." She grinned and licked her lips with her back turned to Tristan. She almost bit her lip when Leah appeared to try hard to hide her smile.

Tristan's face showed recognition as he took her hand and shook it.

"I thought you looked familiar." He smiled. "You're the author of *Frozen* and *When Autumn Comes*. It's an honour meeting you, Miss Winter."

Kate sighed. Her friend looked somewhat embarrassed. Even after several years of being a celebrated author, Leah still wasn't used to all the attention. "Thank you," Leah replied softly as he let go of her hand.

"Visconti is quite an unusual name. Are you Italian, if you don't mind me asking?" Kate asked.

Tristan turned to look at her. "My family comes from Milan, yes, and I was born there, but we moved to England when I was a boy, so I consider myself an Englishman. I visit Milan on a regular basis, though. Have you ever been there?" He looked at her so intensely it made her feel uncomfortable.

"Um, no, but I always wanted to. From what I've seen on TV, it's a beautiful city," she replied politely.

He nodded, and his intense gaze seemed to lessen somewhat. "It is. If you ever have the chance, you should go. I have a feeling you'd like it."

His face broke into a smile, and his features completely changed. It gave him a far more boyish look. Kate found herself feeling at ease instead of uncomfortable, and returned his smile.

"Well, I'd better get these boxes up. It was nice meeting you, Catherine. I hope we'll become more than neighbours."

His dark blue-eyed gaze seemed to glue her feet to the floor. It made her think of indigo and the ocean. Pulling herself together, she just smiled at him, and said, "Time will tell." She started to walk toward the door after she turned around. "Listen, I'm having a Halloween cocktail party this Thursday. You're welcome to join if you're free."

Tristan put one foot between the doors of the lift. "I'd like that. You live in the penthouse, right?"

"Yes," she said, wondering how he knew that.

"Your name is on the doorbell outside." He answered her unspoken question.

Duh, Kate thought. "The party starts at eight," she said. "You can bring someone if you like."

"Thank you, I'll be there."

The lift doors closed, and Kate and Leah walked outside. "Well, that was interesting," Leah said.

A few minutes later, they arrived at Albion. Thankfully, there was no queue so they were seated right away. Leah stretched her legs under the table and let out of sigh of relief.

Kate laughed. "They are worth it, though. They look amazing!"

"I know." Leah smiled. "I bought them as a special treat. All your fault, really. I never used to be a Chanel girl."

"Oh, please!" Kate rolled her eyes. "Don't you dare go blaming me, missy. I'm hardly loyal to any house. Well, Prada maybe, but in any case, I've gone three months without buying anything. So there. I'm just saying!"

Leah rolled her eyes as well. "Okay, let's agree we're both just as bad, and we will probably never learn. Well, with the minor difference that we don't exceed our income like we used to."

Kate had done quite well for herself. Eight years ago, she'd moved to Shoreditch, London. She had an English mother and a Dutch father, and had been raised bilingual, so she was fluent in both languages. She'd studied in Amsterdam, and after her graduation, she'd started her own massage practice, using her own line of massage oil. People had been so satisfied with her treatments that within a year she'd needed someone else to help her run the business. Deborah had been the perfect match. Moving in the same circles, they'd known each other for years, becoming friends along the way. When Kate had offered the job to Deborah, she'd taken it immediately. Then Kate's father had passed away, and her mother decided to move back to England to live closer to her brother. Kate had investigated options of moving to London herself, but had felt guilty about her friend. She couldn't just ask her to leave everything behind and jump on her London train. In hindsight she need not have worried. When "the talk" came, Deborah had just looked at her, went into the other room, came back with her pink suitcase, and asked, "So when are we leaving?"

Kate had been more than grateful. Deborah understood the way she worked like nobody else. Also Deborah knew all about Kate's more special side and wasn't scared or bothered by it. As a child, Kate had noticed that whenever she felt really sad, it rained, and the first time she got really angry because her next door neighbour had stolen her My Little Pony, lightning had suddenly flashed. Her mother had mumbled something about being just like her grandmother, whom she'd never got to know due to an early death, and told her to learn how to control her emotions. So Kate had tried and tried and then tried some more with a lot of patience and support from her mother. In time and with age, she'd got better at controlling her emotions. Her teenage years had been somewhat "colourful," but as she came into adulthood, things started to get better. She rarely lost control nowadays, and really, she could think of few people who would complain about a little extra sunshine when she was feeling extremely happy.

In these same last four years, Leah and Deborah became closer friends as well. With Kate's successful method in massage and healing techniques and Deborah's gift to "see" what it actually was that people needed, their private practice became somewhat of an exclusive item. That had been mostly Deborah's doing. Coming from the music industry, she knew a lot of artists, whether the musical kind or another kind of artist. A high-pressure industry, or so people said, and when word got out that Kate's way of thinking and her techniques had a remarkable effect on body and mind, and that she'd helped several people overcome their drug abuse, various high-profile artists decided to try, as they would called it, "her way or the highway," because Kate had a reputation for not accepting any crap from anyone. It'd meant quite some overtime in the beginning, and that was when Leah and Deborah started to go out for lunch or dinner without Kate, until she decided she had to learn how to delegate or she'd have no personal life whatsoever.

So after due consideration, Kate decided to choose two women from within their own group. Leah sometimes liked to refer to them as the X-men, which according to Kate was still an improvement from the C-men, which sounded way too much like "semen" as Sheldon's friends from *The Big Bang Theory* had pointed out more than once. In all fairness, Leah did have a point, because they were, at the very least, special women. They all were, though some didn't like to have that pointed out. With Meg and Romy on board to help her and Deborah out, Kate's life had returned to normal, with enough free time to spend it with her family and friends.

"Anything to drink, ladies?" the waiter asked.

"Um, yes, please. I'd like an orange juice and a cappuccino," Kate replied.

"Same for me," Leah said with a smile. The waiter handed them menus and told them the breakfast special of the week. "God, I still love this place!" She looked around.

"Well, you haven't been here for at least six weeks, almost two months I think," Kate answered with an accusing glare.

Albion did have a lovely atmosphere. It resided in the larger The Boundary, a French restaurant with the most amazing rooftop terrace. It had this industrial vibe, but with a homey feel to it, and the cooking was exquisite. Though some would say Shoreditch had gone mainstream in the last decade or so, Kate still loved this neighbourhood better than any other part of London.

"Well, out with it," Kate said.

Leah looked surprised. "Who says I have anything to tell you?"

"Oh, please, don't insult my intelligence. You've been bursting to tell me something from the moment we left the building." Kate raised an eyebrow. Leah had always been lousy at hiding secrets from her, even with birthday presents.

"You're right, I do have something important to share, but perhaps we should order first. What are you having?" She looked at the menu for a third time.

Kate grinned. Leah loved the Albion and their menu. She didn't even glance at hers. She knew it almost by heart, anyway, and as far as breakfast went, she usually stuck to her Albion granola with the occasional almond croissant on the side, which was just divine. "My regular. The granola."

Leah nodded. "I think I'll have the same, but with a muffin. I can always save it for later," she said.

After they placed their orders with the waiter, Leah leaned back and stretched her legs again. "Two weeks ago, I got a call from Violet, seeing if I could come down to the office. Since we became friends, we rarely meet there. Except maybe to pick her up when we're going out for a bite, but she insisted I should come down. So I did. There we're two gentlemen there who looked slightly familiar, but I really didn't have a clue. Violet was grinning like a maniac stuck on acid, so I knew it must be something good."

Kate learned forward, her full focus on Leah. "And?"

"They turned out to be producers, and they really would like my approval to start filming *Frozen*."

Kate was completely dumbstruck. This was obviously the news her friend had been bursting to tell her since arriving from New York.

"You're kidding!" she practically shouted. Several people turned their heads toward them. "That is so fucking awesome, pardon my French. Oh, darling, I'm so happy for you. You're going to be a star. Oh, dear, we have to go shopping immediately. You'll need a red carpet dress and everything. Do you get a say in the casting process? How much are they paying you? When are they going to start shooting? Can I come visit? I've never been on a movie set." Kate was almost on the edge of her chair.

"Take a deep breath, darling. Your eyes are glowing. You'll set yourself on fire or bring the sun down in here. I'm pretty sure Albion would be shocked by both events," Leah said.

The woman next to them smiled at Leah's remark, but it brought Kate back down to Earth. Her extreme happiness could get a bit dangerous, though obviously the woman next to them thought Leah had made a joke. She took a deep breath and connected to the earth. It immediately grounded her, and the fire inside her receded to a nice glowing simmer.

"You have to tell me everything. This is so exciting. You could be the next JK Rowling." Kate grinned from ear to ear.

Leah laughed. "Um, honey, I don't think I'm quite there yet, but it does look promising. We've met three times now, and yes, I do get a say in the casting process. Violet can be a complete bitch when it comes down to business negotiations, which is a good thing, because frankly, I don't know shit about the film industry. Fortunately, she does so she bargained a pretty good deal. They're going to pay me a certain amount of money for the rights to make a movie out of my book, but I'm also getting a percentage of all the profits, which I'm told by Violet is certainly no given, so she took pretty good care of my interests. I didn't want to cancel my trip to England, so we're meeting again after Samhuinn in early November. They'd like to start filming early next year, and release it in the summer. Apparently, they have this advertising idea to do this play with words along the likes of, 'This summer prepare to be *Frozen*,' or something." Leah rolled her eyes at that last remark.

Kate gave her a serious look. "Well, that doesn't sound too bad. Actually, that could work, and it's certainly dramatic."

Leah nodded. "I know. It just takes a little getting used to. When I thought writing a bestseller was madness, you wouldn't believe the stuff you have to deal with in this whole film business, but in all fairness, I was rather flattered," she finished with a shy smile.

"Well, of course you were. I mean, I always knew they'd make a movie of your book. It's just too awesome, but the confirmation is very nice indeed. Besides, I like being right," Kate concluded.

Leah rolled her eyes. Her friend was just impossible.

"So, does this mean you're staying until Samhuinn?" Kate asked.

"Of course I am," Leah replied somewhat insulted. "I have this whole schedule, you know. Shopping, because you actually did have a point about the whole red carpet dress thing, catching up with you and Deb and the rest of the group, your fabulous Halloween cocktail party on Thursday and Samhuinn on Saturday. My plane leaves on Sunday night, so plenty of time to pack my bags and stuff after the ritual. About that, I assume you want me on the north again?" She took a sip of her cappuccino.

The waiter brought their order, and Kate waited for him to leave again. "Yes, if you don't mind, that is. Samhuinn is always a bit heavier, so I'd like the most powerful people at the quarters. Deb is representing the south, and Romy is facing the east."

"You're going to be in the west?" Leah asked a bit surprised. "I don't mean anything by it, but it's not something you normally go for," she explained.

Kate smiled. "I know, and no, I'm not representing the west. Meg is strong enough to hold it, and she deserves to test her emotions. She's come a long way this year. I'm actually thinking about trying something new, but Albion is probably not the best place to discuss this." Leah suddenly appeared very interested. "Well, I'm thinking about testing my powers for a change and combining the elements," she whispered.

Leah raised an eyebrow. "Really? Wow, that's really something, darling. You know I always tell you to give it another try, but I thought it better to let it go after, well, you know, the last time," she said softly.

For a second, Kate was lost in her darker thoughts, but before Leah could comment, she snapped out of it and smiled. "I think it's time to say goodbye to my demons, so to speak."

"Well, good for you, honey. Good for you," Leah replied with real warmth in her voice.

After that they enjoyed their breakfast, and when Leah decided she had room for her muffin, Kate ordered an almond croissant and another two cappuccinos.

Kate sighed. "Ahh, this is the great life, kid, I'm tellin' ya, and we didn't even have to rustle up our own grub." She winked at Leah, who laughed as she put the last piece of her muffin into her mouth.

"Ah, yes, something with stress and charmed, I believe," she replied with a wink. It was a reference to her friend's favourite band. "What did you have in mind for today, darling, because if there's any shopping involved, I should run by my flat and put on slightly more sensible shoes."

Kate flashed her a wicked grin. "Then Charing Cross Road it is I'm afraid, because I definitely had some shopping planned. I thought we could have tea at Claridges around four. I made reservations just to be sure we'd get seated."

Leah sat up straighter. "Excellent! I haven't been to Claridges for over a year I think, certainly not for tea. Is Deb joining us?"

"Unfortunately, no, she has our last client around four p.m., but she'll be joining us for dinner. I thought we could go to Suki in Chinatown, have a light dinner there, and Deb can order a bit more for herself."

"Perfect. Shall we ask for the bill and get a move on? This one's on me, because I had something to celebrate." Leah signalled for the waiter to bring them their bill.

"Thanks, hon. Next one is on me then." Kate grabbed her coat and purse and then went to visit the ladies' room while Leah took care of their bill.

Once they stood outside, Kate asked if Lee would mind taking the Underground as opposed to grabbing a cab. "Traffic will be murder this time of day. We'll reach Charing Cross quicker if we just hop onto the tube."

"No problem, darling. I was actually planning on travelling by tube, anyway. I just have to ditch these boots. Oh, and I have to top up my oyster card, otherwise there will be no travelling at all," she finished with a grin.

After Leah had arrived at the airport, she'd taken a cab to her apartment and again this morning to Kate's place, so she hadn't had the chance to top up her card. This was done in seconds since there was almost no queue in the Underground, and then they hopped onto the first train to arrive. One transfer and ten minutes later, they stood outside Leicester Square Station.

Leah lived on Charing Cross Road near Shaftesbury Avenue, and depending where she came from, could exit at Leicester Square or Tottenham Court Road. Tottenham was a tad bit farther away, so they exited at Leicester Square. The sun shone when they resurfaced above ground, and they chatted away until they reached Leah's apartment.

Leah hadn't had a chance to clean or tidy things up since she'd arrived only yesterday, but the apartment looked in pretty good shape, thanks to her weekly housekeeper. Even her plants were still alive, and Marlene, her housekeeper, had put two blossoming orchids on the dinner table to welcome her home again. Leah had good taste in furniture. It was kind of obvious she was a book fanatic, considering the many bookcases that were in her place. It was an odd combination of English library style mixed with Arabian influences, which really worked due to the high ceilings and the almost man-high windows. Comfy sitting cushions and two sofas were centred around a round table with a big hole in the middle where Leah could light a small fire. She didn't have a chimney and had settled for that option. Kate had loved it so much, she'd recreated the same table on her rooftop terrace. The apartment only had two bedrooms, but the master had an en suite bathroom and the living room was rather large with an open kitchen and a bar that separated the two spaces.

Kate sat on one of the barstools as Leah turned around. "Coffee?" Leah asked while laying her purse on the bar and then looked for her coffee beans.

"Yes, one cup would be nice. You can change and then we can decide where we'd like to go."

Leah found the beans before she put them into the coffeemaker. She liked using fresh coffee and the way the scent always spread through the place. "I don't think I have any fresh milk yet," she said while peeking into her fridge. "Hang on, yes, I do. Marlene got me some. Such a sweetheart that girl." She smiled and put the milk into the aeroccino and pressed the button.

A few seconds later, Kate sipped on her cappuccino, and Leah had put on some different boots that were more appropriate for a lot of shopping.

"We've never had a Christmas here, have we?" Kate mused.

"I don't think so, no. I'm usually in New York that time of year, of course, and either you're coming over or I stay at your place. Why? Do you think we should do it here?" Leah considered this seriously.

"Tell you what," Kate said, "why don't we celebrate Christmas at your place this year and then we'll fly back together to see the ball drop at Times Square. How does that sound?"

Leah laughed. "Sounds great, but if you want to see the ball drop, I'd better pull some strings and make reservations to get us a good view at some nice hotel, because, honey, you don't want to be down there in the crowd. It's kind of special, but you'd have to get in line like at three in the afternoon and stay there until after midnight."

Kate's face looked unbelieving. "Really? I didn't realise it was that popular. I mean, could you? Get us in somewhere."

"Darling, I'm a celebrated author. It has to come with some perks, now doesn't it?" She grinned wickedly. "I'll fix it. So, who's coming this year? You, Deb, Meg, Romy. Is Sue coming?"

Kate nodded. "Yes. Her husband is touring Japan. She went with him last time, so she's staying home this year. She already asked me if we we're still on for the holidays. I'll fill her in this Thursday at the Halloween cocktail party that we're having Christmas dinner here and spending New Year's in New York. She'll like that."

Leah fished her iPhone out of her purse and then created a reminder to make reservations for six for New Year's Eve. She looked up from her phone, and said, "I'll make dinner reservations as well at Ruby Foo's, you know, the Japanese place we've been before. The girls will like that."

Kate looked doubtful. "Um, won't it be difficult to get through the crowd to get to the hotel if we have dinner somewhere else?"

"No, sweetie, they deal with this every year. You print out your reservation and then show it to the police on the street, and they will clear a path so you can get to your point of destination. It's all very organised, just as long as you don't wish to cross the street a few minutes before the ball drops, but we'll be in the hotel long before then."

Kate looked relieved after Leah's explanation. She really had no idea what to expect if people were apparently queuing for this event early in the afternoon. She smiled. Something else to look forward to.

"What about family obligations and all?" Leah asked. "You think we should have dinner on Christmas Eve or Christmas day?"

"Christmas Eve, just to be on the safe side. Then everyone can visit their family on Christmas day, and we can kick them out at a decent time. Also a bonus," Kate said knowingly. She'd had her share of organising Christmas dinner parties, and though she loved to organise them, it did take up a lot of her time.

"Will you help me organise?" Leah batted her eyelashes.

"Oh, stop it, you crazy woman. You know I will," she said laughing.

"Well, I guess we could make a start with some Christmas shopping this afternoon. I'm sure Liberty won't disappoint, and we could visit Fortnum and Mason." Kate tried to think of some other suitable places to go.

Leah interrupted. "Liberty was also on my list, so perhaps we should just take it from there and see where it will lead us?" Kate nodded. Leah stood and then put their cups into the dishwasher, turned off the kitchen lights, and grabbed her coat and purse. "Ready then?" she asked.

"Yep, all good to go," Kate replied.

Leah locked up and then they walked down the stairs. The sun shone even brighter and there was a nice warm breeze. It was rather pleasant to be outside, especially for that time of year.

Leah looked over at her friend with a suspicious smile. "Did you have anything to do with this?" she asked.

Kate looked affronted. "What? There can't be any sunshine in London without my interference?"

"Well, you have to admit it's rather unusual for this time of year, and I'm not accusing you of anything. I'm just asking. You know I don't mind, darling. I know you take your gifts very seriously, and you never are the personal gain type, so to speak, anyway, so I never worry on that account."

Kate relaxed. She still got a little defensive when it came to her powers, even with Lee, who'd known her for almost her entire life. She wondered if her happy mood had affected the weather. "Well, if I had something to do with it, it was unconsciously done. And what do you mean, on that account?" she said with an accusing glare.

Leah laughed. "Nothing, darling. Let's just say you could give Fred and George Weasley a run for their money when it comes down to, um … trouble." She grinned.

Kate pretended to hit Leah over the head. "Oh, do shut up." She laughed.

They walked to the Underground arm in arm, still laughing and enjoying the sun on their faces. They spent the rest of the day catching up. Leah needed a skirt to go with her new boots, so they started at Liberty to try to find something in a three-number range, in which they actually succeeded. She also browsed for a red-carpet dress. She walked out of the building with at least three or four ideas, but she didn't want to buy one that expensive on impulse, so she decided to look in other places as well. Kate bought a dark blue scarf she knew Deborah had had her eye on for weeks, and decided it was worth the ninety pounds. It'd be a nice Samhuinn gift to celebrate the New Year.

After a lovely walk through Hyde Park, which was rather nice with the sun shining, they went for chardonnay at Waterstones' 5th View restaurant. Kate had a soft spot for their chardonnay and the view over London, and Leah always liked to be anywhere near books. They spent an hour apart, browsing the shelves at Waterstones to meet again at the counter downstairs.

Kate looked suspiciously at Leah's shopping bags. "How many did you buy?" she asked with one eyebrow raised.

"Yes, well, I could hardly go to the counter with just one book, now could I?" Leah replied, looking like such a thing was unthinkable. In her case it was.

"So, how many?" Kate asked again. Leah mumbled something indistinguishable. "Sorry, I didn't quite catch that, hon," she replied with a wicked grin.

"Ooh, shut it. Five, okay? And I totally needed them all." Leah gave her a look that had a "don't you dare try to contradict me" vibe.

"Darling, you buy as many books as you want, but no moaning if you have to purchase an extra suitcase when you have to fly back." Kate grinned like an idiot. "Again!" she added mischievously.

Leah rolled her eyes. "Fair enough. Just to be clear, you're never gonna let that go, right?"

"Not a high hope in hell, but you know you love me, anyway." Kate batted her lashes.

Leah couldn't help but laugh with her. "You're impossible, love."

Once they were back outside, most of the afternoon had gone by. "Almost four. Time to get our lovely arses to Claridges." Leah looked at her watch, which dangled on a gold chain attached to her pants. Kate always thought it looked very Sherlock Holmes. "What do you think? Cab or tube?" she asked.

Kate raised her hand and whistled. A yellow cab stopped in front of her. "Does that answer your question?" She grinned. They got into the car, and Leah gave their destination to the driver.

After they arrived at Claridges, Leah let out a big sigh. "God forgive me, but I just love this place. It's so choice."

Kate smiled in understanding. She liked it as well. Perhaps even more so for lunch or an afternoon tea than dinner, which was, by no means, disappointing. Their kitchen used to be run by the famous Mr. Gordon Ramsey, but Claridges' menu was perhaps a bit too traditional for her more adventurous palate. Their tea was one of the best in London, though, with maybe the exception of the Ritz, which you'd have to book at least months in advance to actually make it across the doorstep.

A nice lady guided them to their table and then let them have a look at their tea menus before she came back with two glasses of champagne.

Leah whispered to Catherine, "Oh, right, no Prosecco. I almost forgot."

Kate whispered back, "No, no, no, darling, we don't serve Prosecco. We serve champagne." She put her nose up into the air.

Leah giggled out loud. "Does Deb have an intake or a regular customer?" she asked.

"Regular," Kate replied, searching her purse for her iPhone to check if it was on silent mode. "He's a recovering actor with a bit of an attitude, so she always reserves a full ninety minutes just in case." She put her phone back into her purse, satisfied it wouldn't make any noise.

Leah looked interested. "You still have a lot of artists then?"

Kate frowned. "*Pfff*, don't get me started. Apparently, word got out that we have great results, and they all seem to know each other, so yes, we have quite a few now. They're rather high-maintenance people, though. Not that I mind. It's actually quite flattering that they come to us for help instead of their personal trainers, gurus, dealers and what not, but between Deb and me, even with Romy and Meg helping out, there's only so many people we can take on, you know, and I just hate saying no to people. I still suck at that."

"Really?" Leah asked, smiling. "I would never have guessed."

They started with some lovely sweets, and Kate was rather enjoying her oolong tea. A man took a place at the piano and then played a ballade by Chopin, one of her favourites. The man smiled at her, and she smiled back.

"You're not flirting with the pianist, now are you?" Leah teasingly asked.

"Wouldn't dream of it, darling. I'd rather find out more about my lovely new neighbour I think, but I wouldn't mind if he played the piano just as well as this man. Did I tell you Dustin O'Halloran has a new album? It's absolutely amazing. A bit like his project *A Winged Victory for the Sullen*, but also completely different. You'd love it as well. We should check his touring schedule and find out if we can see him live somewhere later this year."

Leah was interested. "You know, I always love to see Dustin play. We should definitely check that out, but, um … neighbour, you were saying?" she asked seriously.

Kate hadn't been interested in a man for a very long time. First with the death of her father, then the move, building her business, and helping people along the way with her gifts had left her with very little time for a romantic life. Not that she felt sorry for herself, she didn't, but sometimes she did miss a male companion. Leah understood that. She'd been living a single life for a long time herself and was very protective of her personal space. She'd told Kate it wasn't until she'd met Ryan that she'd felt she could share her space with someone.

Ryan was an executive officer at Juilliard, the performing arts conservatory in New York. At first, Leah had thought he was a bit of a schmuck, but they'd kept bumping into each other at parties, and Kate observed her friend actually had a lot in common with him. Ryan never appeared to be intimidated by her friend's intellect. He obviously cherished it, and it was that that had made Leah totally at ease with him. Kate knew they were both away from home a lot, but for the last two years, they'd considered Leah's apartment in New York as "home base," and when he'd had an unexpected buyer for his apartment last summer, Leah had encouraged him to sell it and call her place home.

Kate loved Ryan, not because he always got her the best seats to her favourite ballets, but mostly because he made Leah happy. She did miss that sometimes. Tristan had looked promising. She couldn't really put her finger on what attracted her to him, but she felt drawn to him, for lack of a better word. She'd told Leah as much.

Leah looked doubtful.

"You don't like him?" Kate asked.

"Not at all. I don't even know the poor man. I just have a weird feeling about him. He's … I don't know. Intense perhaps, is the word I'm looking for?"

Kate knew better than to laugh. Leah's character judgment had saved her from many would-be embarrassing moments in her life, so she took her gut feelings very seriously.

"I do sort of feel what you're saying, but I still am drawn to him. I promise to be careful, though," she said, giving Leah a sincere look.

"That's all I'm asking for, darling. And as far as eye candy goes, you could do a lot worse!"

They laughed and the mood lightened considerably. After the sandwiches arrived, Kate had forgotten all about Tristan and was getting Leah up to speed on the latest gossip concerning their mutual friends and acquaintances.

They decided to go to Kate's apartment to pick up Deborah. The trip home took a little longer than usual due to maintenance on one of the Underground lines, but they finally made it.

It was divided into two big spaces, each with its own entrance. One led to Kate's private home and her rooftop terrace, the other to her and Deborah's healing practice. It'd been a huge investment at the time, but to this day, Kate hadn't once regretted her choice of buying the industrial penthouse loft. Her financial load had lessened when Deborah had decided to become a full partner, so they shared the expense of the private practice part of the building.

Kate had a real soft spot for natural material. There was a lot of wood and glass mixed into the interior. Leah always said it looked like Tolkien's Rivendell, if Rivendell had been built in the twenty-first century. Something Kate had done with the lighting gave the place a mystical, yet homey feel. She could enter the practice from her own home. Behind the open staircase there was a two-way moss wall, which connected the two spaces. Kate and Deborah only used that entrance, though, when there were no clients around.

The healing practice had an entry hall from which you could reach the counselling room with comfy, squashy chairs, soft lighting hidden in the floor, a magnificent bookcase with a little ladder to reach the top shelves, and a floor to ceiling glass wall with a view over Shoreditch. Another door led to the massage and healing room. There were two massage tables, a massage chair, and a circle filled with seven chakra pillows. In the middle of the circle a big pendulum hung from the ceiling. The third and final room was Kate's pride and joy—her meditation room. She loved working with the elements, and her meditation philosophy was inspired by various ones.

When you looked up, you saw the night sky, which was done almost to perfection. A hidden beamer projected the actual sky across the entire ceiling. In one corner there was a large Jacuzzi, and on the other side there was a rock-shaped formation. Alongside it the entire wall resembled a water wall, where the water softly came rustling down. Inside the rock was an actual amethyst sauna. Kate and Deborah used it frequently, to let their clients connect to their inner self again, before starting on either a coaching, massage, or healing session. It opened even the most introverted people, and that helped a lot to further treatment. The meditation room was very popular among the clients, and many of them often booked an hour just to meditate or relax.

After they entered the apartment and Kate turned off the alarm, she noticed on the panel that Deborah was still in the other side of the building, so she put her bags onto the table, hid the box with the scarf for Deborah, and opened her fridge.

"Care for one glass of chardonnay? I have the 5th View one."

"Sure. Why not. We're not driving anywhere tonight," Leah answered from the window. "Honey, you do know how to create a view."

The sun had already gone, but the sky was filled with pink and orange over Shoreditch. It was going to be a good night.

Once one chardonnay had turned into two, the moss wall opened and Deborah stepped through. "Hey there! I was hoping you guys would come and pick me up!" She walked over to Leah and then gave her a big hug. "It's good to see you again, girl. Looking pretty amazing too," she said, looking Leah up and down.

Leah smiled. "Thanks, darling. Looking pretty good yourself, especially considering you've been working all day."

"You should have seen me twenty minutes ago, when I was still sweaty and all." She laughed. Deborah had short, a-symmetric hair, big blue eyes, and was a classic ninety-sixty-ninety sized girl, which got her a lot of attention on the streets. More so than she liked, but she dealt with it with her usual flair. "Ah, yes, weekend. Finally, I thought this week would never end. We've been busy like crazy, and even Meg put in extra hours. I'm not complaining, though. Business is booming, but sometimes it'd be nice to have some low-maintenance clients, if you catch my drift?" She winked at Kate.

Kate nodded understandably. "Everything go okay?"

"Yep. He actually cried today, which is a really good thing, considering he hasn't done that for over a decade, so we've made some real progress."

Kate looked pleased.

"Anybody I would know?" Leah asked with a smile.

"Ha ha. I'm pretty sure you would, but unfortunately for you, I'm not telling, confidentiality and all that," Deborah replied with a wicked grin.

"Bugger!" Leah looked disappointed and then shrugged. "Oh well, it was worth a try," she said to Kate.

Kate rolled her eyes. While she went into her bedroom to put on something a little more elegant for the evening, Leah told Deborah her great news. Kate heard Deborah's excitement through the door and smiled. She always knew Leah would become a huge success someday, and this was certainly a whole new step. Writing international bestsellers was one thing, having your book turned into a movie by a very famous producer and director was quite another. If it became a blockbuster, Kate wondered if Leah had any idea how big the media circus would become. Not that she doubted her capacity to handle the media. It was Leah's modesty that kept her with both feet on the ground. She extended that capacity to her friends on more than one occasion, but she did struggle with boundaries. Leah hated to disappoint anyone, and Kate always thought she did way too much for the people around her. She slipped a little black Prada dress over her head and then put her hair up with a few strands hanging down. Nothing fancy, but elegant enough for dinner. She decided to wear her Prada boots as well. Besides being practical to walk in, they looked great under a cocktail dress and gave it a bit more oomph.

"How about it, ladies, ready to get going?" Kate asked, walking into the living area.

Leah took one last sip and then put her glass onto the table. "We're all yours, baby," she said with a grin.

"Excellent. I'm starving!" Deborah said, grabbing her purse before putting on her coat. Kate and Leah exchanged looks. "What?" Deborah huffed. "I've been working my butt off while you two monkeys had scones and tea, okay? So shut it."

"We know, darling. It was a guilty look, because we're actually still quite stuffed from this afternoon. We had way too many finger sandwiches, but you know they always keep them coming unless you jump up and practically scream 'no,' so what were we going to do? We're the victims here when you really think about it," Leah finished her plea.

"Wow, hon, you really missed out on a career in politics. You can sell some dazzling bullshit," Deborah replied. They laughed.

Once they arrived at Suki, there were only two couples waiting before them, so they were in luck. The one downside of Suki was you couldn't make reservations unless you were with a large party of people. You just had to try your luck. Sometimes that meant waiting for forty-five minutes, but they were led upstairs in less than a quarter after they waited downstairs and looked over the menu. Suki was a modern Japanese restaurant in the heart of Chinatown on Gerrard Street with a mix of Cantonese, dim sum, Thai, and Japanese food. Their top floor was dedicated to shabu shabu, a special Japanese hotpot. Tonight, however, they were going for sushi. While they waited for their order, they started with a Prosecco and toasted to being together again.

"So did you tell Deb about your new neighbour?" Leah asked after taking another sip from her Prosecco.

"Oh, did they sell apartment 3B? That was fast. It's been on the market for like, what, a week?" Deborah looked at Kate.

"Really?" Kate asked. "Just a week? I hadn't realised that. Well, anyway, yes, it has been sold. At least I presume he bought it. Maybe it's a sublease or something? I actually don't know. You can ask him yourself on Thursday. I invited him to the Halloween cocktail party."

Deborah looked interested. "So it's a guy then. Well, come on, give me the gory details. What do we know? Is he tall, dashing, obnoxiously intelligent and playing Chopin while finding a cure for cancer?"

They laughed. "Kate was rather speechless, I believe," Leah said with a wicked grin.

"Oh, really," Deborah cried. "Well, then he must be promising indeed, if he can shut up Kate."

Kate gave them a murderous look. "Yes, thank you, darling. I love you too," she said to Deborah, then stuck out her tongue. "And for the record, we know very little, except that he's originally from Italy. Though he's way too tall for an Italian, and I'll admit to him being rather appealing to look at."

Deborah huffed. "Well, high praise indeed. I'll be sure to get some juice on him when I meet him this Thursday. On that note, are we baking like crazy this week or did you hire a caterer?"

Kate looked up from the plate of tempura shrimp and vegetables that had just arrived and said that she had hired a caterer. "With Samhuinn coming up as well, I just didn't want the extra work, so they'll serve the finger food and drinks. I was thinking of opening up the living area and rooftop. With the pergola closed, just to be sure in case it rains. Then people can smoke on the rooftop, and I keep the living area as clean as possible. The caterers, John and Chris, by the way," she said to Deborah, who smiled, "can use the kitchen area as well, of course, but just them. Have you all decided on outfits? I'm going to hide in plain sight this year I think," Kate finished with a grin.

"Oh, really, so what does hiding in plain sight look like these days?" Leah asked.

Deborah smiled, having already seen Kate's outfit.

"I'm going as fire. I have a dark red cat suit with red and orange fringes on each side around the legs, and I'm going to weave red and orange feathers into my hair so it looks as if I'm on fire." Kate was rather pleased with herself.

"And what would that represent to the general public, if I dare ask?" Leah asked with a raised eyebrow.

"Well, the theme is 'movies,' so I thought I'd go as Fawkes, Dumbledore's phoenix, duh!" Kate answered wickedly.

Leah shook her head. "Well, if we're going for this hiding in plain sight thing, I should probably dress up like Madam Blavatsky and bring a glass orb." She looked at them as if waiting for their response.

"Brilliant!" they answered in stereo.

"Okay, so judging by your reaction, that's settled then." Leah looked pleased. "What are the plans for tomorrow, by the way?"

"Well, I assumed you'd want to go to St. Paul's in the morning, so I thought we could get together for lunch with Romy and Meg and go over the details for Samhuinn," Kate answered.

"Yes, I'd like to go to the morning service, so lunch would be perfect. Where shall we meet? Do you want to eat out or shall we meet at my place?" Leah asked.

"Your place isn't very practical, hon. You'd have to go shopping before or after church. Why don't we meet at my place instead? I'll bake us some mini quiches, and we'll have a nice platter with olives, bread, and cheeses. How about that?" Deborah cut in.

"That does sound lovely. Are you sure that isn't too much trouble, though? It's your only day off this week," Leah said with real concern in her voice.

"Don't be silly. You know I love to bake, and I can whip those babies up in no time, so no trouble at all. My place it is then. Let's say two o'clock?" They nodded.

"How's your mother doing, Kate? I haven't seen her in ages. I really should pay her a visit sometime this week." Leah looked at Kate.

"I'm sure she'd love that," Kate replied. "Mother's always happy to see you. She's doing rather well. I even think she's found a lasting male friend to go to the theatre with, visit gardens, and drink lots of tea. Nothing serious I think, but I do believe they've become good friends, and she gets out more, so I'm happy for her. She did have an incident a couple weeks ago when Simon, her friend, went for a check-up at the hospital and she pointed out they were looking at the wrong place and should focus on his left knee instead."

The girls laughed. "Oh my, how did the doctors respond?" Leah asked still laughing.

"Forget the doctors," Deborah cried out. "How did Simon respond?"

"I think the doctors just thought she had a medical background herself, so she got away with that pretty easily. Simon was quiet for the entire day, my mother said. I think she was rather shocked herself. She never uses her gift in public. Well, obviously, I should say almost never. They went out to dinner that night, and she decided she should trust him in this as well, so she actually told him she could see people's auras if she put in an effort. His response was quite funny. Apparently, he let out a sigh of relief and said he thought she was into something scary."

Deborah giggled. "How cute!"

Kate smiled. "She even told him about Grandma and me, though not the specifics, but I think she was thinking ahead and thought it wise to give him a heads-up, just in case."

Deborah sighed. "I wish I could see people's auras. I tried and tried, but all I get is a slight golden glow around the body, and that costs me so much effort it gives me a headache."

Leah frowned. "Why on Earth would you, of all people, want to see people's auras? You know how they feel and what they need, anyway."

Deborah tried to explain. "I know, and I don't mean to sound ungrateful, but sometimes it feels as if I can do a bit of both. I 'feel' people's moods, but I'm not an empath, and I know what they need, but I'm not a healer as well. I'm a bit of both, and sometimes I just think it'd have been easier to excel in just the one thing. Does that sound weird?" Leah's face softened. "No, sweetie, that doesn't sound weird at all. I sometimes wish I could see more of the future instead of the present or past. I never understood why it's helpful to see things when they've already happened. It leaves me frustrated, because there's nothing I can do to prevent it." Kate was about to say something, but Leah continued. "Yes, yes, yes, I know what you're going to say. I'm probably not supposed to intervene or prevent it, but that doesn't change the fact it's frustrating. With my hectic life, I only get to help so many people as it is, and when I see something, I'd actually like to be able to do something positive, you know?" She let out a big sigh. "Anyway, also not complaining, but I think we all agree that being gifted is both a blessing and a curse."

Kate and Deborah raised their glasses. "Hear, hear!" they said in unison.

Leah looked at Kate with a sad smile. "Sometimes I wish I could make it easier for you. It must be hard to have so much power and not have someone around who can really show and teach you how to use it. I mean, you've come such a long way, but I know it's still difficult for you, especially because it seems to be tied to your emotions."

Kate shook her head. "No, darling, you've got it all wrong. Of course I still struggle, and I probably always will, but I did and do have people supporting and helping me." Her eyes teared up. "You and Deb and Meg and Romy, Sue, my father and mother, all the others, you've always been there for me. I could never have asked for better support than that. I'm always very aware that my so-called 'gift' is very dangerous, because it is indeed, as you so delicately pointed out, tied to my emotions. It's also a part of me, the elements, I mean. I don't think I could live without them, nor would I want to. The only thing I regret is not really knowing my grandmother. She must have been a remarkable woman, and I'd be lying if I said I wouldn't be interested hearing her thoughts, or her opinion, on how I'm doing." She shrugged and then emptied her drink in one last gulp.

"I never really asked. Was she an elemental as well? I mean, I know she was gifted, of course, but what exactly could she do?" Deborah looked at Kate.

"No, she wasn't. At least not like me. She did have control over fire, so pyrokinesis I suppose you'd call that, and she was also a seer like Leah, but my mother always said she mostly saw the distant future, not the near future, present, or past."

Leah sighed. "So sad she died in a plane crash. Just goes to show that seeing other people's futures won't save you from your own."

Kate nodded. "You know, I always wondered about that. I remember very little of her, and some of it is probably not even my own memories, but those of my mother or from photos, but sometimes I feel as if she's watching over me, as if she's still here. My mother always found it very hard. She couldn't even say goodbye to her. The crash left the bodies in such bad condition they thought it wise to go with a, well, you know, closed casket." Kate cleared her throat.

Leah looked sympathetic. "Your uncle identified her, if I remember correctly, right?

"Yes, he did," Kate replied. "He recognised her from the ring she wore. It was one my mother and he had given her for her fortieth birthday. She never took it off."

She looked at the ring on her left hand. Her mother had given it to her on her twenty-first birthday. Her uncle had no daughters, and they'd both decided Kate should inherit it to remember her grandmother. It had two rubies shaped like a diamante set in gold like a little hourglass. Kate always thought the rubies resembled her grandmother's fire and the hourglass the future. She loved it very much, and like her grandmother, wore it every single day.

Deborah looked at it as well. "I love that ring. It's so beautiful."

Kate smiled. "Yes, it is. I played with it as a child, one of the few memories I have of her. I loved how the rubies catch the light, and I always said to her, 'I feel like the ruby, Nana.' Then she'd smile, and say, 'No, my sweet, you're so much more than the ruby. Always remember that.' When I grew up, I thought she meant I was more important than the ring, but later in life I wondered if she already knew what I was, what I'd become."

Deborah took Kate's hand to have a good look at the ring. "Well, she probably did. I mean, she was a seer. It's probable she would have seen something of your future, don't you think?"

Kate laughed. "Yes, hon, that would be 'probable.'"

Leah and Deborah laughed as well. They all ordered another round of drinks and continued exchanging stories from the past. It was good to get together again and catch up, Kate mused. These were her two best friends, and they would always understand her.

When it was half past nine, they decided to call it a night and head homeward. Tomorrow they had another day to catch up and plan for the upcoming ritual. Leah looked forward to seeing Meg and Romy again and just being in London. Deborah was looking forward to a well-deserved day off and spending the day with her friends.

After they split up while being way too loud and giggly on the street, Kate leaned back into her seat on the tube and sighed contently. It'd been a good day.

She walked the last couple blocks to her apartment, retrieved her mail from her mailbox and pushed the button for the lift to come down. As she was going through her mail to see if there was anything important, it arrived and Tristan got out.

"Oh, I'm sorry!" Kate said, almost crashing into Tristan. He steadied her and then let go of her arm. He bent down to pick up some of the letters, which had fallen to the floor. "Thank you," she said as she felt a blush rise on her cheeks. "How clumsy of me. I guess I was lost in thought. So sorry. Did I hurt you?"

Tristan met her gaze. "Not at all," he said with a soft smile that made her heart skip a beat. "You could make it up to me by joining me for a cup of tea. I was just going to go out to get one. There's supposed to be a really nice place nearby called Albion. I understood from their website they're open until eleven. You could fill me in on the dos and don'ts around Shoreditch?"

Kate hesitated for a second and then nodded. "Albion is really nice. I go there regularly, and I suppose I could give you some pointers," she added with a smile.

It wasn't her habit to go out with a total stranger, but Albion was on familiar ground, and somehow Tristan made her feel safe. Furthermore, tea sounded harmless enough. She was kind of interested to get to know him a little better.

She put her mail into her purse and then looked at Tristan. "Shall we then?"

Tristan held the door for her. "Lead the way, milady."

Kate laughed. As they walked toward Albion with only the occasional streetlamp to guide their way, she took her chance to observe him without him noticing. He was probably somewhere in his mid-forties with half-long dark brown hair. Now that she walked next to him, she noticed he was indeed a lot taller than her, but not as tall as she'd first thought. He had the appearance of being tall, something in his energy perhaps, she mused. She couldn't see the colour of his eyes right now, but knew them to be an intense dark blue. His pace was attuned to hers, but there was a bounce to it that told her she held him back, which made her smile. Tristan was a gentleman. She'd noticed it before when he'd held the door for her.

She pointed to her right. "It's at the end of this street. We're almost there."

Once they arrived at Albion, he held the door for her again, and waited until she was seated before sitting down. He looked around.

"Do you like it?" Kate asked.

"It has a very pleasant atmosphere," he said. "You come here often, you said?"

"Yes, quite often. They're open all day, and they serve a really nice breakfast. So whenever I'm feeling lazy, I go here for it," Kate said with a smile. "Also they have a killer rooftop, part of The Boundary. They do wine tastings, and the view is really nice, especially during sunset." She stopped when one of the waiters arrived at their table.

Tristan looked at her. "What would you like, Catherine?"

"A pot of fresh mint tea for me please."

He looked approving. "Same for me please," he said to the waiter, who then left to get them their tea.

He appeared about to say something when Kate said, "So, have you settled in a bit?" She looked at him. "I'm sorry. You wanted to say something?"

Tristan shook his head. "Not at all. And thank you for asking. All the furniture is in place, so it comes down to emptying boxes now, which is not my favourite chore, but thankfully they're mostly filled with books. It shouldn't take that long to sort them out. I still have a few more days before I have to go back to work. I'd better make the most of it."

Kate was interested. "Do you mind me asking what it is you do for a living?"

"My company helps people and organisations to improve the world. I could give you the details, but I'm afraid I'll bore you to death. It's not very interesting. I do a lot of travelling, though, which makes it rather enjoyable. I always love seeing the world, and my job allows me to see a great deal of it," he finished.

Kate frowned. "That doesn't sound boring at all! So you work for an environmental organisation or something?" she asked.

"Or something," Tristan replied with a grin. She smiled back. "So, what about you?" he asked. "I noticed your apartment is divided into two spaces, and I saw the name Elements outside."

Kate nodded. "Yes, that's the name of our private practice. Deborah and I, a friend of mine, are the co-owners, and we have two more ladies working for us. It's a massage and coaching practice. We treat everyone who needs our help, but our main clientele are people in the music or acting industry. It didn't start out that way, but apparently our treatments have quite an impact," she added with a touch of pride in her voice.

"Elements," Tristan said. "Elements. It has a nice ring to it. I like it. What made you choose that word?"

Kate practically had to force herself not to blurt out that she was an elemental. Confused about her own emotions, she tried to focus on his face instead. "Well," she carefully began, "I have a thing with the elements. You know, earth, air, fire, and water. A theory of mine is that when body, mind, and soul are in balance, the elements inside you are in balance, or in perfect harmony, whatever you want to call it. So I thought it'd be a nice name to represent what it is I do. Also it makes for very pretty brochures when you can work with them," she ended on a lighter note. It was the closest she'd ever come to giving an honest answer to a stranger.

Tristan smiled. "That's a beautiful theory, Catherine. Now I like the name even more."

"Oh, please ... call me Kate. Everybody calls me Kate."

He tilted his head a bit to the side. "Do they? I like Catherine. You're a Catherine to me. Would you mind if I keep calling you Catherine?"

Her name sounded like a caress when he said it, and she suddenly found herself not minding it at all. "No, it's fine. I'm just not used to being called Catherine anymore, except by my mother," she said, laughing. "She always calls me Catherine, so I guess you're in good company."

He smiled. It made her slightly lightheaded, as if she'd had too much alcohol to drink.

"You're an odd duck, Tristan Visconti," Kate said with a smile.

He laughed. "An odd duck? Well, that's something new. What made you say that?"

Kate shrugged. "I'm usually pretty good at reading people, but I find it very hard to make out your character."

He looked incredulous. "Then let me return the favour by stating the exact same thing about you."

Now it was Kate's turn to feel incredulous. "Really? People are always telling me I'm an open book."

Or they could tell by the weather or room temperature, she thought, but she wasn't about to share that bit of information with Tristan. Her mother was always afraid the "wrong" kind of people would find out what she could do, and sometimes it was hard to distinguish the right from wrong.

Her gut feeling told her Tristan was the right kind of people, but she was also sure he hid something from her. It made sense, of course. They were still complete strangers to one another, but she had a feeling he hid a lot of things from people, so she was a bit more cautious than usual.

Also her emotions were in turmoil whenever she was around him. She'd noticed it in the lobby at their apartment building and again now that she sat across from him, sipping her mint tea. No matter how many grounding exercises she did, she still was all over the place. She wondered if it was something she was doing to him or something he was doing to her. A shame, really. This wasn't the type of conversation you could have with the average person. She realised once again how lucky she was to have so many great friends in her life and a mother who understood her.

Her father had as well, and she still missed him terribly. His jewel, he used to call her, or "my favourite gem." He'd always brought her gems whenever he travelled around the world. Her father had been a reporter, mostly in warzones, and his final trip had been fatal. Collateral damage, the paper had said. Amsterdam had never seen such an ugly thunderstorm, and afterward Kate had cried for days while at the same time trying to be strong for her mother. Among his possessions there had been a ruby. He'd never brought her back one, and it'd become her favourite gem. She wore it around her neck, and it matched perfectly with her grandmother's ring. She liked to think of them as little talismans, watching over her. She played with it now, holding it between her thumb and forefinger. She noticed Tristan looked at it.

"You're not an open book to me," he said. "That's a beautiful ruby. It goes well with your ring. Anniversary present?" he asked with a hint of cheek in his voice.

Kate laughed. "Good god, no. I'm not married or anything. They're family heirlooms. The ring was my grandmother's and my father bought me the necklace. What about you? How many little Tristans are roaming the earth?"

Tristan raised his eyebrow. "None that I know of, at least. Over the years, it's come to my attention that my line of profession doesn't really go well with a long-lasting relationship. Women tend to want more than a monthly visit, and I can't say I blame them. I'd want more as well."

Kate absently stirred her tea. "Sounds kind of lonely, Mr. Visconti."

"It does, doesn't it?" He smiled. "Maybe I'm just trying to win your sympathy so you'll feel sorry for me."

Kate leaned back and tossed her hair over her shoulder. "Well, then it's working. I'm a sucker for people who are lonely. Everybody deserves some company in life. I think it's what keeps us sane. Though in all fairness, you don't really strike me as the type people feel sorry for, in general, I mean. You seem very um … self-sufficient is the word, I believe."

Tristan laughed. It was a deep rumbling sound. "Do I now? That was exactly the compliment I was looking for. Self-sufficient." He rolled his eyes.

Kate laughed. "Well, you are rather pleasing to look at as well," she teased.

"Thank heavens, I still have my looks!" He grinned. It gave him a more boyish look when he smiled that crooked smile. "Do you want another pot of tea or would you care for a glass of wine? I'm thinking of having one myself." He looked at the menu to see what they served.

"They have a nice chardonnay," Kate answered. "I think I could do with one glass of wine." She smiled.

"Excellent!" Tristan signalled to one of the waiters, and he came over to their table at once. "Two chardonnay please," he ordered. He looked at Kate. "Would you care for some olives as well?"

"Sure."

"And some olives please." The waiter nodded and then left their table. "So, Catherine, pray tell, what should I expect from this Halloween cocktail party?" Tristan asked.

Kate grinned. "It's good you asked. I almost forgot. It's a theme party, so I hope you have a creative streak inside you."

Tristan pretended to look horrified. "Oh dear, well, that would depend on the theme I suppose."

"The theme is 'movies,' but a TV character is also okay. Perhaps you could go as Shrek," she suggested with a wicked grin. Tristan just stared at her. She grinned even more.

"I'm going to ignore that last remark, I think. So, which character are you going to be?" he asked.

She shook her head. "Nuhuh, not tellin'. You'll have to wait and see, but I'm quite pleased with it."

He sighed in defeat. "Well, obviously, you're not going to share and tell. Are you expecting a lot of people?" He moved a little to the side so the waiter could put down their glasses and olives.

"Give or take a hundred. Not everybody's coming, but this is an annual thing for us, our clientele and friends, so it's become rather popular over the years. Usually, it's no more than a hundred people, though. Fortunately, I have a very large rooftop, which can be closed, depending on the weather. I never have any trouble with a large crowd. And I can always throw some people off the roof when it becomes too crowded."

Tristan looked at her. "And you're calling me an odd duck," he said, trying to suppress a grin.

Kate raised her glass. "A toast, Mr. Visconti. May you approve of Shoreditch, and may Shoreditch approve of you."

Tristan looked into her eyes as he raised his glass as well. "*Cin cin*," he said while they toasted. "So are there going to be a lot of famous people in our building this Thursday?"

She nodded. "Give or take a hundred."

Tristan looked surprised. "I'd hardly consider myself a famous person, Catherine."

She smiled mischievously. "No, but you'll be dressed as one."

Tristan put his head on the table. When he looked up again, he said, "Wow, I fell right into that one, didn't I?"

Kate grinned. "Yep, you did. To give you a more sincere answer, I'm sure you'll see one or two familiar faces in the crowd, depending on your movie, reading, or music knowledge. Deborah knows way more people than I do, though. I always have to ask her what he or she is famous for, so as not to offend anyone, because half the time I don't recognise them. Not even if I like their music. It's easier with actors and actresses, because I see them a lot on TV or on the big screen. With writers or musicians, it's much harder to connect a face to a band or book. Well, for me it is, anyway. She's always drilling me a week before the cocktail party so I won't mix up names and bands." She laughed.

Deborah had already started doing that again last week. She'd gone even further this year and actually had made a whole book with pictures of their clients on the left and what they did on the right. According to Deborah, Kate was a very visual person, so she'd recognise the picture of a band, book, or movie more easily than just the name of said band, book, or movie. Kate had practically rolled on the floor with laughter until she realised Deborah was dead serious. She had pulled herself together, humbly apologised to her friend for all her hard work, and studied "the book." She'd felt like a character from *The Devil Wears Prada*, but credit where credit was due, it worked.

She knew a lot more about her clients. She always knew exactly which problems they were confronting, but other than that, she stayed way out of their personal lives. Ever since last week, though, she'd come to learn which musicians hated each other, who just had an ugly break-up, who was doing who, and that a bad review in *The Guardian* could double the amount of coaching sessions with a certain writer. She was so glad to only be a small part of their world. It seemed like a lot of hard work to her.

People probably said the same thing about her, but she never felt like that. Even though she could only share all of herself with her inner circle, she never felt as if she had to pretend. Over the years, she'd come to realise that being an artist entailed a lot of pretending and pleasing other people. She'd probably be suicidal within a year. Or in jail, for that matter, because she'd most likely kill someone.

She hated pretenders. It was exactly that which made her so successful. She got people to let down their guards and show their true selves. Once she had them at that point, the road to recovery was relatively easy. Relatively because no one was alone in this world. There were people surrounding everyone, influencing, and even though we understand what it is we want and need, others might not. Everybody struggled with that, but Kate did believe it was a bit more difficult for artists, because so many people depended on them and their success. It made the danger of falling back into old patterns more real. Sometimes she invited a manager, publisher, or other band members along for a coaching session, just to get her point across. That had led to some fireworks, but the end results were pretty good. She thought it was worth it. She started when she noticed Tristan was talking to her.

"I'm very good with faces," he said, "but terrible with names. I think I could do with one of Deborah's books. You think she'd make one for me?" He grinned.

Kate smiled back. "I'll ask her, but be careful what you wish for. She's a real drill master when it comes to these things. If you get one question wrong, you won't get a cupcake, and trust me, you don't want to miss out on her cupcakes."

"I'll be sure to remember that," Tristan replied.

"So, are you settling down in London?" Kate asked. "You said your work has you moving around a lot. That must be hard. Never to call a place home."

Tristan stabbed an olive and then held it out to her. Her fingers brushed his when she took it from him. She shivered slightly. He took another one himself and then took a sip from his wine.

"Sometimes it is," he said after a moment, "but I've got used to it, I suppose. I'm not sure how long I'll be staying here, though. I'd like to for a longer period of time. I'd like that very much indeed." He looked straight at her while he said that.

Kate felt a blush spreading across her face. She hated it when that happened.

Tristan smiled and continued. "It all depends on how fast I'll be able to get through to my client. The people I work with have such great influences on our world that often they don't realise how much power they hold. That's where I come in. I have to make them see what they can do, or sometimes can't do. Sometimes that means people have to let go of their power, and most don't even like the thought of that, let alone act on it. Then I have to, let's say, persuade them, to come to my way of thinking, and that's not always a lot of fun."

There was something in his tone when he spoke about persuading people, which made Kate shiver. She didn't think anyone would like Tristan persuading them.

"Fortunately for me, it's the other way around this time. My client needs encouraging, and I really love that part of my job. It's very rewarding. I'm sure you have that as well when you see one of your clients back in perfect balance, out there facing the world again."

Kate nodded understandingly. "That is very fulfilling indeed. Although I don't dare to presume I have that much impact on my clients' lives. Your clientele sounds a lot more, I don't know, heavyweight? Suddenly I have visions of Shell's top dog and such," she said.

Tristan laughed. "I can well imagine," he said. "And you wouldn't be far off, either. Some of our clientele are businessmen, but like you, we get all kinds of flavour." He winked. The waiter came to their table to ask if they wanted anything more from the bar before closing time. Tristan looked at Kate, who shook her head. "No, just the bill, thank you."

"Very well, sir. I'll be with you in a moment," the waiter replied.

Tristan looked at Kate. "Now I still don't know anything about the dos and don'ts around Shoreditch. I'm afraid this will lead to more tea on another day."

Kate was pleased. "I'd be happy to. Well, at least you know Albion now, but Shoreditch has many gems."

The waiter returned with their bill. Kate tried to see the total amount, but Tristan took one look at it and then put it into his pocket.

"I asked you to accompany me, remember," he remarked when he noticed Kate was about to object.

Kate just shrugged. She was used to going Dutch, but if she had to be honest, she kind of liked his old-fashioned manners. She excused herself to visit the ladies' room while Tristan took care of their bill. After she returned, he helped her into her coat.

"Thank you," she said, turning around to face him.

Outside the air was fresh, but not too cold. The warmth of the day still lingered in the streets. A slight breeze brushed Kate's face. It felt nice. She breathed in. She wondered if he'd take her hand, but he didn't. She almost felt sorry he didn't. *Stop acting like a silly little girl,* she thought. *You're not in college anymore, for god's sake.* She sighed inwardly and used her hair as a curtain to sneak a peek at Tristan. He looked relaxed, more so than at the beginning of the night. She debated with herself to take the initiative for their next … what? Date? Of course he'd said he wanted to have more tea to talk about Shoreditch, so it wasn't as if she'd be imposing or anything. She was dying to see his apartment. She could tell a lot from seeing someone's place. *To ask or not to ask, that is the question,* she thought, smiling to herself. She doubted Shakespeare ever had that kind of problem. He'd probably had dozens of women fighting for his attention.

"It's very quiet here for a Saturday night," Tristan remarked.

She nodded. "This part is quiet, but when you walk toward Great Eastern Street, it becomes more crowded and noisy. A lot of clubs are located there."

"Are you a club kind of person?" he asked.

"No, not really. I used to be, but I'm more of a restaurant or cafe kind of girl nowadays. Getting older, you know," she said, laughing.

"And how old is old these days? Though I realise you should never ask that of a lady."

"Then how dare you ask." Kate laughed. "I'm thirty-five if you must know." She wondered how old he was. It was hard to tell.

"A spring chicken then. I'm forty-seven."

Kate was surprised. She'd thought he was older than her, but not by that much. "Really? You don't look it." She was sincere.

"Why thank you. You're being too kind, milady."

They'd reached their apartment building, and Tristan took his keys out of his coat to open the door for them. Kate went inside first and then pushed the button for the lift. "I had a really nice evening," she said. *Jesus, cliché much*, she thought.

Tristan smiled. "Me too. You still owe me another date, though. You promised me the inside scoop on Shoreditch. I can't be trusted out there on the streets on my own, you know." He slightly tilted his head to one side and gave her a pleading look.

Kate doubted if she'd have been able to say no if she'd wanted to, but she had no objection whatsoever to seeing Tristan again. So she pretended to stall a bit, making a show of grabbing her iPhone and checking her schedule.

With a big sigh, she said, "I might be able to squeeze you in on Monday. How about lunch?"

"Make it dinner and I'll agree," he replied with an arrogant smile.

She gave in. "Dinner it is then." Tristan looked satisfied. "I'll even let you choose the place," she added wickedly. "See how you're getting on in Shoreditch and judge if you're able to pick a nice place."

Tristan looked slightly worried, and Kate was satisfied to see the arrogant smirk had left his face. "I'll do my best," he humbly replied. "Shall I pick you up at six thirty?"

They'd reached the third floor, and the doors opened. Tristan held them from closing and turned toward her.

"That sounds good. Six thirty it is," Kate replied.

"Goodnight, Catherine. I'm very glad to have moved to Shoreditch. I had a lovely evening." He took her left hand and bowed over it. Softly he touched his lips to her skin. She shuddered. "Sleep well," he said as he let go.

"You too, Tristan," she replied softly.

The doors closed and then opened again before she stepped out at her penthouse floor. As she closed her front door and then turned off the alarm, she let out a big sigh. It could turn into a very interesting week. A very interesting week indeed.

SUNDAY

KATE SLOWLY OPENED her eyes and stretched her legs. The sun peeked through her closed curtains, and if her hearing was correct, the sound of Placebo had just awoken her. She listened to the radio more carefully. Yep, definitely Placebo. *No mistaking that voice*, she thought, smiling. They were about to go on tour again, and she made a mental note to check their touring schedule. Leah would definitely want to go, and Deborah probably as well.

She just loved that band. Her favourite period was when Steve Forrest, their drummer, had joined. Kate had always been a fan, but since the release of *Battle for the Sun*, she really appreciated them. One look at their new drummer had made her smile. Of course. He'd brought them the sun, and their song writing had been more balanced, she thought. An equal amount of darkness and light. Though they'd most likely never write about puppy love. Probably a good thing too, she mused. *Loud Like Love* had followed, and she'd loved every song on it.

Unfortunately, Steve had left the band after that album. If they'd play in The Indigo O2, that would be nice, but that would be a long shot. They'd probably play in a bigger venue. Oh well, one could always hope.

Kate stretched her legs one more time and wiggled her toes. She hummed along with the tunes and pulled the sheets back. She was in a very good mood. Yesterday had been a most interesting day. She loved having Leah in London, and Tristan was turning out to be quite a fascinating character. He was hard to make out, though. She hadn't been kidding when she'd told him he was an odd duck. She usually had very good senses about people, but he was a mystery to her. Then again, she liked a good one. It wasn't as if she had to figure him out within the week. She had plenty of time, and she had to admit to herself that she was looking forward to Monday evening when they'd go out for dinner.

Poor Tristan, she'd put pressure on him when she'd told him to find a suitable restaurant. She could tell by the look he'd had on his face. Then again, he had it coming with that arrogant statement of her joining him for dinner, so she didn't feel sorry for him for long.

She strolled to her en suite bathroom and then took a quick shower. Once she walked back into her bedroom, wrapping a towel around her head, the clock told her it was nine o'clock. Good, she wanted to visit her mother this morning, and she'd have plenty of time to be back before lunch with the girls.

She started the tedious affair of blow drying her hair, which took her more than fifteen minutes each day, but she just hated walking around with it wet. Fortunately, it was unbeatable, so no matter how many times she used a hairdryer, it still kept growing and had a natural shine to it. She'd cut it off only once in her teens when she'd been going through a particularly rebellious phase. Having no money to visit a hair salon, she'd persuaded her father, who eventually gave in and cut it for her. Her mother didn't speak to her father for a week, and she received the silent treatment for over a month. Looking back Kate regretted her choice, because it'd taken her over five years to grow it out.

Back then she'd been too stubborn to admit that to her mother. She hadn't thought she could live with the I-told-you-so look. It was one of the few times they'd disagreed. She smiled at the memory.

She grabbed another string of hair and moved the hairdryer slowly toward the bottom. It was almost dry. She brushed it thoroughly until it had a nice golden shine, and decided to wear it down today. The Foo Fighters were blasting their way through her radio now, telling her to never surrender, and she screamed along to the music. Standing in front of her walk-in closet, she grabbed a pair of skinny Levis and a black sleeveless Armani top. She browsed her jackets to locate her blue Escada that would go nicely with her jeans. She stopped her fingers and pulled it out. She loved to mix and match, or as her mother would say, mismatch. Her mother thought mixing haute couture houses was a capital offence, but even she had to admit her daughter had a natural flair for picking out the right clothes.

She fished her Prada boots out of the hallway and then put them on. Time for breakfast. Being in a lazy mood, she decided to go to Albion. She grabbed her purse, put some sunglasses in her hair, as it looked sunny outside, and put on her coat and scarf. Downstairs she retrieved her morning paper and then walked toward Albion.

* * *

Albion wasn't too busy just yet, so she sat in the back, which was her favourite spot. The waiter smiled in recognition and asked if she'd like the Albion granola.

She returned his smile and nodded. "And a cappuccino and an orange juice, please."

"Coming right up, miss."

She opened her paper and scanned the headlines. What was the world coming to? Another earthquake in Japan, bombings in Syria, and a local fifteen-year-old who apparently had killed his whole family, including his nine-year-old sister. *Just lovely*, she thought. She sighed. Sometimes she regretted not having any children, but she wondered if she could live with the responsibility of having any in this day and age. It felt as if the world were losing its mind. She comforted herself with the thought that it probably felt that way to every generation, but she often felt as if the world were losing its balance, and she and her friends had to work harder every year to maintain it toward the side of light. Not that people knew that, of course. Influencing the world from a supernatural or spiritual point of view was as old as the earth itself. People just didn't read about those sort of things in the paper. Good thing too, her grandmother used to say, because most people would just want to use them for all the wrong reasons, and then where would we be? She would have been seventy-eight today, and Kate felt a pang of sorrow.

Outside, a cloud shifted over the sun. Kate noticed and shook herself out of it. *No point in wallowing, girl.* The waiter returned with her order, and she dug into her granola. After she finished, she took out her iPhone, which told her it was now almost ten o'clock. Her mother would be up and running by now. She pressed her contact details and waited.

"Mrs. van Dyk speaking."

Kate smiled. "Hi, Mommy, it's me. Are you free this morning? I was just about to head your way, if you don't mind."

"Sweetheart!" her mother cried. "How nice to hear from you. Of course I'm free this morning or I would make time. It's been way too long. Will you be staying for lunch?"

"No, sorry, Mom. I'm having lunch with the girls. Leah is over for a visit. She was hoping to visit you as well this week, by the way, so you can expect her call. I'll hop onto the tube now and be there in about one hour I think. Is that okay?"

"That's fine, Catherine. I'll make us some scones then and put the kettle on. See you soon, darling."

"Bye, Mom!" Kate said before disconnecting.

Her mother lived in Greenford, on Conway Crescent. It was a good neighbourhood, and rather green and quiet, which had been two of her mother's demands in finding a new place. She could easily visit the city when she wanted or needed to, but she'd made a life for herself in Greenford, and liked it there. Kate visited her mother more often in Greenford than the other way around, because the hustle and bustle of the city wasn't always to her mother's tastes. Or nerves, for that matter.

She asked for the bill and then checked her iPhone to see if the central line was operating as it should. The tube status showed her a "good service," so she put on her coat before she left Albion to catch her train. She got onto the tube at Liverpool Street, which was a five-minute walk from the Albion, jumped onto the train to West Ruislip and took a seat.

She searched for her headset and then connected it to her iPhone. After scrolling through her music, she decided to go with Frank Sinatra. The train ride would take about forty minutes, so she had plenty of time to go through her mail and make a head start since she probably wouldn't have time later. As she listened to the song "Witchcraft," there was a young girl sitting across from her in a red coat. She shivered and looked really cold. The early signs of coming down with the flu. Kate took one look at her and let her fire element take over. It floated toward the girl and then went inside her. The girl visibly relaxed and looked a lot better. Kate smiled at her, and the girl smiled back, though appearing a bit confused.

When Kate looked up again, she noticed the next station would be Perivale where she had to leave the train. She put on her coat again and then moved toward the doors. The girl in the red coat gave her another smile as she exited the train. The sun tried to break through the clouds, but it was still rather nice outside, especially for that time of year. Kate enjoyed the walk to her mother's house, which took her no more than ten minutes. The neighbour was trimming the hedges, and she noticed he was also trimming her mother's.

"Hello, Mr. Hadley. Keeping those muscles in shape?" She smiled at the older man.

"Why, Catherine! How good to see you again. My, my, upon my word, you're getting lovelier by the day."

Kate made a dramatic gesture. "Stop it, Mr. Hadley. You're making me blush." She winked. He laughed. "So nice of you to take care of my mother's hedges as well. She's lucky to have you as a neighbour."

Mr. Hadley stepped down from his ladder. "No trouble at all, love. I know how passionate women can be about their garden." He winked back. "Your mother and Mrs. Hadley spend a fair few hours planting, watering, potting and what not, so the least I can do is trim those hedges. They've been growing like crazy this summer, but they'll be winter ready when I'm done with them." He smiled at his own little joke.

"It was nice seeing you again, Mr. Hadley. Please give my love to Mrs. Hadley," Kate said.

Mr. Hadley climbed back onto his ladder. "Will do, will do, my love. You take care now." He waved.

Kate waved back and then rang the doorbell. Her mother opened the door within seconds.

"Catherine!" Her mother gave her a big hug. "I thought I heard your voice outside. Come in, come in, sweetheart, and let me have a good look at you."

Kate sighed in resignation and turned on the spot to let her mother have a look at her.

Her mother smiled. "Oh my, what a lovely shade of pink, and there's more red as well. You've met someone, haven't you? I want to hear all about it over tea, and I'll fill you in on the latest gossip on the street." She went humming into the kitchen.

Kate shook her head and smiled to herself. Sometimes it sucked big time having a mother who could see and read people's auras.

"Well, tell me all about him... or her, which would be fine as well, my dear," her mother said with a wink.

Kate sighed and put another spoonful of clotted cream onto her scones. She had a feeling she'd need the extra scoop. "It's a him, Mom. I know I've been single for a long time, but I'm still in the sausage camp."

Her mother tried to look shocked. "Language, darling," she said, clicking her tongue.

Kate rolled her eyes. Her mother was a real lady, but she doubted if she'd ever be able to shock her. She looked around. She always felt at home there. Even though her mother had decorated the house completely differently from when they'd lived in Amsterdam, she still had several pieces of furniture from that time, including the large bookcase Kate had loved as a child. It had a ladder that went all the way up to reach the high shelves. When she'd been a little girl, her father always had let her climb it while holding the ladder so she wouldn't fall off.

Kate smiled. "Tristan," she began as her mother gave her an approving look, "is my new neighbour in apartment 3B. He moved in last week. We met briefly downstairs when I was going for breakfast with Lee. His surname is Visconti, which sounded very Italian to me, so I asked him about his heritage. He was indeed born in Milan, but he moved to England as a boy. He considers himself an Englishman. He doesn't look Italian, by the way. I think you'd very much approve. He has impeccable manners, half-long dark brown hair and the most beautiful blue eyes I've ever seen. He travels around the world a lot. Something environmental or 'governmenty' I think. I'm not really sure. It sounded interesting, though not to him. I got the feeling he was being modest. His taste in clothing is quite expensive, by the looks of it, so he probably makes a pretty decent salary." She paused to take another bite from her scone. "Oh, and I invited him to my Halloween cocktail party."

Her mother looked impressed. "And you got all this from a minor encounter in the hallway?"

Kate felt her cheeks turn slightly redder. "Um, well, no, not exactly. I met him again that night when I arrived at home. He was going out for a cup of tea at Albion, and he asked me if I wanted to join him. To give him pointers about the neighbourhood," she added as a weak defence.

"Really?" her mother said with a laugh. "Well, he must have made you feel safe. You're usually a pretty good judge of character when it comes to these things, and it's not like you to go somewhere with a strange man." Her voice held no accusation. She just stated her thoughts.

"Funny you should say that, Mom. He does make me feel safe, but I get the feeling he wants me to. Feel safe, I mean. He must have known I'm not the type to go out with strangers, but somehow all my objections sort of faded away. It's a bit strange, really. Don't get me wrong, I do like him. I mean, he's kind of mysterious and all that, what's not to like, but he's also hiding something from me. Maybe not per se from me, but from people in general, so it might be nothing. For now my motto is 'handle with care.'" She gave her mother a smile.

"Sounds very wise, darling. Hmm ... I'd love to get a good look at his aura. That would tell us more."

Kate laughed. "In that case, Mom, I couldn't agree more. We could try spying and get a pair of binoculars and lay in the bushes just beside the building."

Her mother laughed. "Sounds like an adventure, sweetheart, but I'm afraid I'm going to burst your bubble. I can't see auras through binoculars, just like I can't see them on the telly."

Kate looked surprised. "You never told me that. That's interesting. So when your view is somehow 'blurred' it doesn't show the aura anymore. Hmm, kind of makes sense, though. I need fire to make fire."

Her mother looked at her. "I know you believe that, honey, and far be it from me to disagree with an elemental. You know I can't help you find out the way your powers work, but your grandmother always believed you didn't need the elements to make them come to life."

Kate looked the other way. "Do you still think about her, Mom?" she asked. Her mother remained silent. She turned to look at her. "Mom?"

Her mother seemed far away for a moment, but then she snapped out of it and looked at Kate. "Every day, sweetheart, every day."

They spent the next hour gossiping about their mutual acquaintances and her mother's book club, always good for a couple juicy stories, as the club read mostly books that were out of the ordinary, for some reason.

They were now discussing Marquis de Sade, who wasn't a very good writer at all if Kate had to go by her mother's opinion, but the man had caused a nice little upstart when the topic turned to human bondage. Apparently, a friend of her mother's thought it was the only way to go, which had caused all sorts of exclamations amongst the other ladies. Her mother had enjoyed herself immensely. She had even suggested it might be a good idea to read the whole *Fifty Shades* trilogy, but was stared down by most of the ladies. Kate could well imagine her mother adding fuel to the fire, but secretly thought that Marquis de Sade was probably a lot "worse" than anything E.L. James had written.

Then there was the business of discussing the garden. It was very important to her mother, and she always wanted Kate's thorough opinion on each and every plant. As an elemental, Kate could feel what they needed most, and her mother always wrote everything down to make sure parts of her garden flourished at different times, so there would be something to see through the whole year.

As they stood next to the wisteria that grew against the side wall of her mother's house, Kate loved how the garden looked. It was full of little corners and surprises with benches and tree trunks to sit and enjoy the view from different points. At the back her mother had a porch attached, which allowed them to enjoy the garden even in winter, because the area could be heated. It seated ten people comfortably and could be turned to fit sixteen if need be.

"How did the wisteria do this year?" Kate asked.

"Oh, it was a real shame you were in New York. I took pictures, though. It just exploded, darling. I think it covers half the wall now. I'm glad to have it here again."

Kate's mother loved wisteria. Her husband had bought her three different ones for their third anniversary when they were living in Amsterdam to represent the love and growth of their marriage, and it'd been with pain and regret her mother had left the trees behind. They belonged to the house, however, and she knew that. So when Kate had taken her shopping for her fiftieth birthday, she'd arranged to plant a huge wisteria against the house. After they came back and her mother had noticed it, she'd cried like crazy, but as she'd tried to explain to Kate through her sobs, they were happy tears. That was seven years ago, and the tree had got even bigger.

Kate smiled at the memory as they took a turn around the garden. Her mother, unlike herself, really had green thumbs. Kate instantly knew what a plant needed, which was the main and probably only reason her plants were still alive. Well, that and the good care of her housekeeper. She never had the urge, though, to do some real gardening. Other than mixing herbs for her oils, which gave her great joy and sometimes new insights on how a combination could cause a certain effect on the body or mind, she had no interest in the fine art of gardening. She loved nature, but sometimes she wondered if nature loved her back. She enjoyed being in it, as often as she could possibly manage, but every now and then she thought she heard the earth cry, and that scared the living daylights out of her. She'd learned to close herself off to that particular side of her gift, and now only noticed it when she gave it her full attention. There was only so much she needed to know.

"I'm spending New Year's at Leah's this year, so next year I'll be here to enjoy it. She'll be busy as hell by then, anyway, so I probably won't be in New York for quite some time."

Kate told her mother that Leah's first book was going to be filmed. Her mother was very happy for Leah. Leah was her oldest friend, and Kate's mother considered her a second daughter.

"She must be so proud!" her mother exclaimed. "Oh, I do hope she'll find the time to visit this week."

Kate nodded. "I'm sure she will, Mom. As I said, she mentioned it, and she's staying the whole week. Ryan is away on some promotion thingy for Juilliard until Christmas, so we'll be spending Christmas here as well and leave together for New Year's in the Big Apple."

Her mother looked happy. "So you're free on Christmas day? I had hoped you'd want to join me and Simon for dinner. Unless you think it's too soon." She looked a bit timid. It pained Kate to see it.

"No, Mom, you must never think that. You know I like Simon, and I know very well you'll never forget Papa. You deserve to be happy. Father would want you to be happy, and so do I. I'd love to come over for dinner. We're planning a Christmas Eve dinner at Lee's, leaving everybody free for Christmas day, so it all works out perfectly, you see?" She smiled and gave her mother a big hug. "You can get silly ideas sometimes, you know," she teasingly said.

Her mother huffed, but looked a lot happier again. Catherine's opinion was important to her. Since one p.m. was fast approaching, and Kate had a long way back to the city, they walked to the house.

Her mother walked her to the front door. "It was great seeing you again, dear. Give my love to the girls. I hope you'll have a lovely afternoon." She hugged Kate and gave her a kiss.

"Will do, Mom. Maybe when Leah comes for a visit, I'll tag along, depending on how busy Deb and I are this week. I'll be sure to let you know, okay?"

She returned her mother's kiss and then waved goodbye on the street. Once she reached the corner, she took out her iPhone and then connected it to her earbuds. She checked her tube app to see if the central line was still running a good service. It was. She could catch the same train back and get out at Notting Hill Gate, as Deborah lived on Portobello Road.

Kate tried to avoid going to Deborah's house on Saturdays as much as possible, as the Portobello Road Market was held on Saturday. It was quite famous, and a favourite amongst the tourists that came to London. Deborah loved the market and hustle and bustle of the neighbourhood. They'd shared Kate's apartment for a year when they first moved to London, but they'd both agreed Deborah should have her own place when she became a full partner. Becoming one allowed her to get a good mortgage deal on her house, and Deborah had been living there happily ever since. It was close enough to work, but far enough to keep that and her personal life separate.

Kate selected her favourite Placebo playlist, sat back to enjoy the ride and got lost in her own thoughts. Half an hour later, she stepped out at Notting Hill Gate and then walked the last five minutes to Deborah's house. It was a nice two-storey with a small garden at the back, which was convenient, since her friend was a huge cat person and owned three of said monsters. When she'd bought the house, it had a blue front door, which was one of Deborah's favourite colours, but after the third tourist came knocking, asking if this was the house used in the film *Notting Hill*, she'd decided to paint it white instead. The tourists stayed away after the paintjob, and Deborah and her cats enjoyed the peace and quiet again. Inside the house, you couldn't help but think you were in Morocco or perhaps Bali. There were a lot of Moroccan and Indonesian influences with lots of earthy colours, varying from sea-blue to the deep ochre-red of the earth.

As Kate knocked on the door, one of Deborah's little monsters came running toward her to greet her. "Hello, Aini. Did you know I was coming?" She petted the now purring cat.

Deborah's cats were referred to by her friends as the triple As. They all had Indonesian names that started with an A. Aini meant the eye, and she did have a knack for knowing when visitors were dropping by. Asmara, the youngest, meant love. She liked nothing better than to be cuddled all day and sit either just beside you or on your lap. Arya, the name of the oldest and first cat, meant warrior, and she really lived up to her name by bringing back all sorts of prey to Deborah as nice little "gifts."

Footsteps rushed toward the door, and seconds later, her friend opened it. "Hey, girl, you're the first to arrive. Come in, come in. I have to get the mini quiches out of the oven."

Deborah was already gone again, and Kate turned to Aini. "Well? In or out, kitty cat?"

Aini purred and walked past Kate into the hallway. She closed the door behind them and then followed Aini toward the kitchen where Deborah was pulling muffin trays out of the oven. They had the perfect form to bake mini quiches.

Kate sniffed and immediately her mouth watered. "God, that smells delicious!"

Deborah smiled. "I know, right? I made a salmon and spinach batch, and a brie, walnut, and honey batch. I thought it'd be nice to have something sweet and something savoury. Be a dear and find me two matching plates to put them on." She cut the Turkish bread into long slices and then put them into a nice little bread basket.

Kate went over to the Chinese cupboard and selected two matching plates. She gave them to Deborah, who arranged the quiches when the bell rang again. Kate walked into the hallway to get the door. It was Meg.

"Hey, Meggie. Good timing. Did you have a busy day yesterday?" Kate asked as they hugged.

Meg had started working at Elements part-time when Kate and Deborah couldn't handle their clientele between the two of them anymore. She was the owner of a spiritual bookstore near Covent Garden, and she organised workshops on a regular basis for her customers as well. Usually on the weekend, when she didn't have to work at Elements.

"Crazy busy," Meg answered while hanging up her summer jacket.

"I invited Mr. Greyfeather again for a drumming workshop, and we were completely packed. All in all, there were thirty people I think, so it was a good thing I cleared almost the entire space."

Meg had an extra room just next to the bookshop, especially for workshops and meditations. Elements had provided massage workshops at her bookstore as well, for people who took an interest in learning just the basic skills for a partner or friend or relative. With massage tables in the room, they could attend to ten people maximum, and usually allowed no more than six to make sure everybody had enough personal attention.

"Did you use the chakra pillows?" Deborah asked, having overheard their conversation in the hallway.

"Yes, we did, and they're a perfect size, so thanks for that nice little piece of advice. It was kind of funny to see people drawn to different chakra pillows. I asked them to focus on the one they were most drawn to, as you suggested, and I think it worked out perfectly. Mr. Greyfeather said there was 'great power' in the drumming session, and he was convinced it was because people felt connected to the chakra they'd chosen," she finished with a smile.

Deborah nodded. "Makes perfect sense. I'm sorry I couldn't be there. He sounds fascinating, and this is the second time I missed him. Do you think he'll become a regular?"

Meg gave her a wink. "You're in luck then. I just closed the deal with him yesterday. We decided to have a drumming circle around every festival, so eight times a year. It won't be on the exact date, due to our own rituals, but close enough to feel the energy. He was pretty excited about it, as am I. So plenty of chances to get acquainted, darling."

Deborah looked pleased. "Excellent! I'll make sure to arrange a day off next time," she said with a shy glance at Kate.

"Oh, good god, woman, you're a full partner. Get used to it. You don't have to consult with me to take one lousy day off," Kate said, rolling her eyes.

Deborah still wasn't used to the fact they were now co-owners of Elements and that she had just as much pull as Kate did. She was starting to get used to it, and Kate always encouraged her to draw up contracts for new clients or try out new techniques.

Deborah smiled at Kate. "I know. I'll never ask again, okay?" she replied with a wicked grin.

Kate nodded. "I'll hold you to that, missy." Meg asked if she could do anything to help, when the doorbell rang again. "I'll get it!" Kate yelled as she was already walking down the hallway. Leah and Romy had arrived.

"Hey, sweetie. We were on the same train. Are we the last ones to arrive?" Leah said while she hugged Kate.

"Yep. Meg's inside with Deb. Just follow your nose, ladies," Kate said while letting go of Leah to give Romy a hug. Leah took off her coat and then walked toward the kitchen.

Romy pulled her iPhone out of her purse and looked at Kate. "Before I forget to ask, can you spare me the last week of November? The International Fitness Convention is being held then, and they asked me to give a power yoga workshop and a demo with my students."

Kate looked surprised. "Wow, that's really cool. Moving up in the world I see."

Romy was a fitness instructor with a degree in both traditional and power yoga. Kate thought she had the most amazing body. She had long, lean muscles, but she wasn't a "bag of bones," a term Kate sometimes liked to use to describe certain women in Romy's line of work. Romy was also a natural platinum-blonde girl, her hair bordering on white. It wasn't as long as Kate's, which reached almost to her derriere, but it fell well over her shoulders. With Romy's dark grey eyes, Kate always thought she was the embodiment of air, and Romy often represented the east in their rituals. It came naturally to her.

"I'm sure we can manage a week without you. Just remind me to take it up with Deb and Meg later today, so we can plan around your schedule."

Romy gave her a big smile. "Thanks, Kate. That means a lot to me. I know it's kinda last notice, but I had no idea they were that interested in me and my group."

"No problem, sweetie. I'm really happy for you." They joined the rest of the ladies.

Meg looked at Romy. "Did you ask her?" Romy nodded.

"Ask what?" Deborah asked.

Romy looked somewhat embarrassed. "I've been asked to perform at the International Fitness Convention this year with my demo group."

"No way! That's so cool, girl!" Deborah cried. Leah looked pleased as well.

"Thank you. It's in November, though, so we'll have to—"

"Oh, shut it. We'll figure something out," Deborah interrupted. Kate and Meg smiled at her response.

Romy looked relieved. "You guys are too sweet," she said.

Deborah clapped her hands. "Ladies, lunch is served, so please be seated." She had a large wooden dining table in her kitchen, which had a pretty view into her garden. Colourful comfy chairs surrounded the table, and they took their seats while Deborah laid the finishing touches to her dishes. "So, we have salmon and spinach quiche, the other one is a brie, walnut, and honey. On the big plate over there is Turkish bread with freshly made pesto, hummus, aioli, and olives. Then for our sweet tooth we have brownies, carrot cake, and homemade scones. Help yourself to the clotted cream and marmalade, girls, and well, dig in!"

They gave a round of applause. "It looks amazing, Debbie darling. You've outdone yourself," Leah said as she looked over the various plates filled with yummy goodness. Sounds of agreement came from all sides of the table.

Deborah looked pleased. She came back with five glasses on a tray filled with Prosecco, and gave each of them one.

After Deborah sat, Kate raised her glass. "A toast, if you will, to our beautiful hostess for providing such a lovely lunch, and to all you ladies, including Sue, who couldn't be here today, for being your magnificent selves. Without you, my life would be black and white instead of this beautiful rainbow. To us!"

"To us!" the girls replied.

Kate looked at Meg, who was saying something to Leah. Kate felt Meg's gaze on her, but decided to let it go. Meg didn't have empathic abilities, other than her own intuition, but she knew Meg loved her very much, so she was perhaps more attuned to pick up on minor changes than she would with just an acquaintance. Meg's ability was somewhat darker than the other ladies' who were so dear to her. She saw death. Kate knew that had been rather difficult to deal with when Meg was a little girl. She didn't see ghosts, though sometimes they thought that would have been a lot easier to deal with. No, Meg could see the moment people were about to die. Sometimes weeks before, sometimes a day before, sometimes just seconds before the actual moment. She could reverse it as well, especially when the cause of death was some sort of accident, and she'd saved many people from fatal accidents by yanking someone back from an unsuspected oncoming car, pushing them out of harm's way, or helping people choking to death on a piece of whatever in a restaurant.

She couldn't always prevent it, though. One couldn't cheat death, as Meg had learned the hard way when she'd failed to save her own mother from a disease she'd only picked up on when it was too late. "People die when they are supposed to die," Meg had said to her once. Kate knew Meg believed this with all her heart. So if she got a chance to intervene—she believed she was meant to intervene—it wasn't his or her time to go.

Of their little group Meg was the one who had the greatest difficulty to "hide" her natural-born gift. Kate always said she looked like freaking Snow White, and meant that as a compliment, but one could see where that remark came from. Meg had black hair, but pale skin with natural full red lips.

When Kate first made her Snow White remark to Deborah in Meg's presence, Deborah had laughed, and said, "I see what you mean, but you're more like Angelina Jolie to me." To which Kate had replied, "Well, yeah, if Angelina would play Snow White, sure."

Meg and Deborah had rolled their eyes. There was just no arguing with Kate. Deborah was perhaps closer to the mark. With Meg's darker ability, she also had a slightly darker aura around her, not very Snow White-like. People, especially men, were often scared of her, as if they could sense what she could do. She'd got used to that in time, but sometimes it still hurt when she noticed someone avoiding her.

Meg nudged Leah's elbow. "Is Kate feeling okay?" she whispered.

Leah frowned. "Yes, fine. Why do you ask?"

Meg shook her head. "It's probably nothing then. She has a weird … hang on." Meg focussed her eyes on Leah. "You have it too." She looked over at Deb and Romy. "You all have it. Hmm, weird. I've never seen this before. Maybe it's a bug or something."

Leah stared at her. "Oh great, Meg," she whispered back, "that's a real comfort."

Meg sighed. "Forget I said anything. Please don't tell the others. It's probably nothing and they'll only worry."

Leah rolled her eyes, but nodded.

Kate noticed Deborah looked in Meg's direction, probably picking up on the anxiety she felt as well, and she saw Meg relax. Deborah gave Meg a smile and offered the plate with salmon quiches to Romy, who sat next to her.

Conversations flew back and forth across the table. Romy was filling Deborah in on the latest developments in her demo group, and Deb told Romy about her upcoming plans for a new workshop they'd give at Meg's store come January. Across the table Leah leaned toward Meg and asked if she'd heard the latest Kate gossip.

Meg looked interested, especially when Kate rolled her eyes. "No, do tell," she said with a grin.

And Leah was off into a detailed description of Tristan, Kate's new mysterious neighbour. Kate made a show of pushing her chair toward Romy and Deborah, which got a laugh out of Meg and Leah. Aini strolled into the kitchen to see if anything would come her way, but when she got no response from them, she left through the double doors and then laid herself down on one of the terrace chairs in the sun.

They were quite a colourful bunch. Kate's remark about her life being a rainbow, thanks to her friends, wasn't that hard to imagine when you took a good look at them chattering away while they enjoyed their lunch. Kate, with her extremely long hair and bright green eyes, was always a sight to see, even with her small frame and lack of height.

Deborah, with her modern-cut hair and looks was always dressed according to the latest fashion, which usually meant she was one step ahead of the crowd and the catwalk. They often took their cue from her, especially when they had to go somewhere and dress for the occasion, with the exception of Kate, who was just too stubborn and had developed her own style, which seemed to work for her. Even Kate, however, went to Deborah when she wanted to do something special with her hair or makeup.

Romy, the youngest of the group, was also the quiet one in their little sisterhood. Being so active in life as a fitness instructor and working at

Elements, she oozed calm, even though she was only twenty-seven. Today she had her hair pulled up high in a braided ponytail, which bounced on her back with every move. She usually wore tight-fitting clothes—with her figure she could get away with almost anything—but having white hair and grey eyes, she tried to choose something colourful to wear as often as she could, to match with her usual black.

Sue, who wasn't present today, was the only redhead in the group. Being a healer and having a musician as a husband, she travelled the world a lot, which didn't always match with the busy schedules of the rest of the group. She never missed Kate's Halloween cocktail party, though, and they were looking forward to catching up with her.

When the food was almost gone and tea had turned into wine, they moved from the dining table toward the living area where they made themselves comfortable. Kate helped Deborah clean up in the kitchen, which didn't take long thanks to Deborah's organised way of thinking and the trusty help of a dishwasher. Once they were done, they joined the rest of the party, and Deborah put on some music. Kate smiled at the sounds of The National through the speakers. Deborah loved them.

"So, Catherine dear," Meg said with a posh English accent, "pray tell and let us know your divine plans for Samhuinn." The girls laughed.

For the last two years, they'd celebrated each of the eight festivals together, and Samhuinn represented the beginning of the new year to them. It was also the festival when the veil between our world and the otherworld was at its thinnest. Samhuinn was perhaps the darkest of the festivals, if such a term could be used to describe a ritual done by lightworkers, because of its connection with death. It was about honouring the dead, your ancestors, death and rebirth itself. Wiccans celebrated the festivals, as did the druids and other nature religion-based groups. Some of their group came from these traditions. Some from very different paths.

Two years ago, Kate had felt the earth shift. It had cried, and she hadn't been able to shut it out. For days and days it went on until she confided in Leah and Deborah, and they decided to work their combined magic to bring healing to the earth. It had worked. The crying had subsided to a slight humming noise, and Kate could breathe again. It was in that moment she'd realised the balance between light and dark was off, and not in their favour. So they'd gathered their friends and asked them if they'd noticed anything different of late. Almost every one of them had sensed something or had felt uneasy the last couple days. Deborah explained to them what had happened to Kate, and how they'd performed a healing ritual to try to stop it, to increase the balance of the world again.

Meg had jumped up, and said, "We have to do something then. We all have our unique gifts between the six of us, and maybe we can find even more. We have a responsibility to ourselves and our world. We didn't receive these gifts for nothing!"

There had been a big mumbling of agreement. She'd spoken with such passion it'd humbled even Kate, and she'd been immensely grateful to hear her own wishes spoken out loud by the people she loved and cared about. Eventually their group had expanded to thirteen women, friends of her friends, some with gifts of their own, some with a background in magic, but all with love for mankind and the earth.

And so their ritual work, their healing work, had begun. Not just during the festivals, but also on a day-to-day basis. Whenever, wherever, they could help the forces of light, they did it.

Meg, with her powers of seeing death, kept tabs on heads of State and known terrorist groups to see if anything shifted on that side. Leah helped her along with her ability to see the future, which drove her up the wall sometimes, because she couldn't see very far, and with them interfering quite often, it constantly changed. Deborah and Sue often healed people, mostly under the guise of being a mental coach from the hospital if someone important to the course of events was brought in. They had to be careful, though, as Sue had been caught once already when she'd forgotten to pull her hair back and take off all her jewellery. A doctor had found her in a patient's room with her hands hovering just above his heart. With her red hair flaming around her, she'd let her power fade away as fast as she could, but the shocked look on the doctor's face had told her that he'd seen something.

Thankfully, that was where Romy had come in. With her ability to glamour people, she could make them focus on something else. She had been her "guard dog" and her saviour that day, though it'd taken her quite a lot of time to let the good doctor think he'd seen a ray of sunshine instead of a woman with flaming red hair and glowing hands. Sue had been utterly embarrassed, and from that moment on always wore a short, dark brown wig when she was sent into a hospital.

Kate, being an elemental, sent them in all directions, wherever she felt something off, joining her group of women whenever she could or when her particular powers were needed. She'd also been rather busy helping the fire department, since there was a group out there targeting financial companies. So she helped by providing lots and lots of rain to aid them in their efforts, as she couldn't dampen the fire without raising a whole bunch of questions.

All in all, they led quite busy lives, and sometimes the strain got to them. It was moments like these, just getting together for a nice lunch, chatting about life and the universe, that made it all worth it and helped them relax, recharge, and enjoy life in general.

Kate took a sip of her chardonnay and then smiled at Meg. "Well, darling Meg, I do have a special treat for you all," she said with a mysterious smile. A round of "ooooohhhhs" went through the room, and Kate laughed again.

"No, seriously, though, I'd like to try something different, if you all are up for it, that is. Lee is standing north, Deb represents south, Romy will be east, and Meg will hold west." They all nodded. They'd gone over that already. "Sue has agreed to be one part of the portal to the otherworld, and I think she asked her friend, Sheila, to work beside her. They work well together, and I have complete faith in them to hold it up for over an hour."

Silence fell over the living room, and Asmara, who'd been lying on the sofa, stretched, got up and left the room as if to say, "You're on your own here."

"Um, what do you mean for over an hour, Kate? The portal is only opened to invite our ancestors in, right? To join us in celebration and honour them and then they take their leave again." Romy looked around the group for confirmation. Meg and Deborah made noises of agreement, Leah just kept looking at Kate. Kate realised Leah probably had a pretty good idea of what was coming.

"Yes, I'll get to the ancestor part later. I think we should do something before the ritual to honour them, but it's a special year this year. We'll be celebrating under a blue moon, and with the recent positive changes, I think we should try something bigger to perhaps tip the scales of balance toward the side of light. So instead of inviting the ancestors in, I'd like to invite the forces of the elements in, to unite them and send them out into the world."

Leah sent her a soft smile. Deborah looked slightly shocked, but tried to hide it as well as she could. Meg looked quite dumbstruck, and Romy had the same expression on her face.

"Say what?" Meg asked. "The actual elements? As in, we can all see them and shit, not just calling the quarters and having a nice representation of them in the circle?"

"That would be the general idea, yes," Kate replied.

Meg leaned back in her squishy chair. "And you've had experience with this, I presume? I must say, I'm intrigued, but also a bit scared."

Kate noticed Leah and Meg exchanged a glance and made a mental note to ask Leah about it later. Kate hesitated for just a second and looked at Leah and Deborah. They were the only ones, besides her mother, who knew what had happened the first time she tried her full powers. It was time to increase that number. "In a matter of speaking, Meg. Some of you perhaps know that when I was still living in the Netherlands, I was also part of a group of lightworkers."

Meg and Romy nodded. They'd heard this several times, and also that the group had quite abruptly fallen apart.

"The initiator of that group was a man, and one of my dearest friends and partner for quite some time. He had great power. Like you, Meg, he could see death, but he also had empathic abilities, which effectively made him a master of death. He could bend people to his will, if he wanted to. I know this sounds rather negative, but he never used it to manipulate, only to guide and help people see the solution to their own problems. That is until someone tried to hurt his family. After that, he changed, and so did his powers. They shifted. I felt it, and we grew further and further apart. Where once we'd agreed there was a very fine line protecting the innocent and punishing the guilty, he seemed to find more and more reasons to punish the guilty. May the gods forgive me, but I let it go on for too long. I didn't want to accept I'd lost my friend. I tried to make him see the error of his ways, but he wouldn't listen. One day he confided in me that he'd get rid of a man who was responsible for the latest drug abuse increase, and I reasoned with him to just get the evidence and let justice prevail. He scoffed at me for being so naïve. We were way more suited to deliver justice, and I'd do well to come to his way of thinking. I said I wouldn't let him go through with it. I think he mistook my kindness for weakness, and we ended up facing each other in front of his building." Kate took a deep breath. They were all hanging on to her story.

"What happened?" Romy whispered.

"He unleashed death on me. I felt it coming, along with his will to let me die, and I reached inside myself and just let everything out. It was immense, and they just manifested, all four of them—fire, air, water, and earth. They soared his way and smashed into his body. He … He fell to the ground, and when I called his name, he didn't seem to recognise me. I called an ambulance, and they drove him to hospital. I said he'd just fallen, never even told them I knew him. He's been in a mental hospital ever since. I think … I think they took his mind, or his soul perhaps, I don't know. I used my powers that day out of fear, out of survival, not out of love, and I'm sorry for that. I'm not sorry I survived, however. It took me a very long time to reconcile with the power that lies dormant within me. I'd very much like to try to see what my powers can do when love is the great motivator behind them." A single tear glided down her cheek, and when she looked up, they were all crying. Deborah was even sobbing out loud.

"Oh, honey, that must have been terrible!" Meg stood and gave her a great big hug. Kate smiled and gave her one in return.

Romy looked at her in awe. "I can't believe he'd do that to you. You were his friend, his partner. That must have been so hard on you."

Kate looked at Romy. "It was. I had Leah to help me through, though. Deb and I met just after. It came up some years later, so she already knew as well, but before we try something like this, I thought you should all fully understand what my powers can do and what happened. I trust you all with my life," she finished.

"Does Sue know?" Meg asked.

Kate shook her head. "No, not yet. I didn't want to tell her over the phone, so I will on Thursday. She thinks she's coming over a bit earlier to help prepare for the party, but I wanted some quiet time to tell her in person."

Leah looked at her. "So instead of asking the sea for answers, we're going to ask all the elements," she said, smiling. It was a reference to a Placebo song, and Kate looked at her in surprise and gave a short laugh.

"I doubt he meant it that way, but come to think of it, pretty much, yes. Water represents our emotions. It's quite a beautiful phrase, actually. But listen, you all, I won't have any of this if there's just the slightest hesitation or fear or something. We should really talk this through."

Leah sat up straighter. "You know how I feel, darling. I trust you and your powers completely. My only fear was your own, and you seem to have dealt with that particular demon. So without wanting to sound too much like Jodie Foster, I'm good to go," she finished with a grin.

Meg looked around. "Honey, I think that goes for all of us, including Sue and the others. We're not only friends. We also started doing this to make a difference. Now that we may have an actual chance, I think we should use the opportunity. Who knows what we might achieve?"

Kate looked around to check her friends' responses and saw nothing but determination on their faces. Sometimes she still underestimated the love they felt for each other. It sent a warm glow through her. "Okay, tell you what. Let's go with it for now and work out some of the details. Then we can decide later on whether or not we go through with it or just do our 'normal' ritual. How does that sound?"

"Sounds fair," Deborah said while the rest of them responded with similar reactions.

"Okay, first things first. What about location?" Leah asked, always the practical one. "Did you want to go out to London Fields again?"

Kate nodded. "We'll probably have to drive. It won't be practical to travel by public transport, carrying cauldrons and what not. We want to attract as little attention as possible. I'll borrow my mother's car, and I wanted to ask Meg if we could use her station wagon as well." She looked at the latter while saying that.

"Sure," said Meg, "my trusty steed is at your service."

"Then I think we have the wheels covered," Kate said more to herself than everyone.

"London Fields is still closed to the public then?" Romy asked.

"At the far end, yes. They opened up the first area a few weeks ago after the murder incident, but that part is still closed. It's not guarded anymore, though. I checked last week. We won't have any trouble getting there, and there's minimum chance of exposure I think. Worst case scenario, we do get caught and will probably get off with a fine. Also, we can leave the cars near the entrance and then cross the last yard or so on foot. Now, for this to work, it'd be ideal to have all thirteen of us present. Anyone think that's going to be a problem?" Kate waited for their responses.

Romy was the first to speak up. "I know for a fact the twins are going to be present. I spoke to them the day before yesterday, so that's them. You said Sheila was tagging along with Sue, so that's her as well. Which leaves Caroline, Helen, Sam, and Joni."

"Samantha is coming," Deb said.

Kate nodded as well. "Yes, Sam's also coming to the Halloween party, as are the twins. I haven't heard from the others, though. Anyone else?"

Meg came out of the kitchen with another bottle of wine to refill their glasses. As she went round, she said, "Caroline asked me for a ride, so that's a yes, and I'll give Helen and Joni a call tonight. How about that?"

Kate looked pleased. "That would be great, Meg. Remember to remind them of the party as well if you would. I haven't seen them for over a month."

Meg saluted her. "Yes, ma'am. Will do," she said, grinning. Kate pretended to slap her over the head.

"Kate, do you have any idea if and how it'll affect the people representing an element?" Deborah asked.

"I've thought about it, yes, and I can't know for sure, of course, but I think you'll be able to feel the element you're representing through me. However, we have to have a trial run, and seeing as it's Sunday already, that's probably not going to be realistic. Again though, if there's anything uncomfortable during the ritual, we won't go through with it and fall back to our regular one."

Deborah nodded. "That's all fine, but it's a shame, though. I'm actually quite curious to see what would happen, and what it will feel like. How does fire feel to you, Kate?" she asked.

Kate laughed. "Um … it varies, I suppose. To me, fire is warmth, love, and passion. It's also where my anger comes from, so it can be destructive as well. I never feel burned, though. It's more like you're surrounded by flames, but they're a part of you, so they don't hurt you. You feed off its energy. Does that make any sense to you?"

Deborah looked really interested. So did the others.

"Actually, that makes a lot of sense," Leah replied. "I always thought of the elements as a part of you, Kate, but I'm curious to find out if your powers will surge through us, so to speak. It sounds something like a vessel."

Kate looked at her. "I think you hit the nail right on the head there. If everyone is open and true to their element, I think it should be able to go straight through you. More so, I think, with all our powers combined, it'll make mine stronger. So hopefully when it flows back through me, I can send it off into the world full force, so to speak."

There were a lot of excited murmurs going up. Kate felt grateful they were all obviously interested and looking forward to this instead of being scared. Once again she felt blessed to have such good friends.

* * *

The afternoon came to an end, and they were still in the process of catching up, discussing details of the upcoming ritual, theories about what would happen running wilder with the increase of wine, combined with a lot of laughter while Kate shook her head or rolled her eyes. Deborah offered to provide dinner as well, but Romy and Meg were expected home by their husbands, so they'd be leaving soon.

Kate looked at Leah to see if she wanted to stay, but Leah stood up as well. "Come on, we'll help you in the kitchen and then get out of your hair. You've done enough." She picked up a few glasses at a time and then walked into the kitchen.

Meg and Romy followed suit, ignoring Deborah's protestations that she didn't need any help. With the five of them in the kitchen, her place was cleaned up in fifteen minutes. The girls got their coats, and there was a lot of hugging, kissing, "see you soon" and "thank you" going through the hallway.

Meg walked over to her car and looked at the other ladies. "Anybody need a ride home?"

"Well, if it's no trouble, I wouldn't mind one," Romy said.

"Hop in, darling!"

Leah thanked her for the offer, but she'd just take the train. After they waved goodbye to Meg and Romy and started walking toward the Underground station, Kate looked at her friend and asked if she'd like to grab a bite somewhere.

Leah grinned. "I thought you'd never ask!"

MONDAY

KATE SIGHED after she hung up the phone. She was just done with her morning clients, and was looking forward to a lazy afternoon, when a client of hers called. He was on tour and momentarily back in the UK, and if she could please, please, please fit him in for a, what he called, energy session. After the usual back and forth comments about their insane touring schedule and that she couldn't be used as a "personal healer," she gave in anyway. She was sure he'd been betting on that. Bugger, she still sucked at saying no. Just when she was about to start a good sulking spree, Deborah came through the moss wall.

"*Pff* … Man, I could eat a horse! You're lucky to be done for the day." Kate glared daggers at her. "Oh dear, now what?" she asked with a crooked smile.

Kate rolled her eyes and put on a dramatic expression. "He who shall not be mentioned is completely surprised that people are, in fact, not built to last through six touring days in a row across two continents and is now suffering the consequences. If I'd be so kind to fix him up, he'd be good to go and do it all over again on some other continent. I swear to the gods, man plus musician equals moron!"

Deborah looked sympathetic. "Sorry, love, my bad. I brought him in, after all, because I knew you liked their music. I shall refrain from this in the future and only seek out artists whose music you either despise or who have their lives completely in check and just come to us for relaxation. How does that sound?"

Kate looked at her with one raised eyebrow. "Like la-la-land. By all means, try," she finished with a smile. She walked over to her sitting area and let herself fall onto the couch.

"Anything else bothering you, love? You look a bit put out, and I doubt Mr. High Maintenance is solely responsible for that." She sat on the chair next to Kate.

Kate ran her hands through her hair and sighed. "No, you're right, of course. Though I'm bothered by the fact that some people seem to care so little about what happens to their bodies and minds. I'll never understand how someone can write such beautiful lyrics about our world and how we should live in it while neglecting his own needs. No, I just had a bad start today, woke up from a nightmare. Probably because we talked about what happened with Alan yesterday. And now I feel slightly tense about going out for dinner with Tristan, which is just stupid, I know, but still." Kate gave Deborah an unhappy look.

Deborah put her hand over Kate's. "Sweetie, it's not stupid. It's perfectly normal. You lost the love of your life and your best friend to the dark side, and here's this mysterious new neighbour guy who's dark and handsome, and you have a feeling he's hiding something. Of course you feel tense. Do you want to talk about it?" she asked softly. Kate hesitated. "Tell you what, I'll make us lunch, and you talk while I'm in the kitchen," she said as she got up and walked over to Kate's kitchen. "How about I make us a salad?" She poked her head inside Kate's fridge.

Kate smiled. "Sounds lovely." She played with an obsidian stone that lay on the kitchen counter. "It actually started out quite nice. I was out with Tristan, I think in a gallery somewhere, and he was telling me all about the paintings and why they meant so much to him, it felt … I don't know, normal? As if we'd been doing this for quite some time. There was this one painting, a bit like Pyke Koch, except it wasn't, but it had the same dark vibe. It was a corn field with a man standing inside it, and when I looked closer it was Alan. He was trying to say something to me, so I leaned in and suddenly the painting came to life, and he pulled me in. He screamed at me for giving up on him, and how was this guy going to be any different? I tried to pull myself free. He just laughed. 'Silly girl,' he said, 'you're still not seeing the big picture, now are you? So naive, yet so beautiful.' I pulled again with all my might and stumbled out of the painting. I looked around to see where Tristan was, but I couldn't find him. The gallery wasn't there anymore, and I was at the site in Holland where I had my final encounter with Alan. Only the building had a different name. It had Empathy in golden letters, and they glowed when I looked at it. I remember screaming, thinking Alan would come back to haunt me or something. That's when I woke up, sweating like a pig. Oh, and I broke the lights in my bedroom. They all went bust the second I opened my eyes. Probably too much energy floating around." Kate let out another big sigh.

Deborah had a concentrated look on her face while she cut up tomatoes and then stopped to look at Kate. "Hmm, Empathy, huh? Your empathy, Alan's empathy, or was it referring to the possibility that Tristan is an empath? And then there's the whole not seeing the big picture thing. Alan's an empath right?" she asked.

Kate nodded. "Yes, he was, is, I should say. There's no reason to assume he's lost his abilities." She was starting to feel better just by talking about it in a rational manner and trying to figure out what it might mean.

Kate trusted Deb's opinion in these matters. She was usually pretty good in dream interpretation, probably because she had empathic powers herself. And having known Kate for quite some time now, she'd developed a knack to distinguish between Kate's "normal" dreams and more "prophetic" ones. Kate wondered how she'd interpret this one.

"Did you, at any moment, get the feeling Tristan might have empathic powers?" Deborah asked.

Kate flipped through the few moments they'd shared together, letting them appear in her mind. Her mood swings, the uneasiness she'd felt at first and then the complete opposite, her wanting to join him for a cup of tea.

"I'm not sure," she said. "He could have empathic abilities, but he could also just have really good powers of persuasion, if you know what I mean."

Deborah nodded. "Lee didn't 'get' anything when she saw him, I presume?"

Kate shook her head. "No. Well, no visions, anyway. She did get a slight uneasy feeling. She said he was intense, and I actually agree with her on that count. We talked about it over dinner last night. She had me promise to text her the location of wherever we'd end up for dinner, just to be on the safe side." She smiled.

Deborah smiled as well. "Sounds like some good advice."

Kate agreed.

"I could hang out in the hallway for a bit, see if I bump into him," Deborah mused.

Kate laughed. "I think that's taking our presumptions a bit far, darling. You'll have to wait until Thursday, unless you meet him unexpectedly in the hallway, but to go in full stake-out mode is a bit much for now I think," she said with a grin.

Just being able to share her worries with her friend and partner made her feel a whole lot better. She was just knackered from the nightmare, which had brought back old memories she thought she'd dealt with. She put her arms above her head and gave her body a good stretch. "That salad looks great. I'm actually starting to feel hungry again. Thanks for listening to me, sweetie. Just talking about this has helped a lot. I'll see if I can figure out if he has any emphatic abilities, without just coming straight out and asking him, that is. If he does, chances are he's just as cautious as me to let that little fact slip. Oh, Meg called last night. Helen and Joni are coming to the party, and will be available for the Samhuinn ritual."

Deborah put down two plates and some cutlery on the dinner table and then walked back to the kitchen to get a large pitcher of water with two glasses. As they sat, Deborah said, "Great. It'll be good to see them. As for Tristan, sounds like a plan, but handle with care indeed. Some men are more open about their abilities than women, but not many, so he'll have to trust you to tell you anything."

Kate snorted unladylike. "Well, that goes for us both then, doesn't it?"

Deborah put some salad onto their plates and then poured them glasses of water. "You don't think you can trust him?" she asked.

"I don't know. I feel as if I could trust him with my life in a James Bond kind of way. I'm just not sure if I can trust him with my heart."

Deborah looked sympathetic. "I know that feeling for sure, but at least you consider him one of the good guys, and that's a start, right?" she asked, smiling.

"I suppose it is, yes. Perhaps I'm seeing ghosts that aren't even there. What's the worst that can happen? He turns out to be a badass motherfucker, and I blow his ass to kingdom come," she finished lightly. They laughed and then enjoyed the rest of their lunch, catching up on each other's clients.

*   *   *

When it was almost two o'clock, Kate changed into one of her wellness outfits, cleaned up their lunch and went through the moss wall to wait for her client to arrive. On cue, he came through the door after just a couple seconds. Frankly, he looked exhausted, even if he was all smiles.

"Thank you so much for seeing me on such short notice, Kate. I really appreciate this, and I do hope you know that."

She sighed and motioned for him to follow her to the healing area. "Yes, I do. How was Tokyo?"

"Good, good. We had a nice response from the audience. Glad to touch home base for a couple days, though. This is the part of the tour where we get little to no rest. With all the travelling and such, it makes it harder to adjust, you know." He looked a bit timid.

Kate looked him up and down. Fire was totally off, almost empty. Earth was out of balance as well. Hardly surprising. Air was holding up rather impressively, and water was a complete mess. Probably more to do with his state of mind, as water was connected to our emotions.

He stared at her. "Well, how bad is it?" he asked with a look that said he expected the worst.

Kate smiled. "It could have been worse, I guess. Your energy level is extremely low, though. We'll fix that with a nice healing session. I'm also putting you back on grounding exercises. That will take you five minutes before you wake up and five again before you go to bed. Don't skip them. I'll know next time I see you." She had a stern look on her face.

"Wouldn't dream of it, ma'am," he said, grinning.

Kate looked sceptical. "Furthermore, I'm going to teach you something that will help you maintain your energy. It'll take some practise. It's what we refer to as a healing flame exercise. It's used in various forms of nature religion under different names." He looked interested. "I want you to perform it every night before a gig. Now what I'm about to say isn't criticism, just observation, okay? So just hear me out." He nodded. "You give too much to the audience. It's something you do automatically. Lots of artists do it. There's nothing wrong with it, but it can literally drain you. Sometimes the vibe of an audience is so good, and you're so open to them, they give their energy back to you. That can feel really rewarding, but it can also confuse the hell out of you, as they aren't your own emotions."

He looked surprised. "That's exactly how I feel sometimes!" he exclaimed. "Sorry, you were saying."

Kate smiled. "I know, that's why I'm saying this to you. What the healing flame exercise will do for you, is put your body in a nice little bubble. Some people see it as white light, others as golden or yellow. It doesn't really matter. Whatever comes naturally to you. I'm going to teach you how to do it. After some practise, you can put it up in just a few seconds. Just ask the bubble to stay with you through the entire concert, and it will stay with you. When you're done, thank the energy for helping you. You can also give thanks to God or a god or goddess or the universe. Well, you get the point. Whatever you believe in. If you don't believe in anything, just thank the energy. That will work just as well."

"Is it like a healing session with you?" he asked.

"I guess you could see it as a form of one, yes. Only performed by yourself," Kate replied.

"I won't detach myself from the crowd?" He looked a bit worried.

She smiled. "No, not at all. General positive vibes will still get through. It'll just protect you from what we call 'high emotions.' It'll also protect against negative emotions, though with so many young people liking your music, I don't think that's a bad idea." She winked.

He raised an eyebrow. "Hmm, good point."

Kate went to the massage table. "Okay, so first things first. Let's get you energized again. You may leave your t-shirt and underwear on, and lie down on the table on your back." She pulled the curtains closed to give him some privacy and then walked to the little stereo. "You like piano music, right?" she asked over her shoulder.

"Depends on the piano music I suppose, but generally, yes."

"Dustin O'Halloran okay?"

"Oh yes, that's nice. I have his work."

She heard him climbing onto the massage table. After she selected some of Dustin's early work before she pressed play, she grabbed a warm fluffy towel and then walked over to the curtain. She pulled it back before she draped it over his body, making sure his feet were completely wrapped as well. She put a roll-shaped pillow under his knees and then slightly lifted his head to put a small pillow underneath.

"Are you comfortable?" she asked. He just nodded, his eyes already closed. "If at any point the heat becomes too intense, or you experience something unpleasant, just say so, okay?"

He nodded again. They'd gone through several healing sessions together, but she always went over the procedure with her clients, just in case someone forgot or wasn't completely in the moment.

Kate focussed on the fire element inside her and let it come to the surface. Now she looked for the part where the energy came from. There it was, like electricity building. She let it roll through her body to her hands, and took a deep, grounding breath.

"I'm going to start at your feet," she let him know.

She first held her hands above his feet, to let him get familiar with the heat emanating from her. After a few seconds, she lightly put them on him. He let out a sigh and relaxed. Slowly, she worked her way up, moving from his ankles to his knees. Then to his thighs and respectfully hovering her hands above his genitals. She placed one hand on each hip and moved up toward his tummy and to his chest. She lingered at his throat and lungs, giving them a bit more attention. She noticed him slightly tensing.

"Breathe in," she softly said and watched him respond. "And breathe out again." She waited a few seconds and then repeated the movement. "Breathe in ... and out again."

His breathing hitched, and she felt the emotions inside him battling to come out. He was having difficulties letting go. He trusted her, but it was still hard for him. Our fifth chakra, also known as the throat chakra, often became blocked. When, metaphorically, at least, we feel as if we can't use our voice or we feel as if we're not being heard, we choke up. As a singer, that was always going to be both his strong side and his weakness.

She decided to turn to earth as well to help him ground and feel safe. She reached inside herself to connect to that part of her, lying in the hands of the Great Mother, feeling protected, warm and safe, and let it flow through her hands toward his throat and lungs. He relaxed again and a tear slid down his cheek. Gently, she wiped it away and then moved around the table to stand in front of his head. She covered his ears, let earth fade away and focussed on fire to do its work.

She moved her hands to hover over his eyelids. Once she was done, she went back to one side and laid them over his heart. She felt his heartbeat. It was a nice steady rhythm, and she smiled to herself. She looked at his body with her inner eye and noticed his energy level was back to approximately ninety percent. The rest would return on its own in the following days, if he heeded her advice.

A good thirty minutes had passed, which Kate had expected, seeing as his energy level had been so low when he'd walked into the building. Softly she laid a hand on his head, and said, "When you feel ready, you may open your eyes and slowly get up. I'll get you some water. Take your time, okay?"

He stretched his legs as she pulled the curtains around the table again. Kate walked into the reception area where there was a fridge with cold water and energy drinks. She took out two bottles of water and then returned to the massage and healing room. She sat on the red chakra pillow, which resembled the first chakra of the body, and waited for her client to come out. After a few minutes, he took a seat on the blue chakra pillow, and she smiled to herself. He'd chosen the fifth chakra, the throat chakra. She always loved how that worked. She gave him his bottle of water.

"You have to drink it all," she said, smiling.

He smiled back. "That was different," he said.

"How are you feeling?"

"Good. Way better than just one hour ago." He laughed. "I feel oddly 'together' I guess. And safe, for lack of a better word." He looked a bit embarrassed now.

"That would be spot on," Kate said. "You know I work with the elements, right?" He nodded, though by the look on his face she could tell he didn't exactly know what that meant.

He wasn't the only one. Many people just accepted what Kate could do, because it did wonders for their health. Understanding how it exactly worked, or that she was an elemental, was a whole different ballgame. There were a few clients who moved in spiritual circles who had an inkling, but not many.

"Well, what you felt was the energy of earth, which is very different from fire. The energy I use to get you back on your feet, so to speak. If you think about it, earth is where we all come from. Mother Earth, the womb and all that. So it's perfectly normal you felt safe. In the arms of Mother Earth, if you will."

He looked relieved to hear his reaction was a completely normal one. People were always afraid that something was wrong with them. "It also felt, I don't know, normal. As if it was a part of me?"

Kate looked up. "Can I ask you what your star sign is?"

He looked surprised at her question. "Taurus, why?"

Kate smiled. "Because people usually have a deep connection with their own element. Taurus is an earth sign. Didn't you know that?"

He laughed. "No, I'm not really into that, but I'll take your word for it."

He looked much better. His eyes were bright again, and Kate felt pretty pleased with herself. This was the rewarding part of her private practice, the reason she still loved what she did.

"Now that your energy is holding up again, are you ready for a little exercise?"

"Bring it on, sweet cheeks!"

Kate grinned. *Getting back to his usual self indeed,* she thought. "Okay, in order for this to work properly, we start with grounding while breathing in and out with purpose."

"That's the tree-thingy, right?" he asked with a look of concentration.

She laughed. "Yes, the tree-thingy, as you so eloquently put it. Sit up straight and imagine your spine is the trunk of a tree. Your roots go deep into the earth. With every breath you take, you let the life force of the tree flow into your body. When you breathe out again, let all your worries go, let it seep into the earth. You breathe energy in and tension out again." Kate attuned herself to his breathing rhythm and breathed in and out with him. After two minutes, she said, "That's good. Just keep breathing in and out at your own pace. Close your eyes. Now I want you to visualize a nice glowing light around your navel. This is the easiest place to start, as it's near your solar plexus and is called that for a reason." He smiled while he concentrated on his breathing. "You're doing great. Can you see a little ball of light?"

"Yes, it's very bright, like gold-yellow or something."

Kate nodded, even though he couldn't see her. "That's perfect," she said. "Now I want you to expand the little ball of light. Just let it stretch until you're completely inside it." She concentrated on her fire element again to see what he saw, and was pleased to notice his ball of light expanding quite rapidly. Apparently, he was a natural.

"Wow!" he said. "Is it always like this? This is pretty awesome."

"Pretty cool, huh!" she replied. "To answer your question, a true healing flame is like this, yes. Apparently, you're quite a natural, because I expected to practise a lot longer than this. Now try opening your eyes and see if you can hold it."

He concentrated again as he slowly opened his eyes. It was still there. Kate could see it and apparently so could he. He smiled.

"Well done!" she said, smiling.

He looked really pleased. "It doesn't feel like hard work. I expected this would be way more difficult."

Kate nodded. "For a lot of people it is hard work. Everybody can learn this, but it does help if you have a certain flair for it. You seem to be one of those people."

He looked at her with quite a serious expression. "You live in an interesting world, Miss van Dyk, I have to say."

Kate smiled. "I could say the same about you. Now, let it reduce to a small little ball again around your navel and then let it disappear altogether. Be sure to thank whatever it is you wish to thank."

He concentrated again, and she watched as his healing flame reduced to a small light hovering over his navel and then disappeared completely. She gave him a few more moments, and wondered who he'd be thanking. She didn't really know much about his personal life, nor did she need to. Sometimes she wondered, though, when people had a natural gift, if they'd want to enhance it had they chosen a different life.

He opened his eyes again. "Do you think this will hold an entire concert?"

Kate nodded. "With practice, yes. Probably not the first time, but you'll feel a difference all the same. If you work on it every day, I think you'll have it down pretty quickly, and your energy level will remain stable much longer."

He looked relieved. "Good, because I won't be anywhere near London for the next month or two, and I was getting pretty worried I'd have to cancel gigs."

Kate was thoughtful for a moment. "Tell you what, and don't take this lightly, but if, and only if, you feel really bad and the healing flame isn't working, you give me a call. I'll be able to help you from a distance."

He looked shocked. "You can do this from afar?"

"Yes. Though it works slightly different, and I don't want this splattered across music land. I hope I'm making myself perfectly clear on this." She gave him a very stern look.

"No, bejesus, of course! You have my word. I'm really glad you offered me something like that. I mean, I hope I don't need it, but it's comforting to know there's help out there if I really need it. Thank you. I mean really, thank you."

Kate grinned. "Don't thank me just yet. Wait until you see my bill."

He laughed. "You're well worth it, Kate, as I'm sure you're very much aware."

They got up and walked over to the reception area. Kate gave him another bottle of water and told him to drink it on the way home. "Good luck on the rest of the tour, and remember your homework," she said.

"I'll let you know how it's going," he replied.

"No, you won't," she said, laughing. "And that's okay. Just as long as you take the time to practise."

He looked a bit sheepish. There were rumours that Kate could read people's minds, and at this moment she could tell he wondered if they were correct. She couldn't. However, she just knew enough about the daily life of an artist to know they hardly knew in what country they were playing, let alone keep in touch with someone, and she understood that.

"I will. I really will, and thank you again," he said and gave her a big hug.

Kate was surprised for just a moment. He usually wasn't the touchy/feely kind of person. She returned the hug. She saw him outside and waved a last goodbye as the lift doors closed.

Kate returned to her healing room, cleaned up, and cleared the room with an abalone shell filled with burning sage. After that, she opened the windows to let in fresh air. Looking around and checking to see if the room was "neutral," she nodded to herself and then closed the door behind her.

She sat in the reception area and updated her paperwork for today. She put her letters and bills in the letter tray that was marked "outgoing mail." Deborah would add hers and mail them at the end of the day. Last one in the building was responsible for outgoing mail. It was now half past three, and she'd have plenty of time to take a shower, relax a bit, and then get ready for her date with Tristan. She hoped he'd found a nice place. Kate was looking forward to seeing him again. She left a note for Deborah, saying she was at home taking a shower and would either see her tomorrow or Deborah could drop by for a bit if she felt like it.

After stepping through the moss wall, she closed it behind her. If Deborah wanted to drop by, she'd ring the bell. Kate walked over to her bedroom before she took off her clothes, which she dropped into the hamper. She turned on the lights in her bathroom and then walked over to her docking station and connected her iPod. Scrolling down, she finally decided to go with Ella Fitzgerald. She loved listening to Ella while soaking in the tub. Slowly moving to the music filling the apartment, she unbraided her hair and waited for the tub to fill. Her hair brushed her buttocks while she made a spin. She loved the feel of it on her back, and closed her eyes, listening to the music, letting her body respond to the tunes.

After a few minutes, she went back to the bathroom to see if the water level was high enough. It was more than half full, and she dipped a toe in to see if it was the right temperature. Satisfied, she sank into the tub until her head was under as well. She leaned over to the side to grab a bottle. She added some pink bubbles and then rested her head back to hum along with the music.

Once her fingertips were wrinkly, Kate got out of the tub before she grabbed a fluffy towel. She wrapped a smaller one around her hair and tied it in a knot. At her wardrobe, she suddenly felt nervous again. What to wear? She had no idea where Tristan would be taking her. Should she dress in something fancy or just go for casual?

Oh god, how stupid, she should never have left that to him. Kate hated being over or underdressed. Sighing in defeat, she decided it'd be better to be underdressed than overdressed, so she selected her dark blue Prada dress. It was just above the knee and had a nice lace trim at the bottom. Going through one of her drawers to find a nice-looking pair of panties, she selected one of her Marlies Dekkers lingerie sets. She carelessly threw everything onto the bed and then blew dry her hair.

Twenty minutes later, Kate looked at her reflection in her man-sized mirror. She turned around and decided to braid one string of hair from the left side to the right in a waterfall braid so it wouldn't irritate her face during the evening. After sitting in front of her dressing table, she braided it.

It was always easier to do someone else's hair, but Kate had learned to braid her own many years ago. Satisfied with the result, she put her necklace back on and her ring. Just a touch of mascara, a bit of perfume, and she was done.

She went to the living room, poured herself a glass of water, and retrieved her iPod from the bathroom to connect it to the docking station in the living room. She was done listening to Ella, but not quite in the mood for loud music. She scrolled through her playlists until she found one that read "Placebo soft songs." She hit the play button and an acoustic version of "Breathe Underwater" filled the room.

She pulled her knees under her on the couch and then picked up the book next to her. She was rereading Jane Austen's *Pride and Prejudice* for the millionth time. After reading two chapters, Kate's iPhone bleeped, and she saw she had a text from Deborah, wishing her a magical evening and that she'd want to hear all about it tomorrow. It was almost six thirty, and Kate was getting nervous again. She stood to check her reflection in the mirror and noticed her eyes were bright green at the moment. "Hmpf, how appropriate," she huffed as Placebo sang about tearing the sun in three and lighting up eyes. "Good grief, woman, it's just a date. Relax." With two minutes to spare, her doorbell rang. *Showtime*, Kate thought.

She opened the door and had to hold back a way too obvious "Wow!" Tristan was looking quite dashing, and like some synchronistic miracle, his jacket matched the dark blue of her dress. His hair wasn't tied back, but fell round his face, which made him look younger.

"Do you want to leave straight away or would you like to come in?" Kate asked.

"I'd love to come in, but the car is waiting for us downstairs, so perhaps some other time? You look truly beautiful, by the way, Catherine. Blue becomes you." He looked at her with a warm expression.

Kate felt herself blushing. "Thank you, Tristan. You look very handsome as well. And we match, it seems," she finished, smiling. She grabbed her coat and purse and then locked the door.

"I was rather hoping we would," he said mysteriously.

Kate fidgeted with her keys and didn't know what to say. She was glad when the lift doors opened and he stepped aside to hold it for her.

"After you, milady," he said.

"Thank you," Kate replied.

Once they arrived downstairs, Kate noticed a silver Mercedes, which was obviously waiting for them. She looked at Tristan, but he just opened the door for her and then got in beside her on the backseat.

"Evening, Mr. Visconti," the driver said. "Where to this evening?"

"Hakkasan at Hanway Place, if you'd be so kind, Charles. And may I introduce you to Miss Catherine van Dyk. Catherine, this is Charles Hayley. He's been my personal driver for quite some time now."

Charles looked in his rear-view mirror and smiled. "Nice meeting you, miss."

"Nice to meet you too, Charles," Kate replied.

She was a bit overwhelmed by the fact Tristan had a personal driver. She didn't even know that many famous people who had one. Personal assistants sure, but personal drivers? Not so much in her world. True to her word, she texted Leah with just the words, *Hakkasan at Hanway. Now sod off ;-)*.

"I hope you'll forgive me for not picking a restaurant in Shoreditch, but I took a chance and thought you might like Asian food, and this place excels in it, or so Charles has promised me. So if you hate it, you have to blame him, you see, not me."

Kate rolled her eyes. "Well, as long as Charles promises me to show me your bat cave, I think you'll both be safe since I'm quite fond of Asian food."

Charles appeared to try to hide a snigger. "I think I like her already, sir," he said before driving off into town.

It took a while to get through traffic, but since it wasn't the weekend, it wasn't too bad. Kate had heard about Hakkasan, but had never been there. She liked to try new places, but was also loyal to the ones she really liked. So when going for Asian food, she often went to Suki's. After they arrived at the restaurant, Tristan was out of the car before she even blinked and came to the door for her.

"Just let me know when you want to leave, sir. I'll be here. Enjoy your evening, miss," Charles said.

"Thank you, Charles," she replied.

They walked to the restaurant and then headed down the dimly lit staircase, surrounded by cooling slate walls filled with tiny crimson lights. Tristan gave them his name at the desk, and a waitress came to lead them to a table in the back. She pulled Kate's chair back for her to take a seat. She asked if they'd like anything to drink. Tristan looked at Kate.

"A chardonnay for me please, and some water perhaps?"

Tristan nodded. "Make that a bottle of water and two chardonnay. Do you prefer still or sparkling, Catherine?"

"Still, if you don't mind," Kate said. The waitress handed them the menus and then left to get their drinks.

Kate looked around. The restaurant was bathed in a mysterious icy-blue light. Carefully placed screens provided an air of intimacy and subterfuge, further enhanced by the shadows created by the many candles. She really loved what they'd done with the lighting. It sort of created the same atmosphere she had at home.

Looking over the menu, she noticed they had mixed traditional Chinese cuisine with the modern world. It sounded exciting. The whole place had a sort of sexy vibe, for lack of a better word. Yes, she definitely liked this place. Tristan had chosen well. She was already thinking of asking Leah to join her there someday.

Tristan noticed her looking around. "Do you like it?" he asked.

"Very much. If the food is as good as the atmosphere, this is going in my top ten list I think," she said truthfully.

Tristan looked pleased. "I'm glad you like it. I wasn't sure what kind of cuisine you liked. I completely forgot to ask. Nerves I suppose. I'm pleased I did something right, at least."

Kate hesitated before she said, "Well, if you must know, I stood for half an hour in front of my wardrobe, realising it wasn't very smart of me to have zero idea of where we were going. I was worried I'd be over or underdressed."

Tristan gave a soft laugh. "I changed three times," he said.

"Oh, good, then I'm not the only loser here," Kate said, grinning.

She started to feel more relaxed. Tristan was easy to talk to, and she had the feeling he was trying to be open with her. She felt the need to return the favour.

"Did you have a nice Sunday?" she asked.

He looked up from the menu. "Rather dull, really. Well, besides stressing over finding the perfect restaurant, of course. I played some cello, though. That was nice. It's been a while since I've been able to play."

Kate was surprised. "You play the cello? I love the cello. It's such a beautiful instrument. I play the harp. Lever harp, not pedal harp. Goes really well with the cello, by the way."

"Does it now?" Tristan asked with a laugh. "Then we must perform as a duet someday. I didn't know you were musical." He looked as if he were trying to remember something, but came up short.

"How could you?" she replied. "The harp is a fairly soft instrument. You wouldn't hear me even with the windows open, and I don't play as much as I used to. Busy, busy, busy. You know how it is. Do you play other instruments as well?"

Tristan nodded. "Piano, but when I started travelling so much, I moved it to my parents' house. They moved back to Italy when they both retired. My father plays as well, so it's put to good use."

"Do you visit them often?" she asked.

"Not as often as I'd like, but every chance I get, yes. My family is important to me. What about you?"

"I'm very close to my mother, and I have an uncle I'm very fond of. My father died several years ago, and I'm an only child, so it was just me and my mom. She moved back here to live closer to her brother, and I decided to move closer to her within the year."

Tristan smiled. "I thought I heard the tiniest accent. Dutch?"

"Good guess. Yes, I'm half Dutch by my father's side. Sometimes I still miss Amsterdam, but I visit friends over there quite often, so I'm quite reconciled with living here now. Leah's of Dutch origin as well. We've been friends for as long as I can remember, and though we always speak English to one another, we still swear in Dutch," she finished with a grin.

He laughed. "I can relate. Swearing is apparently a primal force. I often swear in Italian."

"You speak Italian fluently?" Kate asked.

"Yes. We moved to England when I was young, but we always went back to visit family and friends several times a year. And my parents thought it'd benefit me to speak both languages, so I was raised bilingual," he finished with a smile.

"What are you going to have?" Kate asked, looking at the menu. There were a lot of good things as far as she could tell.

Tristan looked at the menu as well. "Do you like dim sum? We could order a dim sum platter for two to start."

Kate nodded. "I love dim sum. I'm okay with that. I think I'll go for the fish, then, as a main course. This sha cha seafood toban sounds rather good."

Tristan leaned over the table to read what Kate showed him. "Hmm, scallops, prawns, squid, it does sound good, but I think I'll go for something that used to be a cow."

He gave her that boyish grin again. Her heart missed a beat. The waiter came straight to their table as soon as they put their menus down. Tristan placed their orders with the waiter and asked Catherine if she'd like another chardonnay.

Kate looked at her almost empty glass. "Yes, please."

The waiter looked at Tristan. "Another one for you as well, sir?" Tristan nodded. The waiter took their menus and then left.

"I always wanted to learn a foreign language like French or Spanish or Italian," Kate said. "I just never found the time. A shame, really, but you can't have it all I suppose."

"Oh, I don't know. I consider Dutch to be a very foreign language. It's a very difficult language to learn, you know. I tried once, but gave up after a couple months. I think the only thing I remember is *dank u wel* and *goedendag*. Oh, and something I learned off the streets. *Goedkoper dan bij de Hema*, but I never really understood what that means."

Kate tried very hard not to laugh too loud. His pronunciation was terrible for starters, and that last remark was just too funny.

He looked rather sheepish. "Did I say something offensive?"

"Oh, god, no. It's just a very touristy remark," she said still laughing. "In England it'd be the same as saying something like, 'Cheaper than at Boots.' Your 'thank you' and 'good day' were correct, by the way. People almost never get the 'g' right, though."

Tristan frowned. "Well, that explains why I heard it on the streets so much when someone tried to sell me something. They always said it at the end, so I thought it must be a kind of parting remark. Shows what I know." He rolled his eyes.

Kate tried to stifle a giggle. "It's not so bad. It could have been much worse. We're not exactly known for our subtle nature, you know."

Tristan smiled. "Now that, I know."

The waiter came back with their chardonnay and their dim sum platter. He explained the different dim sums and then left again after saying, "Enjoy your dinner."

Kate raised her glass. "Cheers, Tristan. Even though it's not in Shoreditch, I dare say you picked a very nice place."

He grinned. "Good. Cheers, Catherine. I'm very glad you're willing to take a chance on your new neighbour."

Kate smiled mischievously. "Well, it's only the neighbourly thing to do, you know," she said. "No, but really, I'm glad you asked me out. You seem like a really nice guy. We're neighbours now, and frankly, it's been a while since I went out with, well, you know, a man." She felt herself slightly blushing.

"Too busy with work?" he asked seriously.

"That's part of it, yes. Or that used to be part of it. Now I'm just using that as an excuse, to be honest. I don't have the greatest track record when it comes to successful relationships."

And this would be the moment to stop talking, you idiot, Kate thought.

"I already told you that most women don't fancy a man who drops by only once a month, so you don't have to justify your choices to me, Catherine. I understand. You sound sad about it, though. Do you miss being in a relationship?" He held out a dim sum for her, and she lifted her plate so he could put it on there.

"Sometimes, yes. Don't you? I mean, getting together with your friends isn't the same. You share something special with a partner. Not that my friends aren't special, they are. Very special indeed," she said with just a hint of sarcasm in her voice. If he only knew how special.

Tristan nodded. "I do know what you mean. A partner is the first person you see when you wake up, and when you return home. You can share daily life with your partner like no other, not even your parents. Being in a relationship is a magical thing I think, but it's also something I'm not really good at. With all the moving around, I mean."

Kate wondered if he was sending her some kind of warning. Like, don't fall for me, I won't stick around. She was quite shocked to realise she didn't really care. Boy, she really had been alone for too long.

"You're here now, right?" she asked, picking up her dim sum with her chopsticks.

He smiled. "Yes, I'm here now, and I hope for quite some time. I like it here."

"London is a beautiful city," Kate agreed.

"London is nice as well, yes," he replied with a crooked gin.

"Are you flirting with me, Mr. Visconti?" Kate asked, pretending to be shocked.

Tristan looked at her. There was a smile on his lips, but his eyes were serious. "That depends."

"On what?"

"On whether or not you'd like me to flirt with you."

"Oh. Um. I'm not quite sure how to respond to that." She let out a nervous laugh. "You can be very direct, you know." She stared at him accusingly.

He shrugged. "I guess I don't see the point in beating around the bush. Don't get me wrong, I like a good chase as much as the next man, but I'm not blind. When I meet a beautiful and intelligent woman, why hide my interest? You could be running off with another neighbour, for all I know. I'm not about to let that happen if I can help it." He looked at her rather intensely.

"I don't think you have a lot of competition at the moment, Tristan," Kate said rather shyly.

Tristan raised an eyebrow. "Really? Hmm, follow me around the room then. Two tables across from us there are two businessmen. The one in the dark suit wants you desperately, I'm absolutely sure. Then there's the group three tables on your left. The girl with the brown hair just had an argument with that young man sitting opposite her. He checked you out several times before she said something about it. He's been sulking ever since. Should I continue?" he asked with a smile.

Kate felt herself blushing deep red now. "Please don't. And I'm sure you're wrong. You can't possibly know that businessman is interested in me."

"Not quite how I put it, Catherine, but believe me, I know. I'm a pretty good judge of character, and I've learned to trust my instincts."

Oh, my god, Kate thought. He's a vampire. He can read minds, and I'm suddenly in *Twilight.* Instead she said, "Sounds as if you have a pretty handy skill there."

"It does, doesn't it," he said. "I'll tell you mine, if you tell me yours." He grinned.

Kate had to laugh despite herself. "So you think I have a handy skill as well, huh?"

"No, I know you have a handy skill. There's a difference. I'm just not sure what it is, and that, I have to admit, puzzles me. No pressure. I have a feeling you'll either tell me yourself or I'll find out soon enough."

"Is that so?" she asked. "You sound pretty sure of yourself. My 'skill' might not be something you like, you know."

"Impossible," he said with absolute certainty in his voice. "I may not know what it is you're gifted with, dear Catherine, but I am, however, sure you're a force of good. So whatever skill hides within you, it won't scare me away."

Kate was lost in thought for a moment. He'd referred to her skill as gifted, so he probably did know what he was talking about. She felt strangely pleased that he wouldn't go running if he did find out. Well, so he claimed, anyway. The fact remained she knew very little about him. It was time to turn things around.

"And what makes you a good a judge of character, pray tell?" she asked with a smile in her voice. "If you believe me to be a force of good, then you must have no reservations sharing your particular gift with me."

"Ah, clever," he said. "And you're convinced I'm going to explain why I can't tell you. Not at this point, at least, but someday soon. I'll look mysterious while saying this, of course, and you'll feel disappointed, but accept my explanation. Only I'm not one for playing games, remember? If you're asking, I'm telling. I'm an empath. It's a curse, really. Ever since I was a young boy I never knew if children wanted to play with me because they liked me or because I'd somehow made them like me. I learned to block my gift during my teens, but I guess that wasn't a really smart thing to do, because I had terrible headaches and worse. Go figure. So after a while, I accepted I was a little freak and let the emotions back in. I'm able to filter them now, though, so I don't have to feel everyone around me."

Kate was puzzled. Tristan was an empath. She'd suspected as much, but up until this moment, she hadn't been sure. Furthermore, he spoke about his gift with contempt and ridicule. Alan had revelled in his gift, his power to control people. Later in life, at least, and she'd never heard him complain about it. Not once.

"You're not a freak," she said softly. "Don't ever say that."

Tristan looked concerned. "I didn't mean to imply that you're any kind of freak, Catherine. Please forgive me if you thought so. I only referred to myself."

"I know that, but I still don't like it. Being an empath can be something wonderful. Yes, it can be terribly dangerous and manipulative as well. Believe me, I know. And it must be hard to always doubt people's motives to want to be around you. Did you try to make me like you?" she asked with a frown.

"Of course I did, but not in the way you think. I turned on the charm because I wanted to get to know you better. I never interfered with your free will. You were a bit nervous around me when we first met. Sometimes you still are, like now." He smiled. "I can help you relax without losing your focus. It's supposed to even help you think clearer. Watch."

Tristan appeared to focus for a moment, and Kate felt as if she were wrapped in a warm safety blanket, not unlike the feeling she'd created earlier today with her earth element. Her whole body relaxed, but her mind remained remarkably clear.

"See. How could you possibly be a freak if you can help people in such a way?" she asked, smiling.

He returned her smile. "Thank you, Catherine. That means a lot coming from you. I don't know why exactly, but it does. It's strange, you know. I usually get all sorts of emotions from people when I put in an effort, but every time I focus on your emotions, I either almost get burned or I feel as if someone dropped a bucket of water over my head or something." He laughed. Kate stared at him. "What?" Tristan asked. "Did I say something wrong?"

"No, you said something right I think. The reason you probably felt elements is because I'm an elemental," she said with an expression that said, "Brace for impact."

Tristan looked not as surprised as Kate thought he'd be. "I figured as much. So, you can control fire and water? Two elements. That's rather special, you know."

Kate was confused. "No, that's apparently just what you felt up until now, Tristan. I can control all four of them, of course."

Now he did look shocked. "You can control all the elements?" he asked in a whisper. "How is that even possible?"

Kate felt even more confused. "You don't seem to be very surprised by me being an elemental. Why would you be surprised that I can control the elements? Isn't that what being one is all about?"

Tristan shook his head. "I'm sorry. I should explain. Over the years, I've met quite a few people with gifts, and sort of researched what kind of abilities there were, so to speak. I've come across elementals before, but never one who could control all of them."

Kate looked at him. "But one element is not the same. You have pyrokinesis for instance. They have control over fire—"

Tristan shook his head and interrupted her. "No, you misunderstand me. Pyrokinesis is not the same as being an elemental. You. You are fire. They can only control fire. There's a difference. And you're the other elements as well, as it turns out. Sorry, I'm still a bit shell-shocked by that little fact. No wonder you're so careful around people. You should be. I know people who'd like to dissect you like a frog." He smiled, but there was also a serious undertone there.

He probably did know people who'd want to dissect her. "You seem to know more about my gift than I do," she replied softly.

Tristan looked at her. "In theory yes, but again, I've never met someone who could control all four. You have no idea how good that makes me feel. I think there might actually be some hope, after all, for this planet," he said, smiling.

"You speak in riddles, Tristan Visconti." Kate stared at him, feeling slightly mystified. The waiter arrived with their main course, and they fell silent until he left again.

"I know I am. Did you forget? I like to be mysterious, remember?" He winked. "Catherine, I think you just made my whole year."

Kate rolled her eyes. "How could I forget? Well, *bon appétit*, mystery man." She held out her glass to him. Tristan raised his to toast with her.

"*Bon appétit*, indeed!"

Someone seemed to have cheered up quite a lot, she mused. Oh well, better to let it go and just enjoy her evening. She'd weasel it out of him one of these days. He hadn't seen her manipulative skills yet. Two could play that game. A smile spread across her face.

TUESDAY

"WELL, DID YOU snog him or what?"

Kate almost jumped out of her skin. She pushed the sheets back and looked up to see Deborah leaning over her.

"You freak of nature! You scared the living shit out of me!" she cried. Rubbing her eyes, she yawned and got out of bed. "What time is it, anyway?"

"Almost ten, sleepy head. It must have been an all-nighter, right? Good thing you don't have any clients this morning," she said, grinning. "Here, I made you a cup of coffee. Consider it a peace offering."

Kate huffed. "The least you could do, yes. Besides, I'm sure you would have woken me up if I did have any clients, much to my chagrin, I might add." She walked toward the bathroom, coffee in one hand, iPod in the other. She looked over her shoulder to give Deborah another vicious glare and then disappeared into the bathroom.

Deborah just laughed. "You're not getting away that easily, you know. I still wanna hear all about it."

Kate mumbled something incomprehensible that wasn't in the Oxford dictionary or the Van Dale, for that matter.

She let the water run and selected some music before she stepped into her shower. The spray hit her back. She closed her eyes at the first sounds of Chopin's *Etudes* filling the bathroom. Tristan liked Chopin, he'd told her so last night. Actually, he'd told her quite a lot of things, she mused. She'd never expected him to be so open with her, but as the evening had progressed, she'd understood why he liked talking to her so much. She understood him. Really understood him, and she had the sad feeling very few people ever had.

No, she wasn't shocked to find out he was indeed an empath. She'd expected as much, anyway, and was just a bit scared because of the power it implied. As an elemental, she knew quite a bit about having to deal with power, and Alan ... Well, he obviously had failed to handle his power. In the end it'd backfired and driven him mad. Tristan was so the complete opposite of Alan. It took her by surprise. It was almost as if he'd expected her to reject him the minute she'd found out he was an empath. She didn't think Tristan had a lot of friends.

Obviously, his family was very important to him. Being Italian would only add to that. Family was very important to Italians in general, as far as she understood it, but she wondered if he had any real friends in the here and now. She couldn't remember seeing anybody in the building helping him move. Then again, she'd been away or busy in her practice during the day, so that was hardly any indication.

She added conditioner to her hair so it wouldn't be a tangled mess when it dried, and thought about what he'd said after they'd arrived at the apartment building. A part of her had hoped he'd come up to join her for a nightcap, but she'd also been scared she wanted more than she was emotionally ready for. Being an empath, he had, of course, picked up on her mixed emotions, and she'd felt a sudden sensation of calm and acceptance, which she knew to be coming from him. She started to recognise his signature, so to speak. Tristan could really make you feel better and more focussed about yourself or a situation.

She was actually both frustrated and relieved by her own actions, or better put, lack thereof. He'd kissed her, though, and when she thought back about that particular moment, her lips still burned. She'd sighed softly to herself in resignation and turned toward her door when Tristan had grabbed her hand and pulled her gently to him. She'd looked up at him, and his hand came round the nape of her neck. His eyes had been a glittering dark blue, and she'd thought her knees would collapse just as he'd released her and moved his hand to the base of her back, supporting her. He'd looked into her eyes, searching for something, her permission perhaps, and she'd hesitantly smiled. It'd seemed to be enough, because he'd lowered his head and softly brushed her lips. By no means had she been prepared for the onslaught of feelings that had flowed through her the second his lips touched hers. She literally felt what he'd felt, and it was so intense it almost consumed her. She'd automatically reached for the earth within her to help her ground, and was equally surprised to notice it embraced him as well.

Tristan had pulled back gently and gave her another kiss on her forehead. He'd leaned closer as he'd brushed her ear, and said, "*Tutto a suo tempo, miei elementi.*" He'd let go of her and waited until she was inside, then she'd heard the lift doors close.

Shaking her head to get back to the present, she washed out the conditioner and then stepped out of the shower. She'd looked up the Italian phrase, of course. It meant something like all in good time, my elemental. All in good time, indeed. After grabbing a towel from the rack, she rubbed herself dry before she wrapped it around her head. Fifteen minutes later, she appeared in the living room fully dressed and with braided, still slightly wet hair.

Deb was still waiting for her, hanging on her sofa like some slouch and with a catlike grin. "So?" she asked. "On a scale from one to ten, how did the first official date go?"

Kate rolled her eyes, but replied seriously. "I'd probably give it eight out of ten."

Deborah smiled knowingly. "That's good. So probably no full-blown sex then, but apparently he did something right."

Kate had to laugh in spite of herself. "I barely know the man, Deb. Did you really think I'd just melt into his arms and let him have his way with me after one date?" She looked at her friend with a raised eyebrow.

Deborah looked a bit guilty. "No, of course not. I was just teasing. Though, under the circumstances, I wouldn't blame you, you know. You're not some slut inviting men into your bed every other week. Having a one-night stand once in your life isn't a capital offence I think."

Kate smiled. "I know, hon. I was actually teasing you. In truth, I was tempted to invite him up to my place, but I don't think it would have been wise, and I guess he knew or felt that, because he didn't ask. He did kiss me, though, and if that's anything to go by, the future in that course looks very promising, indeed."

"Does it now?" Deborah asked with a grin.

"It does indeed, and that's all the information you're getting, missy," she finished with a teasing glare at her friend.

Deborah appeared to object when the intercom rang. Kate walked over to the hallway and saw Leah standing outside. She smiled and pushed the intercom button. "Hi, sweetie, come on up." She pushed the button to give Lee access to the building and then opened the front door just a bit so Leah could let herself in. Deborah stayed just long enough to say hello to Leah as she entered the living room and gave Deborah a quick hug.

"Enjoy your day, ladies. Think of poor me when you're having fun," Deborah said while giving Kate a wave, and she disappeared behind the moss wall.

"I'm not getting you into trouble taking all these days off on my account, am I?" Leah asked.

Kate looked incredulous. "Really? Of all the things you could be worrying about, this is what you come up with?"

Leah gave her a soft push. "Oh, shut up. I guess not then. Speaking of things to worry about, though, did I miss something going on in New Zealand?"

"New Zealand?" Kate repeated. "What makes you say that? I'm not aware of anything going on there, no."

Leah appeared to be lost in thought. "Hmm, maybe it's nothing then. I just had a vision of lots of heads of state and royalty gathering in New Zealand. I thought there was maybe like a big anniversary thing going on, and it kind of confused me why I'd see such a trifle thing, but no then."

Kate looked surprised. "Well, again, not to my knowledge. We could Google it, if you like. What was the feeling behind your vision?"

Leah shook her head. "I already Googled it and didn't come up with anything special. And to answer your question, nothing much really. As I said, it looked, and also felt, like a gathering, but it was definitely New Zealand. I'm sure."

"Do you want to pursue it or let it go for now?" Kate asked.

"Let it go for now. If there's more to it, I'm sure I'll get another one if it's really important. You're still keeping tabs, health wise, on our prime minister?" She looked at Kate for confirmation.

Kate nodded. "Yep, still anxious, but otherwise she seems to be doing better. More accepting I think. Maybe it was just a minor bug."

She'd noticed their prime minister's health had faltered quite a bit this last month, and she'd sent Sue on her tail to check up on her. Sue had sent her healing powers whenever she got the chance. Kate had sent her earth energy to help her ground and relax the one time she'd seen her in passing. She could work from a distance, but her powers did have more immediate effect when nearby. It wasn't easy getting close to high-profile politicians, because of the increase of security surrounding them. Royalty even more so, but thankfully standing near the building was close enough for Kate's and Sue's powers to have an effect.

Leah agreed with her. "Probably a bug then. Maybe she was worried about travelling to New Zealand for this big social event we seem to be overlooking and had no idea what to wear. She does have a terrible boring sense of style, you know," she said with a wink.

Kate laughed. "Who knows."

She kind of liked their prime minister, as far as politicians went, anyway. She never understood, though, why women holding a certain kind of power seemed to turn into these androgynous sort of people. Thereby almost disguising the fact they were, in fact, women. The world had come a long way, though. England had a female prime minister again, and America had its first female president. Kate had never seen her up close, but Leah had during some highbrow benefit party, and had declared her a complete and utter bitch. She'd finished her statement by saying she was her kind of bitch, though.

"Want to check her out today just to be sure?" Leah asked, meanwhile browsing through Kate's fridge. "Do you have any milk?"

Kate turned on her espresso machine, pushing Leah aside to find the milk, and thought about it for a minute. "Why not? It can't hurt to give it another go and help her along. I haven't planned anything, so it could be a wild goose chase. She might not even be in. What do you think? You're the one with the all-seeing eye here," she finished with a grin.

Leah concentrated for a moment. "I think we have a good chance of catching her inside the building. She has an important decision to make, but she hasn't decided yet. Until she does, I think she'll stay put. God, it does make you curious, doesn't it? I mean, I'm glad I'm not a politician, but in a way it must be quite an adventure. Knowing stuff other people don't. I'd dread the responsibility."

Kate glared at her. "Yes, because our lives are blissfully devoid of any kind of responsibility."

Leah laughed. "Point taken. It's different, though. We have a choice to do what we do. And, of course, there's a sense of obligation. To each other, to the world, but mostly we do what we do because we want to, and because we can. It must be hard to do things you don't want to but have to, because otherwise you won't get where you want to be in the long run. I always get the feeling politicians sacrifice so much of their morals they lose a little piece of their soul along the way. It saddens me, you know."

Kate nodded. "I know what you mean, and I'm glad I'm not in their position, either. Okay then, we'll drop by Downing Street later this day." She speculatively looked at her friend.

"What?" Leah asked.

"Well, I'm actually amazed you haven't asked me anything about Tristan yet," she said.

Leah smiled. "Honey, I know you well enough by now to see Deb has bothered you already with questions, so I thought I'd wait until you told me yourself."

Kate huffed. "Oh, well, that's just ... peachy." She had to laugh. Leah knew her way too well.

"Not that I'm not interested, love. Of course I'm dying to know how it went." She smiled. "Oh, and thanks for texting me. I did find that oddly reassuring. It looked like a very nice place. I looked it up on the Internet."

"It was. You'd love it. We'll definitely go there together some time. He does lead a strange life. I'll have you know he has a personal driver." Kate looked at Leah.

"Does he now?" Leah whistled. "Must be some job."

"Yes, he's quite evasive when it comes to the job description. Not so much on his personal life. He was pretty revealing on that account. Tristan is, indeed, an empath. He also knows I'm an elemental, by the way."

Leah frowned a bit after hearing that piece of news. "Really? Did he guess or did you tell him? You seldom tell anyone."

"A bit of both actually. He sort of guessed, and I told him the rest. Well, actually, I corrected him. He knows quite a lot about elementals. Well, perhaps not elementals in particular, but people with special powers in general. Anyway, he explained the difference between controlling an element and actually being one, which I thought was quite fascinating. I never realised there was a difference."

Leah frowned again. "Neither did I, for that matter, but it does have a true ring to it now you've put it like that."

"He was, however, very shocked to learn I'm all the elements."

"Why would he be shocked by that?" Leah asked.

"My thoughts exactly. Apparently, I'm the only one he's ever come across who can control, oops … I mean, who's capable of being all of them at once. There are a few people who are fire elementals or air, even fewer who are water or earth, and there's never been one who's all of them. Well, according to his knowledge, anyway."

Leah laughed. "So you mean you're special? Well, what else is new?"

"Har, har, very funny," Kate replied. "What was really interesting is that his whole mood changed after that little piece of information. He suddenly seemed very happy, and I don't know, full of hope or something. As if I were the second coming. It was really weird. He couldn't stop grinning, and he even said something along the lines of, 'There's hope for this planet, after all.'"

"That doesn't sound so bad," Leah mused. "How was it just to be with him? Did you feel comfortable around him?"

"Actually, yes. More so than I would have imagined. Aside from the fact it was really nice talking to someone who doesn't only understand my powers but actually knows more about them than I do, it was really nice to talk to an empath who's so … white. He's nothing like Alan, you know. I think he grew up with very few friends, and even felt like a freak, an outcast who didn't fit in. He said he found it very hard to decide whether people liked him for himself or because he'd done something unconsciously to make them like him."

"That's so sad," Leah said.

Kate nodded. "I thought so too, and it wasn't his intention to make me feel sorry for him. I could tell he didn't even like saying those things to me."

Leah looked at her. "You really like him, don't you?" she asked softly.

"Well, it's very hard not to like him," she started, frowning a bit. "That's not what you meant. If you're asking whether or not I'm falling for him, then I think the answer is yes. I know I've only known him for a couple days, but he's the first person I'm really interested in since, well, since Alan. I have no idea where this is going and if it's going anywhere at all, but I'd like to spend more time with him. Yes, I think I'd like that very much." She smiled.

"And I really hope you'll get that chance, sweetie. You deserve it. Did he kiss you?"

Kate smiled. "Yes, he did. I had the feeling we both wanted more but weren't ready, though perhaps for different reasons. The kiss was very promising, but also a bit weird." She felt a blush crept up to her cheek. "I was kind of … thrown by the moment, so I grounded myself by using earth energy and immediately it flowed into him as well. It was … really intense. I never had that before."

"Not even with Alan?" Leah asked.

Kate snorted. "Hell no. Alan was scared shitless of my powers. He coveted them, but stayed a mile away from them, nonetheless. He always put up walls to make sure I couldn't infect him with my elements." She was disgusted just by the memory.

"Frankly, I always thought he worshipped the ground you walked on," Leah said.

"Oh, he did, in his own fucked up way. Just as I put him on a pedestal at first as well. I thought he was God, or the Messiah at least. God, I was so naive. Even when it was too late, I still thought I could save him. How presumptuous of me, but how do we say that? *Hoogmoed komt voor de val*, right?"

Leah smiled. "Something like that, yes. Although I don't think you were so arrogant to think you could save him. You just still cared too much and really wanted to. So arrogant or proud? No. Naive, yes. And we live and learn. Thankfully, you lived. It could have ended really badly, and I'm still very thankful it didn't."

"As am I, my friend, as am I. Enough of this. How about we get moving? We can drop by Downing Street first, just to get it out of the way, and then I thought we could drop by the National Gallery? They have an exhibition this month, featuring early art from Peru. I thought you might be interested in checking it out." She looked at Leah.

"Sounds lovely. That would be nice. Perhaps we could have lunch there as well then?"

"Sure, we could drop by the National Cafe or have coffee at the espresso bar," Kate replied.

"Have you made any further plans to meet with Tristan?"

"Actually, he invited me over to his place tomorrow afternoon. He plays the cello, and I convinced him to play for me under the condition I'd bring lunch. I'm really curious to see what he's done with the place. A home can tell you so much about a person."

Leah nodded. "That sounds nice. I think I'll visit your mother tomorrow then. Remind me to give her a ring later today to set it up. The cello, huh?" She grinned. "You do know how to pick them, don't you? And will you just be admiring his um … cello?"

Kate smacked her over the head. "Stop it, you dirty girl. Yes, I'll only be admiring his cello. And his house perhaps. Maybe a bit of rolling biceps, but that's it. I swear." Leah just grinned at her. "Although it has to be said, he has a very nice arse as well," Kate finished, feeling a slight blush.

"Indeed?" Leah grinned. "No, I shall no longer tease you. Come on, honey, let's go. I have plenty of time to make your life a living hell later on."

Kate scowled. "Oh goody, I'm so looking forward to that!"

Leah just laughed.

* * *

Downing Street. Home of the English prime minister, and therefore, home of the paparazzi as well. Kate suddenly realised it might not be as easy to walk there with Leah after her book had been filmed. She wondered if JK Rowling could wander the streets without being hassled. The Dutch were far more relaxed about celebrities. They pretty much left them alone. Leah always said the Dutch sucked at swooning over anything. In England, however, not so much. It was one of the few things she really hated about this country. Well, that and the plumbing. They might have invented it, but they hadn't done anything to improve it since then. Her whole house had been done by a Dutch contractor, and she was thankful for that every day.

They couldn't actually enter Downing Street, because after the '91 bombing, security had been increased dramatically. However, they seldom needed to. The one time Kate really needed to get close, she had Romy glamour the policemen into believing they had business there. It'd been tricky, and she'd rather not do it again. Thankfully, with

Leah's skills to see the immediate future, they had a huge advantage, and actually caught a glimpse of the prime minister. When they'd arrived, Leah had insisted they have coffee first. Trusting her friend's instincts, they'd settled in a nice coffee shop nearby. After twenty minutes, Leah suddenly wanted to leave, and Kate jumped up to take care of their bill. They walked toward Downing Street again. Leah grabbed her by the arm and dragged her the other way to Whitehall. They went around the block and were just in time to see a familiar car approaching the gate.

"Well done, love," Kate whispered.

She immediately homed in on the prime minister inside the car and checked the elements. Air was fine, earth as well, but water and fire were off. She focussed on those two and a turmoil of emotions washed over her. Wow, that woman had some serious issues to work out. Kate was almost thrown off balance, and grounded herself and concentrated on the fire element instead. It was almost non-existent. As if the prime minister had lost all passion for life.

A bit shocked by that feeling, Kate pulled back. She let the fire build inside her and then guided it gently inside the car. She saw the golden flames working their way in. Good thing she was one of few people who could actually see her elements working like that. She could make it visible to her friends if she wanted to, and sometimes she did just to explain how something really worked. Having a visual was helpful. Kate felt the fire reach its destination. It almost dissolved immediately. Damn, she must be running really low. She tried again and this time something stuck. Good thing too, as the car was disappearing around the corner.

"And?" Leah asked.

Kate motioned Leah to follow her. Once they were a few blocks out of the way, she started talking. "I don't know what's wrong with her, but it's been a long time since I've come across someone so utterly devoid of emotion. Not that it isn't there, it's just all bottled up inside, bursting to explode. Maybe she lost someone close to her?"

Leah walked in a slow pace. "Perhaps. Loss of a loved one can cause quite a bit of turmoil. It's also something that wouldn't necessarily reach the papers. Somehow I doubt it. Maybe I'm getting paranoid."

"No, I'm with you on this one. I don't think it has anything to do with loss, either. Point is, I haven't got the slightest as to what it might be. Ugh, frustrating much! I have this feeling it's important, you know? You're not getting anything else?"

Leah shook her head. "Zip. Perhaps we should let Meg have a go. See if she catches anything death related?"

Kate thought that over. "Yes, that might be worth doing. Hang on, I'll give her a call now." She fished her iPhone out of her purse and then scrolled through her contact list. Seconds later, Meg answered.

"Hi, sweetie, it's me. Look, Lee and I just visited Downing Street to check up on our prime minister, and she's really off. Water and fire especially, as if she's devoid of all passion. We thought she might have lost someone dear to her, but we're not really sure."

Meg interrupted her. "And you want me to check if I catch anything death related?"

Kate smiled. "If you could, that would be great, Meg. She's out now, but I'm sure she'll be back later today. You don't have to be close, right?"

"Not really, no, but I can't look through buildings, darling. It's no problem, though. The president of India is visiting England. They're having an important meeting today, maybe even as we speak. It was in the morning paper. Anyway, I'm sure there will be pictures, and I can check those."

Kate looked relieved. "Oh, great. I forgot you can see death through pictures as well. My mother can't with auras, apparently, so I wasn't sure anymore."

"No," Meg replied, "that's not a problem for me. I think with death you either have it or you don't. It doesn't constantly change like auras."

"Interesting theory. I'll mention it to Mom. Thanks for the help, Meg. Sorry to bother you at work."

"No problem. I'll let you know if I get anything, okay?"

"Thanks! See you Thursday, hon." Kate disconnected after Meg had said goodbye as well.

"Well, not much more we can do for her now, is there?" Leah asked.

"Nope. Come on, let's go to the National Gallery. I'm sick and tired of all this gloomy stuff. Let's see some colours."

The National Gallery was peaceful and quiet today. They had to pay a small fee for the Peru exhibition, but the rest was free admittance as usual. They walked over to the Peru section first. Leah began on the left side while Kate started on the right. They liked to browse on their own, sometimes exchanging opinions, sometimes just sitting in front of a painting for a while, enjoying the quiet.

Kate went on to the next room and then stopped abruptly in front of a dark painting. It was a corn field. It was the one from her dream. She got goose bumps and shivered. "Leah?" she asked as quietly as she could.

Leah walked into the room. "What is it, love?"

"I know this painting. I didn't tell you yet, but I had a nightmare yesterday about Alan. He stood in the middle of a corn field. This corn field. When I stepped forward to take a closer look, he dragged me inside the painting. It was awful."

Leah took Kate's hand and moved a few paces back, her gaze on the painting. "Best not test that theory then, shall we?"

"No," Kate said, mesmerized by it. "I'm still not seeing the big picture. What big picture, though?"

"Kate?" Leah looked at her with a worried expression.

"Sorry. Something Alan said to me in the dream. He said I still didn't see the big picture. And he was very angry about me giving up on him. As if he knew about Tristan, and wasn't too pleased to learn I'd found someone new in my life."

"Well, it's reasonable to assume Alan wouldn't be pleased at all to learn you'd found someone new. However, seeing he's almost reduced to a vegetable, I can't see him doing you or Tristan any real harm. Having said that, one can never be too careful. Not when Alan's involved." Leah took a step closer to the painting and squinted. "Nothing. No man with long, white waving hair and black eyes. I'm pretty sure he'd be hard to miss. Unless he's hiding in the corn."

Kate had to laugh, but it came out a bit nervous. "Good. Can you see a name on the painting? What does it say on the card?"

Leah moved to the right side of the painting to read the card. "It says, Sacred Valley of the Incas, also known as Urubamba Valley, located in the Andes of Peru, by Carlos Vargas. Doesn't ring a bell, but that's not very surprising. I know zero Peruvian painters."

"Sacred Valley of the Incas. Sure, why go for a normal corn field when you can have a sacred Inca one?" Kate looked irritated. "So it's a real place then?"

"Well, the card does imply that, yes. Located in the Andes of Peru. Why? Did Alan ever go to Peru?"

"I'm not sure. He visited lots of sacred places. I know he was fascinated by the Incas, but then again, who isn't? Oh, I don't know. Maybe I'm reading way too much into this. I just don't like it. Perhaps it's Samhuinn coming up. I've been feeling off for almost a month now. It's stronger than other years. Maybe opening up to Tristan triggered something inside me, and this is why all this Alan stuff is coming back to haunt me or something." She said the last part timidly.

Leah looked at her sympathetically. "Oh, sweetie, don't think that. What? You don't deserve some happiness in life, you don't deserve to be with someone?"

"Yes, well, not to be a bitch, but I don't have the best track record when it comes to men in my life. My father died without me being able to do anything about it, and the only man I ever truly loved turned Lord Voldemort on me and is now in a mental institution, probably talking to fish."

"Okay, time for coffee. This is getting ridiculous. You need a reality check. Come on." Leah dragged her in the direction of the espresso bar since it was still a bit early for lunch. After they sat and ordered two cappuccinos, she continued. "Now you listen to me. Alan was a great and wonderful man until he went bonkers. There was nothing you could have done to prevent that. You do realise that, don't you?" Kate nodded. "Good. Given the chance, he would have killed you, you know? And I'm pretty sure he wouldn't be pining away over you had it been the other way around. How do you think we feel about this, Kate? Meg saw your death, for god's sake, and I'll never forgive myself for being in New York when I saw you facing him at some construction building." She had tears in her eyes.

"You can't always be there to save me, Lee, nor should you be." Kate reached for Leah's hand and held it. "You have nothing to feel guilty about, and neither does Meg or Deb or any of the others. As you said, Alan went bonkers, and this is his responsibility. In my mind, I believe that. Only sometimes it's difficult to convince my heart I'm not responsible. I'm just on edge, you know. Hopefully it'll pass when Samhuinn has come and gone." She released her hand and sat up straight. "Okay, enough of this. I still have a cocktail party to plan, so let's focus on something nice."

They ordered two more cappuccinos and then both took a sip. "Okay, so what's on the checklist?" Leah asked.

"I have to drop by the caterer today to see if everything's in order. Also I have to sample some of the appetizers. John and Chris are expecting us round two o'clock. We can go there after we have lunch or just before. And I'd like to visit Holywell. Some of my spare harp strings are running low. They're open until five. We could do that later in the afternoon. If you don't mind, of course. Did you have any plans for today?"

"None," Leah replied. "I'd love to hear you play, by the way. I haven't heard it for such a long time. It's been weeks!"

Kate laughed. "How dreadful. I don't know how you survived this long."

Leah grinned. "Simple really, I recorded you last time and that's now on my iPod."

Kate looked outraged. "You did not! You sneaky little bitch." She played really well, but aside from a healing harp meditation CD for Elements, she'd never performed for the public. A few artists had asked her if she'd be willing to compose some harp arrangements to their music, but she'd always declined, stating she was way too busy with other things. She had three lever harps in her home. Two big ones. A white Salvi Ana, which she'd ordered from Holywell, because they normally didn't come in white. After some serious negotiations and a lot of extra money, she did get her white Salvi. Her other harp was a Starfish Mamore, made of walnut, and if she really had to, it was just manageable in the lift. She had a small Camac Bardic harp especially for playing somewhere else, because she did perform for her friends. Her repertoire was limited, however, on the Bardic, so sometimes she dragged her Starfish along for special occasions like Christmas. Her mother always demanded a private Christmas concert, and it'd become somewhat of a tradition over the years with her mother singing along with her lovely soprano voice.

"Hmm, I'm not sure you deserve a private concert then," Kate said to Leah.

"Oh, sod that. You know you'll forgive me, anyway. Just be glad I didn't get the damn thing mastered and printed."

Kate glared at her. "You wouldn't."

"No, I wouldn't, but it's nice to see you squirm, nonetheless. You really won't write something for a band?" she asked.

"Nope."

"Not even if Placebo asked you to write something?" Leah knew it was Kate's favourite band.

Kate almost spilled her last sip of cappuccino. "Are you nuts, woman? Especially not if Placebo asked. I'd die of embarrassment, would have to sell my house and move to another continent. Besides, Placebo and a harp? I don't think so."

"Well, why not? They have plenty of violin in their music," Leah said.

"Yes, but that's different. The violin goes really well with rock music. That, and Fiona is a goddess on one. She just gets Placebo. Her strings are a real asset to their music. Well, in my humble opinion, anyway," she finished with a grin.

Kate knew Leah was trying to distract her mind from the painting incident, and appreciated the effort. It helped.

"So that's a no then?" Leah grinned.

Kate laughed as well. "Yes, that's a definite no. Come on, let's stroll through the standard collection and then find us some lunch." They paid their bill and left for the gallery again.

*   *   *

After another hour, they'd seen enough and decided to have lunch near Westminster where Kate's caterer resided. They agreed to drop by the caterer first, since they had to sample taste and didn't want to be stuffed with lunch. They could always decide on a light lunch afterward.

John and Chris, the owners of the store, were the best caterers London had to offer, and Kate just loved them. She'd met John a few years ago at a summer barbeque party organised by a friend, and though it'd been nice enough, she'd really fallen for the appetizers. She'd momentarily forgotten her manners and had declared she'd died and gone to heaven out loud, still chewing on one. John had been delighted, and had shouted there and then that if he ever changed teams, he'd immediately marry her. It was by the look on Chris's face she'd realised they must be a couple.

They'd spent hours talking, and Kate had never laughed so much in one night. John was much older than Chris, and had started the business. Chris had still been studying back then, and John had loudly proclaimed to anyone who'd wanted to hear that he was pleased as punch to put his sweetheart through college. After Chris had graduated and got his degree, he'd joined the business full-time, handling the financial side of things and their locations as well, for they had several now. John was in charge of their personnel and interior decorations. They both developed new appetizers, and sometimes had quite dramatic discussions about that, which Kate had been witness to several times.

In private she called them the Vagina Whisperers, as they both claimed to know whenever a woman was having her period. At first, she'd thought they were pulling her leg, but Kate had tested their theory several times since then and they'd never been off the mark, so far. It always made her think of the book *Das Parfum*, and she'd asked more than once where they hid the bodies. They'd just glared at her and asked if she wanted full details on their special gift. After a serious "Hell no!" from Kate, they'd all laughed, which had turned into a rather girly giggling fit. She'd never had another caterer since.

"Kittycat!" John said to her, opening his arms for a hug. "Don't you look smashing? And what kind of treat have you brought with you today?"

Kate smiled and gave him a big hug and two air kisses. "This is my dear friend, Leah Winter, the celebrated author. You may now gush."

Chris came over as well to hug Kate and have a good look at Leah. "Really?" he drawled. "My, my, aren't you a pretty thing," he exclaimed.

Leah blushed.

"Oh look, Chris, she blushes! So cute!" John cried.

Leah appeared hardly to know where to look, and Kate stomped both John and Chris. "Give the girl some time to adjust to you two monkeys, okay?" she asked, laughing. "So where is all the yummy stuff? Show me the food, baby!"

Chris rolled his eyes. "God, you're so easy to please, Cat. You really should raise your standards, you know. I realise our food is divine, but sometimes a girl needs some of the bulging biceps as well." He winked knowingly.

Kate sighed. "You're insufferable!"

"Yes, darling, but you love us anyway, so let's not pretend that you don't."

Kate let her shoulders drop. There was just no point arguing with those two. She'd never win.

John offered Leah his arm, which she hesitantly took, and he guided her to one side of the working bench made of lovely teak wood. Several mini glasses, small plates, and twisted spoons were laid out before them, all filled with various things. It certainly smelled lovely, but it looked absolutely amazing.

"I think we've outdone ourselves this time, if I say so myself. We actually had an emotional moment this morning." He let out a big sigh. "Sometimes it's hard, you know, being this great."

Chris stood next to Kate, shaking his head. "Well, if John is done slobbering all over himself, I'll explain what you're about to taste. We decided to spice up your theme night a bit, so we have appetizers representing different movies. Here on the mini plates you can see James Bond." As she looked at the left side of the table, she saw some kind of mousse in the 007 shape. It looked really good. "Eel with raspberries and a little cognac mixed into a mousse. The little flowers on top are, of course, edible. Give it a go." He handed them both a small spoon, and they each scraped an entire 0 off the plate.

Kate closed her eyes in delight as the mousse melted on her tongue. She was in her happy place. After she opened them again, she saw Leah had a somewhat guilty look, and Kate wondered if her friend didn't like the mousse. She was about to ask what was wrong when she noticed the plate was now empty.

"Why, you little cheat! You ate the rest of it!"

Leah tried to look guiltier, but failed and just grinned sheepishly. "Sorry, hon, you know better than to bring me anywhere near good food, and this isn't just good food. This stuff is pure heaven."

"Oh, I see why you like her, Cat," John said. Chris looked pleased as well. "So Mr. Bond can stay, I presume?" he asked.

"Mr. Bond is definitely joining the party, yes," Kate replied. "Though we should probably keep an eye on Lee the entire evening if recent events are anything to go by," she finished with a frown toward her friend.

"We'll bring handcuffs just in case she gets naughty ideas," Chris said with a catlike grin toward Leah, who looked slightly uncomfortable again.

"Okay, okay, I'll behave. I promise." She raised her hands in surrender. Trying to change the subject, she moved over to the small high glasses. "So what's in this one?" she asked innocently.

John smiled. "Very smoothly done, my dear. You might make us proud yet. It's a gazpacho with a twist. You sip it in one go." He handed them a glass. Kate kept her gaze on her friend this time and downed her glass in one sip.

Leah mimicked her movements and then appreciatively licked her lips. "Does it taste more sweet than usual? I've had gazpacho before, but I can't remember it tasting this sweet. I like it. What do you think, Kate?"

"Definitely sweeter, but not too much."

Chris clapped his hands. "Very good, ladies. You're spot on. We've added strawberries, which isn't uncommon for gazpacho, and grapes as well. You like it?"

Kate and Leah nodded.

"Very much," Kate said. "Um, what does this one resemble, though?"

John rolled his eyes. "Well, duh. *What's Eating Gilbert Grape*, of course!" They all laughed.

"Brilliant!" Kate said. "Just brilliant."

They went through six more tastings and were actually pretty full when they were done. Kate had declared all of them bloody brilliant. While she and Chris decided on numbers, John poured them a glass of Prosecco to wash it all down. Wrapping up and then handing them her spare key so they could set up whenever they pleased on Thursday, she thanked them again for their excellent work.

"Thank you, darling," John said. "You stuck with us from the beginning. We don't forget."

Kate always got the "friend discount," which was really good. After they said goodbye, and Leah had to accept the fact she'd been deemed huggable, John and Chris waved at them until they were out of sight.

"Honey, you really know some interesting people," Leah said.

Kate just smiled. "I know."

Having eaten way too many appetizers, they decided to forego lunch altogether and just have coffee instead before they went to Holywell. While Kate ordered, Leah dialled Kate's mother and set up her date for tomorrow afternoon. They decided tea would be most convenient, and Kate's mother finished by saying she was really looking forward to seeing Leah again. She asked if her daughter would join them, and Leah explained Kate already had a lunch date with her new neighbour.

Kate heard her mother's reply through the phone. "Oh, indeed?" She raised her eyebrows at Leah, who bit her lip not to laugh. After Leah confirmed the time of her arrival, she promised to give Kate a hug and then disconnected.

"God, she'll drill you, you do realise that, don't you?" Kate asked.

"Yep, but I can handle your mother. I love her a great deal, you know. Besides, gossiping about you will keep the attention away from me."

"Ha! In your dreams, darling. She'll probably start by asking why you're still not married to Ryan, and make meaningful remarks about biological clocks ticking." Kate rolled her eyes.

"Oh, sweetie, my mother isn't any different. And she still hasn't forgiven me for moving to New York. She hates to fly, and even though she can reach London by boat or train, she still thinks it's really selfish of me to have moved so far away. I have no compassion for her poor nerves."

They laughed. Kate and Leah were big fans of the whole Jane Austen oeuvre, and quoted quite a few things in daily conversation. One coffee turned into two, and Kate felt far more relaxed after their tasting visit. She was no fool, however, and she knew that at some point she'd have to face the fact there were too many things going on right now to be a mere coincidence. Besides, she didn't believe in coincidences, not really. She said as much to Leah, who nodded.

"I was thinking the same thing. I'm not saying everything's related, but a lot has been going on lately. The strange mood of our prime minister, your dreams, my visions, Alan showing up on the grid again. Meg's been acting weird as well. She probably doesn't think I've noticed, but I did.

She's been checking up on us since Sunday. I can see it and feel it. And then there's Tristan, of course, our new mystery man. It might not be anything at all, but there is something telling me to keep my head clear and focussed."

Kate looked at her with a speculative gaze. "So you noticed it too, huh? Meg, I mean. I thought I was just being paranoid, but I felt her as well. Do you think there's something she's not telling us?"

Leah shrugged. "Maybe, probably with good reason, but it does give me the creeps. We'll have to trust her to tell us in her own time. I wouldn't like to be pushed either if it comes down to my visions."

Kate's iPhone vibrated, and she checked to see if it was something important. She smiled at the text message.

"What are you smiling about?" Leah asked.

"One of my clients. It says, 'Guess what? Practice does make perfect! Who knew? Thanks again xxx.' I showed him a version of the healing flame exercise to keep his energy grounded. He gives way too much during concerts, and is running low at the end of them or ends up stuck with a lot of other people's emotions. I'm actually quite surprised he texted me. I must have made an impression. He's not one to stay in touch, you know. Not that I mind. That's not what I'm there for, but I'm pleased it seems to be working for him. Hang on a second." Kate quickly typed a message back to him, saying, "See, you're a natural! Well done! X." She put her iPhone into her purse again and then emptied her cup of coffee. "Shall we go to Holywell's? And I think you're right about Meg, by the way. We should let her decide when to tell us, if at all. She's a sensible woman, and she knows when to ask for help. So enough with the paranoia crap. All in good time I guess." Kate frowned to herself. Oh great, now she was quoting Tristan already. She made no mention of the exchanged glances between Leah and Meg at Deb's lunch gathering. Leah didn't seem to notice and got up to take care of the bill.

*   *   *

Leah browsed the store at Holywell's while Kate ordered different sets of strings for her harps and was seduced into ogling the new hard case for the Salvi Ana with little wheels for easy travel. She never took it anywhere, but that looked very handy, indeed. Leah rolled her eyes at

Kate's almost helplessness over the owner's sales pitch. The owner promised to deliver it to her door for the same price, because Kate was such a good customer, and she finally gave in.

Handing over her credit card, she turned to Leah with a look that said not a word from you.

Leah just grinned and remained irritatingly quiet. Kate was also bullied into playing one of their new pedal harps. It was a new Salvi Rainbow version, Electro Acoustic, with forty-seven strings. Though Kate always played lever harp at home, she did have an education for both, and every now and then she liked to play on a pedal harp. Giving in to both the owner's and Leah's pleas, she sat and decided to play one of her own compositions. It was a piece she'd composed for Samhuinn, so it was quite dark. It began slowly with an almost dragging sound, which grew stronger by the minute. As the music continued, her right hand went up higher and higher until it was almost crying. At the end she slapped her left hand flat onto the strings and let them resonate through the room. Her audience looked quite shell-shocked.

"Wow, that's a really magnificent piece, Miss Catherine," the owner said.

"Thank you," she said with a smile. "It's called *Samhuinn*. The piece is actually about a baby being born into this world, yet again. It's a story about life, death, and rebirth I suppose."

Leah wiped away a tear. "I love it! It's beautiful. And I have to say, it sounds really well on that harp."

Kate laughed. "Yes, well, it does help if you don't have to rearrange the levers all the time. It has a magnificent sound, by the way. I bet it'll become a favourite amongst harpists." She lovingly stroked the polished wood.

The owner thanked her for playing the piece, and reconfirmed the delivery date for the hard case. They said goodbye and then left the store.

Leah clapped her hands. "Yippie, I got to hear you play!"

Kate gave her a soft push. "You silly girl. Well, I'm happy for you. You got your wish and I have a beautiful hard case. And not one word."

"My lips are sealed. Although, I will say this. Now you have a hard case, there's no excuse not to bring the Salvi every now and then to one of your private concerts." She grinned.

"Hmm, I guess not. I'm sure my mother will be thrilled. This might actually turn out to be one of my purchases she won't have any objections to," she finished with a knowing smile. Leah was about to comment when Kate's phone rang. *Meg,* Kate mouthed to her after a look at her display. "Hi, sweetie, what's up?" She listened for a few seconds and then replied, "Sure, no problem. We'll leave now and be there in fifteen minutes, I think. See you in a few then." She hung up.

"What was that all about?" Leah asked.

"I'm not sure. She said she found something regarding the prime minister, and she didn't want us to worry, but she'd rather talk about it in person. She asked if we could drop by her store. I said we would. That's okay, right?"

"Sure. Let's go then. See, I told you she'd tell us in her own time," Leah said.

"Yes, well, that's hardly fair play, vision girl," Kate replied.

"Hey! I didn't get a vision on this, okay? Tsss, insufferable presumptions!" She smiled.

Fifteen minutes later, they stood inside Meg's store. "I'll be in the back for half an hour, Shawn," Meg said to the young man behind the counter. He nodded, and they followed her to the back. This was where the kitchen area was, with a large table and comfortable chairs. "Tea, ladies?" Meg asked. They nodded. She filled a large pot with herbs and then put a tea cosy on the table. After they each had a steaming glass in front of them, she looked at them. "I still don't know if it's something important, but after my latest discovery, I can't ignore it anymore, either." Meg glanced at Leah and continued. "I should start by saying I don't think the prime minister is in any immediate danger. Having said that, I'm not really sure either."

"Well, that's good, right? At least that's something. So no death?" Kate asked.

Leah was still looking at Meg. "You did see something, didn't you?" she asked.

Meg looked at her. "Yes, I did see something. Point is, it's the same thing I'm seeing everywhere. You all have it as well. I do too."

Kate tried very hard to stay calm, because water and fire stirred inside her. "Okay, so what does 'something' mean? What is it exactly you're seeing?"

"I'm seeing a greyish sort of mist around people. It's hard to notice at first glance, and I have to focus to even be able to see it, but it's there." She hesitated.

"What is it?" Kate asked. "There's more, right?"

Meg looked concerned. "It's slightly stronger around you, Kate. I don't know why. Maybe because you were the first person I could see it around, maybe because your powers are stronger than ours. Again, I don't know. It isn't like anything I've ever seen before. Death itself is different. Of this I'm absolutely sure, but it does have the same feel. I have to be honest here."

While Kate was still mulling over Meg's revelation, Leah sat up straighter. "Okay, let's go at this from a factual point of view. There's a grey mist thingy hanging around people. Meg is sure it's not death, but it's probably death related. It's slightly more prominent around Kate. This could, indeed, be power related. I can't stress enough that I haven't seen either of us die, and I'm pretty sure I'd see such a minor little detail," she added sarcastically. "It could be Alan," she continued.

Here Kate looked up. "What? No way. That's absurd, Lee. How could this have anything to do with Alan?"

"Oh, I don't know, because he's a master of death!" Leah said with a glare.

Kate sighed. "Fair enough, but even you have to admit this is reaching. Alan's not capable of doing anything right now. How could he have an impact on so many people? Sorry, I'm just not buying it." She faced Meg. "Could you be seeing a potential death? That it's somehow connected to the choices we make or are about to make?"

Meg seemed to think that over. "Actually, that does make sense. I think you might be on to something here." She looked at Leah as well. "What do you think?"

Leah sighed. "I'm not saying no, and certainly you're the expert on your own feelings and how you experience them. I have something to add to that as well. I had a vision of heads of state and royalty gathering in New Zealand. I already told Kate, and didn't think much of it, but maybe it's related to this mist thing. Just for the record, I'm not ruling Alan out. I think it'd be wise to check up on him."

"Check up on him? You want me to check up on Alan? What? Just call the mental hospital and ask how he's doing?" Kate asked.

"Why not? You could say you're family from out of town, wanting to visit. I'm sure they won't give you specifics, but they'll probably let you know something. I could do it for you if you don't like the idea. I mean, I get that." She looked sympathetic.

Kate sighed. "No, I guess you're right. It'd, at least, help to rule out something, right? Is there somewhere I can call in private, Meg? I need some privacy for this."

Meg showed her to her office on the other side and then closed the door behind her.

Kate put down the phone in a daze, still trying to process the information she just received. She heard her friends talking to each other and tried to pull herself together.

"I shouldn't have made her make the call," Leah said to Meg. "I should have called myself. It's probably nothing, and now she's reminded of Alan again, while she was just starting to let him go."

"Don't beat yourself up about it. Kate's a big girl. I'm sure she'll be just f …"

They looked at Kate, who closed the office door softly behind her. She felt as if she'd just heard the world was about to end.

"What?" they asked.

"What is it, Kate?" Leah asked again. "Is there something wrong with Alan?"

Kate laughed a bit hysterically. "That depends on how you look at it, I suppose. I'm sure the general opinion would be that Alan is just fine. More than fine, actually. He left the hospital over a month ago, his health fully restored. So no, I wouldn't say there's something wrong with him. Mind you, there might be something wrong with me right about now."

The water in the teapot boiled once more on its own accord.

WEDNESDAY

KATE WOKE UP to a tremendous headache. One look at the clock told her it was after eleven. God, what a night. It'd been way after three when she'd fallen onto her bed, exhausted, but slightly less worried. Leah had called everyone in their inner circle to tell them about Alan's recovery and all the other stuff that had been going on as well. Sue, Romy, Deborah, and the twins had come over to Meg's store while the others called Kate to sympathise and check whether or not the cocktail party was still on for tomorrow. Kate had answered that it'd take a whole lot more for her to cancel it, so she'd see them tomorrow night.

After Meg had closed the store, they'd all gone upstairs to her apartment, and she'd whipped up a big bowl of soup with bread and some cheeses. They'd stayed deep into the night, talking about what the hell was going on and whether they'd have to consider Alan a possible threat. Kate had almost got into a serious argument with Deborah, who hated Alan's guts for hurting Kate.

Leah and Deborah were the only ones who'd actually met Alan when they were still living in the Netherlands, and even Deborah only in passing after Kate and Alan had broken up. The others just knew him by hearsay or from Kate's own stories. Deborah could get a little overprotective when it came down to her friends, and Kate needed her friend and business partner level-headed instead of becoming another factor to worry about.

When she'd said as much, Deborah had burst into tears (probably also compliments to the wine) and Kate and Leah had had to calm her down. Sue had been awfully quiet the entire evening. Leah had talked to her a bit, and she'd told Kate that Sue felt guilty about not having foreseen this. Kate had been confused. Sue was no seer, after all. She was a healer. Leah understood, though. She'd explained that Sue was probably going through the same emotions Leah had when Alan had first attacked Kate. She hadn't been there. And now Sue hadn't been there for Kate, or at least, she felt as if she hadn't been there.

Kate had walked over to her friend and just put an arm around her. Sue had smiled. Kate told her that she was always there when she needed her to be. As for the times that Sue expected herself to be there, well, that was just stupid, Kate had explained. Sue had laughed and joined the rest of the group at the table after that.

They'd made a plan to find out if Alan was anywhere near them, and they'd call each other at the end of the day for the next week. Kate had thought that was exaggerating a bit, but the others had insisted, so eventually she'd agreed.

Meg had opened three more bottles of Amarone, an Italian wine to go with the Pecorino cheese and mountains of olives, and eventually the talk had turned to the upcoming cocktail party and their outrageous outfits. The Amarone had a rather high alcohol percentage, and Kate remembered at least four glasses. That would explain her current headache.

She had to get up and somehow get rid of it. She'd promised Tristan homemade lunch, and she wanted to be clear-headed for their afternoon together. She went through her medicine cabinet, which was mostly stocked with her self-made salves, oils, and pastes. She needed the hard stuff now, though. After a few seconds, she found the little pink pills she looked for and then took two with a large glass of water.

After a nice hot shower, Kate started to feel a whole lot better. Breakfast would probably do her some good as well. She had a craving for something sweet, and decided to indulge herself with two cinnamon Pop-tarts. She put them into the toaster and then poured a glass of milk. She also checked her fridge and freezer to see if she had all the ingredients to bake a quiche and make a nice salad to go with it. Satisfied that she still had plenty of stuff to last her a week, she pre-heated the oven.

At almost one o'clock Kate was rather pleased with her results. A golden-brown quiche filled with salmon, shrimp, capers, and olives sat on the table, still hot. She'd made a nice fish salad to go with it, and decided to bring along a bottle of chardonnay as well. She had an old-fashioned picnic basket that she put everything in, keeping the wine in a little bottle-shaped cooler.

Deciding this was just a casual lunch, she put on some skinny jeans, selected one of her Placebo t-shirts, and fished her Dr. Martens out of the hallway closet. After sitting down, she divided her hair in to two strings and braided both sides just halfway. She brushed the rest and then looked in the mirror. A bit girly, but fuck it. This was also her. She jumped up and retrieved the basket from the kitchen table before she grabbed her keys. She locked up and then activated the alarm system. She closed the front door behind her before she walked down two flights of stairs.

Tristan opened his door almost immediately after she rang the bell. She smiled. He wore jeans and a t-shirt. "Someone ordered lunch?" she asked, grinning.

Tristan took the basket from her and then gave her a quick kiss. "Come in, Catherine. Perfect timing, I just finished setting up the dinner table." He walked toward the kitchen before he emptied the basket and shook his head. "You didn't have to bring the wine, silly."

"Hey, when I provide lunch, I provide it well," she said, looking around.

Funny. It was nothing like she'd expected, yet it was as well. There was way more colour than she'd anticipated, for instance. One wall was painted dark orange and on the opposite one, which was painted off-white, two squares of the same orange came back. Each square had a picture in black and white. One contained two Italian-looking people, probably his mother and father, Kate mused. The other was a picture of Tristan with his cello. He had his eyes closed, and a beam of sunlight caught his face. Whoever had taken the picture certainly knew their job. It was beautiful.

Tristan smiled. "Go ahead, look around. I don't mind," he encouraged. "I'll get these on a plate and then pour us some wine while you have a peek."

Kate returned his smile and moved through the living room. In one corner there was his cello. It looked old but magnificent. Tristan also owned a lot of books, she was pleased to notice. She hated men who didn't like to read. She knew the outlines of the apartment from other neighbours, of course, but she just loved walking into a home and seeing what people did with their own personal space.

He'd placed the sitting area near the windows so people could look outside. Two couches in chocolate-brown dominated the space. In front of them were two little teak side tables, functioning as one with just a tiny space between them. Underneath them there was a big rug, which Kate suspected to be some long-haired sheep. There was a book on one of the couches, and she leaned over to read the title. Hmm, the latest Neil Gaiman. Who would have thought it?

The dining area, which was connected to the open kitchen, was done in the same colours. A large teak dinner table stood in the middle, surrounded by six comfortable-looking chairs in matching chocolate-brown. The kitchen itself was very light with a light wooden counter and off-white doors with tin knobs. It had a rural look. In fact, the whole place had a bit of a rural look to it. She liked it.

"Lunch is ready," Tristan said. He waited for her to sit at the table before he sat as well. "Well? Do you like it? Does it resemble my soul?" he asked with a slight smirk.

"Your soul, no less? I don't know about that, but it does suit you. In a way. I'll admit, I didn't expect such a country vibe, I guess, but I really like it."

He smiled. "Ah, you forget my Italian roots. My parents live in the country, and I guess I'm always trying to recreate a bit of home. I'm glad you like it, though. Lunch looks delicious, by the way, Catherine. Thank you."

"Do you want me to explain what's what? The quiche has a salmon and prawn filling with little capers and olives as well. The salad is also smoked salmon with homemade croutons, anchovies, cherry tomatoes, some baby leaf spinach and some rocket. I added a bit of freshly made horseradish mayonnaise as a dressing. I hope you like it."

He raised his glass to her, and simply said, "I love fish. *Bon appétit*, Catherine. May this be the first of many homemade lunches."

She laughed. "I'll bet, but you'll be doing as much cooking as me, mister. It's your turn next time." Their glasses touched in toast and then Tristan sliced up the quiche.

"Did you have a busy day yesterday?" he asked.

Kate hesitated. She wondered if she should mention Alan or not. Usually, she'd forego any mentioning of exes so early on in a new friendship, which might or might not evolve into something else as well. Tristan was different, however. She really did feel as if she could tell him anything and he wouldn't be spooked. Furthermore, being an empath he might actually have some interesting insights.

"Not busy really. It was a rather interesting day, though. I said I knew quite a lot about empaths, right?"

Tristan nodded at her questioning look. "Yes, you did."

"Well, that's mainly because my ex was an empath as well. I met Alan at college. He was one of my professors. Yes, how cliché, I know. We didn't start dating or anything, however, until way after my graduation. Um … look, this isn't going to be a light story. Are you sure you wanna hear this?" Kate played with her glass of wine.

Tristan leaned over and covered her hand with his. "I have a feeling I should feel honoured you trust me enough to tell me this, Catherine. So yes, I'd like to hear the story and what happened yesterday, because obviously, it has something to do with Alan."

Kate felt a rush of gratitude. There was no accusation, no jealousy or anything in his voice, just plain interest and a bit of concern.

"Thank you, Tristan, just for being you." She gave his hand a slight squeeze before she let go and then took a sip of wine. "Alan, being older than me—he's about your age, in fact—knew what I was or what I could do from the beginning. He's not only an empath, you see. He can also control death, and he recognises other people's gifts. A dangerous combination, but I thought he was the world. He taught psychology, which must have been a walk in the park for him, as he could tap into anybody's mind to see what their current problems were and deal with them accordingly. I was very interested in how the human mind worked, and so was he, although perhaps for different reasons. Those first years, though, Alan was a really nice guy. Yes, he did use his powers a lot, but always to the benefit of others. That changed after people hurt his family. He wasn't there, and I think he never forgave himself for that. Anyway, he became very bitter after that, and as much as I tried to be there for him, he wouldn't let me in anymore. He started drinking and blocked my powers, so I couldn't heal or ground him, and we grew further and further apart. We had a lot of arguments about punishing the guilty and all that. He just wouldn't listen, and accused me of being too soft. Alan did a lot of things under the guise of 'for the greater good.' I let it go on for far too long, may the gods forgive me. I wasn't ready to give up on him. It would be my failure, you see. At least that's how I saw it back then." She gave him a small smile.

"Did he take people's lives?" Tristan asked softly.

Kate took a deep breath. "Yes. Yes, he did, though how many I don't know. Let's just say I didn't stick around to find out. I know about one, at least. That's when we had our first big fallout. The man was a child molester and he'd murdered a little girl in our block. Alan knew her, and went completely mad. Don't get me wrong, I understand the impulse. I do. A part of me wanted that guy dead as well, and the Netherlands isn't exactly known for its severe punishments, so he'd probably be out again in ten years or so. That was what Alan screamed at me, you see. 'Do you want such a man back on the street in ten years?' Of course I didn't, but taking a man's life … just like that? It felt so wrong. I never went to the police, though. He told me it was clean and quick. Being a master of death, Alan can just stop your heart. He never had a sadistic streak as far as I could tell. I moved out of our apartment that night. He was out with some of his friends, and I stuffed all my clothes in a suitcase, grabbed some personal items, and moved out. I stayed at Lee's for a few weeks until I got my own apartment. We did keep in touch, but he didn't trust me anymore, not completely, anyway. He knew I didn't approve of his way of life, even if I didn't turn him in. One day, though, I learned of his plans to kill another human being. Some kind of industrial hotshot. I'm sure he'd done a lot of bad things, but I couldn't let this one go. Not in advance. With the child molester, I only found out afterward, but I couldn't claim plausible deniability with this one." Kate gave him a weak smile.

"You stopped him, didn't you?" Tristan's face was full of sympathy.

Kate let out a small cry. "Stopped him? Yes, I guess you could say that. Actually, until yesterday I thought I'd destroyed him. I set out to prevent him from killing that man, and we ended up facing each other. I felt death coming toward me, and I was sure I was going to die. In a moment of total panic and pure will to survive, I let go of all the elements, and they manifested all at once and smashed into him. He immediately fell to the ground. I rushed over. He was still alive, but didn't recognise me, or himself, for that matter. I anonymously called an ambulance and told them I was just passing by. They took him away, and I later learned they'd transferred him to a mental hospital. He's been there ever since.

Until a month ago, that is, because I called them yesterday. Apparently, Alan is fully recovered, and left their institution a month ago. Where he is now they could, or would not, tell me. Well, that's pretty much it. Some story, huh?" She leaned back and watched the man across the table. He still didn't seem very upset, just concerned.

"Again, thank you for your confidence, Catherine. It must be difficult to share this with me, though I'm glad you did. I won't say I understand Alan's choices, because I really don't. It does, however, give me a better understanding of your reluctance toward empaths." He raised his hands in defence as Kate was about to reply. "Hang on, that's not me being judgemental, just an observation. And you have every right to be on your guard. I would be as well, and I can tell if I'm being lied to. You don't have that advantage, so I understand. Really, I do. What does concern me, however, is his present whereabouts. You called the hospital for a reason, I assume? So you must have thought you saw him, or didn't you?"

Kate had to smile a bit. Tristan was rather quick on the uptake. "You're right, of course, I did have a reason. Though I haven't seen Alan. Not in real life, anyway. I dreamed about him, and without going into detail, when I visited a gallery with Leah, the dream suddenly became very real. The girls became paranoid and bullied me into calling the hospital. Good thing they did, as it turned out, because their paranoia was justified. But really, he could very well be in the Netherlands. As far as I know, Alan has no connection to England."

Tristan looked at her. "Besides you, you mean."

Kate shifted in her chair. "Yes, well, there's that. I don't think Alan's on a killing spree or something, out for revenge." She laughed a bit nervously. "I know he has every reason to hate me, but somehow I don't think he does. This might be naive of me, I know. Anyway. I'm sure Leah would, um …" Kate stopped abruptly.

"See him coming?" Tristan finished for her with a grin.

Kate looked at him a bit sheepishly. "You knew?"

Tristan smiled. "No, but you just confirmed my suspicions."

Kate rolled her eyes. "Just peachy. What is it with you and honesty?"

Tristan refilled her glass. "Well, I don't know, Catherine dear. Perhaps it's my stunning appearance. It might be my killer smile, which makes you spill the beans. Or perhaps you just trust me?" He gave her a genuine smile.

Kate laughed. "Odd as it may be, I think you're right. I do trust you, but I've trusted the wrong people before, you know," she finished rather sadly.

"I promise I will never lie to you, Catherine. I may hide the truth from you at times, because of my work, or because I think you're not ready for certain things, but I will never lie to you. You have my word."

Somehow Kate really believed him. It made her feel better about Tristan's mysterious side. He pretty much just admitted to not telling her everything, and she was even more convinced now that his work involved a great deal of privacy or even secrecy. Maybe she'd even get him into trouble if she pushed too much on that front, so she decided it didn't matter. As long as he wouldn't lie to her, anyway.

"Thank you, Tristan. That means a lot to me."

"Are you worried?" he asked.

"About Alan, you mean? No, not really. I was quite upset when I found out he was out of hospital. Okay, I was in hysterics, to be honest. The more I think about it, the more relaxed I am about it. Tristan, can I ask you something?"

"I thought you knew. You can ask me anything. If I can't, or don't want to answer, I'll tell you."

"Well, the past few weeks have been somewhat crazy. World wise, I mean, not just Alan. I mean, let's just say Leah and I aren't the only ones with, um … gifts. Have you, as an empath, noticed anything different lately?"

Tristan sat a bit straighter and seemed to consider his answer.

"Look, if you can't say anything, I'll understand. Just forget I asked." Kate suddenly felt a bit foolish.

Tristan actually laughed. "Will you, for once, be patient and let me think for a minute before you jump to any conclusions? Good grief, woman!"

"Sorry," Kate mumbled.

"I think I know to what you're referring. This has been a crazy year at the very least. Something big is just around the corner, but the outcome isn't set yet. Do you believe we create our own future, Catherine?"

Kate looked at him in surprise. "Of course I do. The future isn't set. It's what we make of it."

Tristan nodded. "I agree. A lot of people don't, however, and they're starting to lose hope. Maybe that's what you and your friends are picking up on. Despair is a very strong emotion. It can be felt by more people than just empaths."

"Losing hope? I think you're right. That's what we've been picking up as well. Question remains, why? Oh, and does going to New Zealand sound familiar to you?"

Tristan gave her a rather piercing glare. "Why do you ask?"

Kate shrugged. "It might be nothing. Lee saw lots of important people in New Zealand, that's all. I thought it might make more sense to you."

"Does any of this make sense?" he replied. "New Zealand is a beautiful country. It's an island. It's the farthest from England." He just looked at her.

Kate stared back at him. "You know something."

A flash of annoyance crossed his face. He looked at her again with a slightly unhappy expression. "Yes."

Kate frowned. "I'm sorry. I shouldn't push. I know you're being as open as you can. This has to do with your job, right?" She could see by his face she was right. "Okay, so farthest from England. You're obviously trying to tell me something. England will be in danger? Is that why they're moving important people to the other side of the world? That's it, isn't it? Something's going to happen. And you're here to help? Or to prevent it from happening? Oh, my god, is your client the prime minister?"

Tristan burst into a laughing fit. "The prime minister? Whatever made you say that? I can honestly say my client is not the prime minister, Catherine. Though I agree with you the poor woman could do with some help. Alas, it won't be from me or my company. As for the rest, no comment." He smiled.

Kate smiled as well. "Okay, I'll take that as a yes then. Can I do something about it, Tristan?"

Tristan gave her another smile. "I think you should continue doing the things you already plan to do."

"Hmm … well, tomorrow we're having the cocktail party. That will go through as planned. And Samhuinn coming up, of course, this Saturday."

Tristan looked interested. "Yes, I've heard some people mentioning it as well. I'm sorry, I'm not really familiar with nature religion. What exactly is Samhuinn?"

Kate felt her enthusiasm rise to the surface. She loved explaining about her way of life and smiled. "Samhuinn is the beginning of the new year," she began. "It was, at least, for certain people many years ago. We still treat it as such. It's also the darkest festival we celebrate, because it's connected to death and rebirth. The veil between our world and the otherworld is at its thinnest, and we honour our ancestors during our ritual. We actually open a gate so they can celebrate with us. To me, Samhuinn is also about the goddess, in her form of the Cailleach, the dark one with her burning cauldron. Many fear her, but she always makes me feel safe and loved. Somehow being in the arms of death can be very comforting. We write something down on a piece of paper. Things we want to let go of, and we burn that in her cauldron. It's also a time to set in motion new things or wishes, to let it simmer, so to speak, so it can seed at Imbolc in February."

"So it's quite a powerful time, this Samhuinn?" he asked.

"Oh yes, I'd say the most powerful. Even more so this year, as we'll be under a blue moon as well. It only occurs once every few years, and almost never on Samhuinn. It's the second blue moon in a month, you see, and it's been a while since we had it on Samhuinn. So 2020 is turning out to be quite a special year for us." She smiled.

"And you always celebrate the festivals?"

"Yes, always. Sometimes not as extensive as we would like to, but we always celebrate. It's our way to keep connected to the turning of the seasons I suppose. Being an elemental, it's very important to me personally. It'd feel like neglecting nature, and thereby myself, if I forego the festival celebrations."

"London must be a difficult place to celebrate nature, though," he said with a frown.

"Why? Because it's not bursting with trees or lack of a coastline? We have plenty of parks, you know. Besides, honouring nature is inside us. A beautiful place helps, yes. I suppose it's the same for Christians. Having a beautiful church can be very helpful to put you in a certain state of mind, but you can find God everywhere. I think it's more about sharing the feeling and experience of community than a place of power or worship. That's my personal opinion, of course," she said, giving him a small smile.

"I think I can relate to that feeling. So, you do celebrate outside? Don't you worry about other people seeing you?"

Kate laughed. "Why? Afraid we're going to be locked up?" She grinned. "Sometimes we do have people watching us. We are, however, careful in choosing a place for ritual work. And most people are just interested. We've never had any disturbances during a ritual. Afterward, though, sometimes they come up to us and ask what it was we were doing, because they felt moved. That's a good thing, I think, and we always explain what it is we do. Do you know London Fields? Just beyond Shoreditch?" Tristan nodded. "That's where we'll be this Saturday. Most of it is still abandoned. They opened the front side again, but the back is still closed to the public."

Tristan raised his eyebrow. "And I suppose you don't consider yourself a part of the public?"

Kate grinned. "On the advice of counsel I decline to answer."

"Hmm … indeed. Good thing I don't represent the law then, Catherine."

Kate stared at him. Shit, she hadn't thought about that. She shrugged. Tough luck then. She was pretty sure Tristan wouldn't send the cops after them for celebrating a ritual. So she smiled rather mischievously, and said, "Good thing, indeed."

After their lunch, Kate helped Tristan clean the table and insisted they do the dishes together. He objected, but finally gave in, and they quite enjoyed sharing such a domestic task together. He made them a pot of tea and then filled a plate with chocolate biscuits. As she snuggled herself on the couch, ditching her boots, he went to pick up his cello.

"A promise is a promise, of course," he said. "Is there anything in particular you'd like to hear, Catherine?"

"Do you compose as well?" she asked.

"As a matter of fact, yes. Would you like me to play something for you?"

"Very much. I mean, I love some of the masters, but if you compose yourself, I'm dying to hear it."

Tristan sat in front of her so she had a good view and then played. Kate loved the sound of the cello. Or the violin, for that matter. She'd love to play the cello herself, but she was way too impatient for such an instrument. The harp suited her much more, as did the piano.

Tristan had his hair in a ponytail, but during lunch a lock had escaped and now fell across his cheek. Kate thought he looked dead cute and bit her lip. He had his eyes closed and seemed to be lost in the music. She wanted to close hers as well, but she was captivated by the look on his face and the way he played. It was pure beauty. As the music came to an end, he opened his eyes again and gave her a shy smile.

"Wow," Kate said. "Just wow. There's no other word for it. That was beautiful. It's like air or something, so soft and swift. What's it called?"

"*L'aura è tua messaggera,*" he said with a smile.

"That sounds beautiful the way you pronounce it, but I have no idea what that means."

"It means the breeze is your messenger. I wrote it when I first arrived in England. I lived in Brighton for quite a while when my father was still working here, and I just loved the smell of the ocean. The way the breeze catches your face ... That first night when I was sitting in my new room, still surrounded by unpacked boxes, I wrote this piece. It's still one of my favourites. I'm glad you like it. I had a feeling you'd understand."

Kate gave him a warm smile. "I love it. And I wasn't far off either with my air comment. Can you say it again?"

He laughed. "*L'aura è tua messaggera.*"

She closed her eyes for just a second. "It really is a beautiful language. I won't try to repeat it. I'm sure it'd sound even worse than your Dutch," she finished with a grin.

He raised one eyebrow. "Really? You were laughing pretty hard as I recall, or my memory must be faulty."

She looked at him with an innocent expression. "I have no idea what you're talking about. Now shut up and play something else for me."

"Yes, ma'am!" And he played again.

After Kate had her third cup of tea, she finally took pity on Tristan and allowed him a break and poured him some tea. He put the cello in its stand and then sat next to her on the couch.

"It is a beautiful instrument, Tristan. It looks very old. Not that I know much about cellos."

He took a bite of his chocolate cookie and looked at her. "Well, it is very old. Eighteenth century, to be exact. It used to belong to the Italian composer Nicolò Paganini."

Kate almost choked on her tea. "Eighteenth century! Like what, it's a Stradivari or something?"

Tristan smiled. "Not or something. It's a Stradivari, yes. Why, Catherine, you look positively shocked?"

Kate looked a bit embarrassed. "Yes, well, I mean … they're supposed to be really expensive. I mean, I certainly don't own an Erard harp, and they're not anywhere near the prices Stradivari go for."

He looked at her with a knowing smile. "Aahh, you think I stole it?"

Now she looked even more embarrassed. "No! God, of course not. They're really rare, aren't they?"

He nodded. "Yes, they are. I believe there are only about sixty left in the world. I consider myself very lucky to own one. It's my most treasured possession. It was a gift from my parents. Obviously, I come from money. Though they always taught me to take care of myself. When they moved back to Italy a couple years ago, my mother wanted me to have something that would remind me of them, so they bought me my cello. I had one, but it had a little accident when I was thirty-eight. I was so busy with work back then I quit playing altogether for a couple years. Needless to say I was quite moved when they left me with this beauty." He lovingly touched his cello.

"I can well imagine. And I'm glad your parents gave you such a magnificent reason to play again. Damn, I hope my harp doesn't get a complex, should they ever meet."

Tristan laughed. "I'm sure my cello will be on his best behaviour."

When she noticed it was almost five o'clock, she got up. "My, look at the time. We've been chatting away, haven't we?"

"We sure have, but if it were up to me, you'd stay here all day."

He walked to the kitchen to retrieve her picnic basket and then put her belongings inside. She followed him, still a bit dazed by that particular comment.

"You'll see me tomorrow, though," she said, just to have something to say.

"True, but then I have to share, and I hate to share, Catherine. I just have to make sure you won't forget about me, won't I?"

Before she could respond, Tristan's mouth was on hers. As her eyes fluttered closed, his tongue pressed against her lips, demanding access. She opened and let him explore. A small groan escaped his throat as she gave in to him. Her arms went up around his neck, and suddenly her back was pressed against the wall. As their kiss deepened, Kate softly nibbled on his lower lip, which made him pull her even closer. She felt his arousal, and fire surged through her like crazy. As he took possession of her mouth again with his, she felt like molten lava. Once he finally let go of her, she felt slightly dizzy and noticed her lips were rather swollen.

"I'm pretty sure I'll remember your name tomorrow," she said, her voice a bit shaky.

"Good," he replied with a smile, but his eyes still reflected the fire burning within. "See you soon then, my elemental." He handed her the picnic basket. "You'd better go now before I decide to keep you here."

She laughed a bit nervously. She didn't think she'd mind if he kept her there, but it was better to take things slow. Yes, she'd go about this in a sensible way, all mature and shit. With a big sigh, she gave him another smile and stepped into the lift. As the doors closed, a thought crossed her mind that being responsible and all sucked big time.

*   *   *

After Kate had been reading for a couple hours on her couch with another cup of herbal tea, her phone rang. One look showed her it was Leah, probably checking in.

"Hi, hon. What's up?"

"Hello, darling. God, I'm exhausted! I stayed way too long at your mother's, and we had a blast, but damn, that woman can talk!"

Kate grinned. She'd had a feeling her mother would pump Leah for every bit of information possible. "Well, I hate to say I told you so, but you have to admit there was truth in my reasoning."

"Yeah, yeah, yeah, your logic doesn't resemble our earth logic. You're sublime, now bite me. Are you going to feed me or what?"

Kate laughed. "Oh, poor baby. That bad, huh? Sure, sweetie. You're more than welcome. I was thinking of making pizza. Would that be acceptable?"

Leah grunted. "More than acceptable. The Underground is completely swamped with those annoying beings they call humans, though, so it might take me an hour, at least, to get there."

"No problem. I'll start on the dough. With a bit of luck, the pizza will be ready when you arrive."

Leah let out a big sigh. "Thanks, hon, you're a lifesaver! See you in a bit."

Putting her words into action, Kate started on the pizza dough to give it time to rise. She was done in ten minutes and then put the dough into a bowl with a towel on top. She checked her fridge to see what she'd put on the pizza. Hmm … tomatoes, garlic, of course, some mozzarella, basil, olives, and parmesan. That would go well together and perhaps another one with fish. She had some salmon left, anchovies and capers as well. Yep, that would do. Satisfied, she nestled herself on the couch again and took up her book.

When the doorbell rang, she'd just put both pizzas into the oven. She pushed the intercom to let Leah in and then opened the front door. Anticipating Leah's need for alcohol, she poured two glasses of chilled chardonnay.

"Hi, hon. God, can I just say that sometimes I hate the fucking Underground. Aarggh!" Leah kicked off her boots in the hallway before she walked over to Kate to give her a kiss. Kate smiled and handed Leah her glass of wine.

"Oh yes, baby, come to Mama!" Leah took a large sip and sniffed the air. "That smells delicious. I'm actually starving. Those scones were lovely, and I ate way too many, but I skipped lunch because I almost missed my train, and you know how I get when I skip meals. Your mother sends her love, by the way, and wants to know all about your lunch with Tristan so be prepared."

Kate huffed. "Why am I not surprised? How much did you tell her?"

Leah shrugged. "Not that much actually. Just that he's the first man since Alan you're really interested in, and I think that was enough, to be honest."

"Yeah, I imagine it would be. I think I'm in big time trouble, by the way. I'm really falling for this guy. Not good, not good."

Leah laughed. "Oh, come on, love isn't a bad thing, you know. It's just complicated sometimes." She frowned. "I mean, Ryan and I really love each other, but the distance thing can be somewhat challenging. I'd imagine Tristan comes with the same problems, but I'm sure you'll find a way around that, if it evolves into something serious."

"Solid advice, hon, though we're not quite there yet. I mean, I'm pretty sure he likes me, but love is a different matter. Though honestly, I wouldn't mind shagging him senseless." She grinned. Leah laughed at her remark.

Once they finished their pizzas and decided they were in desperate need of their best friends, Ben and Jerry, they happily took turns dipping their spoons into the bucket of ice cream. Kate had just put another spoonful into her mouth when her phone rang again.

"Hi, Deb," she said, her mouth still full with chunky bits of dough.

"Hi, hon. Am I disturbing you during dinner?"

"Nope, just eating disgusting amounts of Ben and Jerry with Lee here, that's all." She could practically see Deborah's expression, and she grinned at Leah, who grinned back.

"Oh. Well, anyway … I asked around to see if I could find out Alan's whereabouts, but so far nothing. Meg and Sue are on it as well, but we figure he'll most likely watch you or try to contact you, me, or Lee, as we're the only ones he really knows, right?"

Kate nodded. "Sure, makes sense, if he's in England at all, which I'm not so sure, but let's not rule anything out," she added to satisfy Deborah's need for planning and controlling things.

"My thoughts exactly. Look, I'll keep you posted, okay? If we hear anything new, I'll call again. Give my love to Lee."

"Will do! See you tomorrow, hon," Kate said and then disconnected.

"Any news?" Leah asked.

"No, of course not. I don't know what we expect to find. Alan's not an idiot. If he's here, he'll be careful not to reveal his current whereabouts. Trust me."

"He must be curious, though, to see you, I mean. It wouldn't be unthinkable he'd want to catch a glimpse of you, right?" Leah took another spoonful of ice cream.

Kate licked her spoon clean. "No, not unthinkable. Still, highly unlikely, but that's just me. In all fairness, I have no idea what he's like now, let alone how his mind works. So, for all intents and purposes, he could be here."

"You don't seem too worried about it," Leah commented.

"I'm not. Look, Lee, I'm not trying to be bold and brave here. Fact of the matter is, I did defeat him once. If it turns out I have to repeat that act, I know I'm able to. I'd really rather not, but knowing that I can gives me peace of mind. That, and my complete paranoid friends, who are acting like freaking bodyguards," she ended with a laugh.

"Hmm, maybe I should consider a career change. What do you think?" Leah asked with a grin.

"I think you'd be fabulous. You could just stare them all down and scare the crap out of people by predicting terrible futures." They laughed at that.

After they'd finished the entire bucket, cleared away the dishes and put them into the dishwasher, Kate asked her friend if she'd be interested in seeing a movie on Leicester Square.

"There's a new Tim Burton. It might be interesting," she said.

"I'm always willing to give Burton a go. And it's Wednesday, so it shouldn't be any trouble getting tickets. Yes, let's do that. It's been a while since I've seen a movie on the big screen, and I do love the Odeon. It's a date!"

Kate was in a good mood. She had her best friend in London again, there was an interesting new man in her life, tomorrow they'd have a great party with lots of people to catch up with, and tonight she was going to enjoy a quiet night with a big bag of popcorn and a good movie. Life was turning out pretty great.

Just before they turned the corner, Kate sensed they were being watched and looked back. The street was completely deserted. Letting go of her moment of paranoia, she put her arm through Leah's and smiled. *Good thing I'm not losing my head over this,* she thought.

THURSDAY

"KATE! YOUR DJ'S on the phone. He wants to know if he can come over an hour earlier," Leah yelled to Kate, who stood in the kitchen with John and Chris.

"Tell him that's fine. If we're not here, John or Chris will be able to open the door for him," Kate yelled back.

She heard Leah confirming what she'd just said and focussed her attention again on the conversation at hand. John and Chris were already in a heated argument about how to present their food to the guests, and Kate had been one second away from stepping in when she realised they seemed to have finally reached an agreement.

"Now, boys, can I leave you two alone for an hour or two without killing each other? Lee and I need to pick up our costumes, and frankly, I could do with a Starbucks as well. If you behave nicely, I might bring back something for you two monkeys."

"I think we can just about manage that, yes," Chris said in a huff. "And you better bring back the good stuff. Hot, searing hot."

"Yes, yes, yes, you diva, I know what you like. Now, the interior decorator will be here at four. She knows what to do, so do try to let her do her job. Just because she's straight doesn't mean she has no sense of style, okay?" She looked at the pair of them, knowing full well her little speech was completely pointless, but wanting to give it a go, nonetheless.

"As if we'd do such a thing. Really, Kittycat, the things you accuse us of. It's shocking. We'll be way too busy setting up our own things. Far more important, if you ask me, than some frilly little things to cheer up the room. Perspective darling, perspective," John said with a superior look on his face.

"Of course. How silly of me." Kate rolled her eyes. "Well, that's settled then. We'll be back before dinner, so round six o'clock I should think. Will that be okay?" She looked at them to make sure there would be no complaints.

"That's fine, sweetie. Honestly, don't worry. We have everything under control," John said more seriously.

She smiled. "Thanks, John. You guys are the greatest."

Chris messed up her hair, petting her head, and then gently pushed her out of the kitchen. "Go!" he said. "We'll manage."

Looking at Leah to see if she was ready to leave, Kate grabbed her purse and keys. "Shall we go then?" she asked her friend.

Leah grabbed her purse as well, and said, "Yep, all set."

Together they left the apartment and the building.

"Good grief," Leah said. "If this is any indication for the rest of the day, I'm tired already."

Kate had to smile. "I know. I think I'm a bit out of practice as well. Or I'm just getting older, but I also caught myself wishing to just fast forward to tomorrow, instead of entertaining a hundred or so people for an evening. On the other hand, it's probably going to be great, and in the moment I usually come around. As will you, darling."

"You're right, of course. I'm just being whiney. I'm not at my best in a crowd of unfamiliar faces."

"You'll recognise lots of faces. The girls will be there. Tristan's coming, and you could catch up with some of your fellow authors. Quite a few are coming, you know."

Leah looked a lot happier. "I hadn't thought about that. Hmm, yes, that might be nice. Okay, so I might be able to do some serious mingling, after all. Still, I'd rather have you just to myself," she said with a wicked grin. "I hate to share."

Kate wacked her purse on Leah's back. "God! I should never have told you. I thought it was cute, okay!" She sent her a murderous look.

Her friend just kept grinning. "And so it was. Still, if you tell me such things, you know the rules. I get to see you squirm, so tough titty."

"Please don't say anything to John and Chris. I'll never hear the end of it. Or my mother, for that matter. Come to think of it, don't mention it to anyone."

Leah laughed and stuck her arm around Kate's. "Come on, sweetie, your secrets are safe with me. I promise. Let's get our outfits."

When Kate had told Leah about her plans for a fire-like cat suit, and Leah had made her pun about going as Madam Blavatsky, Kate had called her seamstress to see if she could squish her friend in as well. It hadn't been a problem, but the seamstress had come up with the lovely idea to perhaps dress up like Professor Trelawney instead. She was also from the Harry Potter books, so it'd fit nicely with the idea for Fawkes.

Leah, who'd loved that idea even more, had happily agreed. So half an hour later, both of them stood in a fitting room, laughing like crazy. Leah wore glasses at least a centimetre thick and a Trelawney-like wig. Her dress, which was made of five different layers in all kinds of purple, made little bell-like noises every time she moved. Kate looked like a freaking phoenix on fire. The kind lady had made her a headdress as well with waist-long feathers, which she could put on top of her hair. Little clips were attached to several layers, so she could easily arrange the feathers on top later that evening. The cat suit was a dark red, turning lighter at both sides of her body where red, orange, and deep yellow feathers were attached. There was also a bit of feather fluff on her wrists and ankles.

"I feel as if I should have wings or something," Kate said while looking in the mirror.

Leah pretended to stumble over and said in a dark voice, "Yes … Yes, my dear, I see wings in your near future. I'm afraid it's not good. It's … it's a deadly dragon!"

Kate laughed so hard she actually had to sit. "Oh, my god, you're brilliant!" she cried. "Who would have thought it? I loved Emma as Trelawney, but you could have given her a run for her money!" She wiped the tears from her eyes.

The seamstress looked pleased. They were having so much fun with their costumes. "You both look amazing, I have to say. You picked really well. It suits you," she said with a smile.

Kate and Leah exchanged meaningful looks. "I should bloody well hope so," Leah whispered to Kate when the seamstress walked to the counter to help another client.

Kate stifled a snigger. They took off their costumes and then changed into their own clothes again. The kind lady put their costumes into protective covers, which were easy for them to carry, and then printed out their bill. Kate insisted on paying her a hundred pounds extra, for her quick delivery. First, the seamstress wouldn't hear of it, but when Leah and Kate expressed their gratitude, she gracefully accepted their gift and wished them a lovely Halloween.

Satisfied and in a very good mood, they left the shop with their costumes, in search of a Starbucks. There were less of them since the recession, but thankfully London had seen the worst of it seven years ago and was starting to get back on its feet. After turning a corner or two, the green lady with the stars around her head was in sight. Settling for two pumpkin spice lattes—it was the season again—and two muffins, they took the last comfortable purple chairs in the corner near the window.

"Ah, bliss," Kate sighed. "I love these chairs. They're the best." She draped both costumes over the other chair and then laid her purse on the seat as well. "Remind me to order two searing hot lattes when we leave," she said.

Leah nodded. "Will do." She stretched her legs and sighed. "Is it just us and John and Chris for dinner?"

"No, Deb's joining us as well, and I told the decorator she could join us if she wanted to, but I don't know if she will. She might be gone already when we get back. She's really good at her job, but not really the mingling type. The DJ will be there at seven, as you know, as will my hostess. She'll open the door and check the invitations. Sue's coming over to help, of course. Well, that's what she thinks she's coming to do, but I have to fill her in on all the latest developments. John and Chris's staff will arrive at seven thirty. They'll be wearing spotted suits, after the *101 Dalmatians*." Kate rolled her eyes.

Leah grinned. "They really are quite a pair, aren't they?"

"Yes, they are. They're the best, though. Not just in terms of food. Despite first appearances, they're really well organised as well."

Her friend laughed. "They do seem to bicker quite a lot."

"All in good fun, well, most of the time, anyway," Kate said. "You know, I'm finally looking forward to tonight. There's always a certain amount of planning and things that go wrong. You get to a point where you wonder if this was such a good idea," she said laughing. "Now everything's coming together. I think a night of Halloween fun will do me a world of good."

Her friend smiled. "And thankfully we don't have anything planned for tomorrow, so we can have a bit of a lie-in and get ready for Samhuinn on Saturday. I'm also looking forward to that, you know," she said with a wink.

"As am I," Kate replied. "It might be wise to actually try out some parts of the ritual tomorrow. Like a trial run. To see how it goes. Not in the morning, of course, but perhaps later in the afternoon, if some of the girls are up for it."

"Sure, why not," Leah agreed. "I don't think the girls will object to that. We're all kind of curious to see what our powers combined can do when we release them full force."

"No shit, Sherlock, as am I." Kate winked.

Once it was time to head back to the apartment, Kate ordered two searing hot lattes to go while Leah waited outside to soak up some late afternoon sunshine. They hopped onto the Underground and then walked the last bit through Shoreditch. The interior decorator had indeed already left, but she'd done an amazing job. Even John and Chris were in awe, though reluctantly. Building on the Rivendell vibe of Kate's apartment, she'd created a very ghostly atmosphere with lighting, crystals, and fountains with swirling white smoke all over the place. What Kate loved the most was that it just looked beautiful, not at all tacky or Halloween-like. It was, however, a bit spooky.

"Wow!" Leah exclaimed. "I gotta have her number. How the hell did she do this? And how much money did you spend on it? This must be quite costly with the fountains and all."

"Oh, come on. It's once a year, and Deb and I can afford it. It's rather great, isn't it?" she said, still looking around with a smile.

"Honey, I'm gutted to admit it, but yes, it's very pretty. We even had a short chat with her to check if she could drop by our place and share her thoughts," Chris said.

Kate turned around, looking surprised. "Well, that's a first."

"Yes, and let's leave it at that," John said with a smile, joining them in the living room. They all laughed.

"Whoohoo, weekend!" Deborah said, appearing through the moss wall.

A woman with long, wavy dark red hair followed her. She wore a lot of earrings in each ear and was dressed in a tight black shirt and a pair of black jeans. Apparently, Sue had arrived.

One look at Sue's face told Kate that Deborah had already filled her in. Sue came over to hug her. She squeezed Kate tight, and whispered into her ear, "I won't let him hurt you, you know. Not again."

Kate gave her friend a soft smile. "Thanks, hon, but I'm not even sure Alan has anything to do with this. I'm glad you're here." She gave Sue another hug.

While Leah and Sue greeted each other, Kate looked at Deborah. "Hey, darling, everything locked up?"

"Yep, I waited until the cleaners were done, so everything's spotless for after the weekend," Deborah answered. "Oh, man, three whole days of fun and sleeping in. I'm in my happy place." She stretched like a cat and gave Leah a wink. She turned to John and Chris to give them a kiss. "Great to see you ladies again," she said teasingly.

John rolled his eyes. "Oh please, you just like us for the food," he said, but returned her kiss with a big hug.

Chris pushed him aside so he could have his turn. Deborah gave him a big hug and then stuck out her tongue at John. Sue was introduced to John and Chris, and besides some gushing over her long, red hair, they behaved pretty decently.

"Well, ladies," John said, "dinner's ready. So let's get a move on, then we'll have plenty of time to change into our outfits after that."

There was a lot of mumbling, and they all walked over to the kitchen table, which John and Chris had set, and took a seat. Once everyone had a full glass of chardonnay, they toasted to a successful evening. Dishes were passed around the table, and for a moment, they were just enjoying each other's company. There wouldn't be much time to catch up once the party got started, and Deborah hadn't seen John and Chris for quite some time. It was nice to see them again. When everyone had a full stomach, they helped John and Chris clean up, and after that everybody went to change or take a quick shower.

Kate had two guestrooms with en suite bathrooms, so John and Chris took one while Leah and Deborah shared the other. Kate and Sue went to Kate's bedroom to change and take a quick shower. Once

Kate was done drying her hair, she straightened it and got into her costume. She put on the headdress and then attached the little clips to her hair. She applied a hint of dark red and dark orange eye shadow and the blackest mascara she could find. A touch of dark red lipstick and she was done. Looking in the mirror, she was pretty pleased with herself. Her cat suit was boot cut, so she decided to wear her ankle boots under it. They were pretty high heeled, but she'd be able to walk around on them the entire evening, which wasn't unimportant.

Sue came out of the shower and whistled. "Wow, you really look like a phoenix!"

Kate grinned. "Then we'll be a couple phoenixes, won't we?"

Sue was going to dress up as Dr. Jean Grey from the X-men. With her natural dark red hair, it wasn't much of a stretch with the right outfit. As Sue used to be a seamstress, she had designed her own outfit, and it looked amazing. Pretty pleased with themselves, they returned to the living room.

John and Chris had already changed, and looked more dashing than Kate would have expected from men wearing white suits with black polka dots. She decided it was probably their natural arrogance that made it look natural. She and Sue received a lot of wolf whistles from the men, and they turned around to let them admire their outfits. After a few minutes, they were joined by Leah and Deborah. Leah was already in character and calling out ridiculous prophecies, stumbling through the room, which made them all laugh. Deborah looked quite stunning as Elektra.

"Good grief, Deb, is that spandex?" Chris exclaimed.

"No, it's very tight leather. Mind you, I'm not kidding about the tight part. I can hardly breathe. Why did I think this was a good idea?" Deborah asked with a rather unhappy look.

"Are you nuts, woman? You look freaking gorgeous!" John cried out.

Deborah smiled. "Thank you, John. I guess I'll suffer for one night then. Breathing is highly overrated, anyway." She winked at Leah, who was now prophesising an untimely death due to spandex.

Kate rolled her eyes. This was going to be one hell of a night. She took a few minutes to consult with her DJ and gave him a list of all the artists that were going to be there tonight to make sure he'd play at least one song from each of them, so as not to offend anyone. John and Chris were giving instructions to their crew, and when she passed through the kitchen, they all looked ready. She went over the guest list with her hostess and pointed out Leah and Deborah to her, in case she had trouble locating Kate during the evening. Yep, they were all set for the night.

*   *   *

"Good grief, this partying thing, I'm definitely out of practice!" Meg yelled over the music to Rezna. "Great party, though!" she added with a grin.

She wore her long, black hair in a French braided pony tail and was dressed in a tank top and shorts with high army boots. Two guns were attached to her hips. It wasn't hard to figure out who she resembled. Rezna wore a sarong, and a red dot graced her forehead. Gezna had on the same outfit, and they both had wigs with really long, sleek black hair. When Meg had asked who they were supposed to be, they'd both rolled their eyes, and said, "Haven't you read Harry Potter, woman?" And that was all the explanation Meg was getting.

Romy and her husband walked around as Galadriel and Celeborn, gliding through the room, looking very serene, catching everybody's attention. Romy was probably glamouring the crap out of everyone. *Clever girl*, Kate thought when she saw them taking another turn around the room.

Deborah came to find her and told her the hostess had asked for her. She rushed to the hallway to find quite a spectacular sight. The hostess looked at her, and said in a very formal manner, "The Miss Bennetts have arrived, milady."

And indeed, five Bennett sisters stood in front of her. "Oh, my goodness, look at you! You all look amazing! Who is who?" she asked excitedly.

Sheila pointed at herself, made a curtsey, and said, "Miss Jane Bennett, ma'am." She pointed along the line of waiting ladies, and continued, "Miss Elisabeth Bennet, Miss Mary Bennett, Miss Catherine Bennett, and Miss Lydia Bennett."

Caroline, Sam, Helen, and Joni each made a curtsey and smiled at Kate. "Pleased to meet you, Miss van Dyk," they said in chorus.

Kate laughed. "Oh, just call me Fawkes tonight, ladies." They all grinned, momentarily falling out of character.

"Pretty cool, huh?" Joni asked. "Sue helped us with the outfits. We all made them ourselves."

"Wow, respect!" Kate said, amazed. "Well, enjoy yourselves, ladies. No chaperones, I've noticed? That could become tricky, for I think I remember seeing at least one or two Mr. Darcys walking around, and I'm pretty sure one of them was accompanied by a Mr. Bingley, so take care, ladies, take care," she said with a wicked smile.

The girls went into the room where they immediately received some refreshments from one of the *101 Dalmatian* crew. Kate was about to walk back into the room herself, when two more guests arrived. Her heart skipped a beat.

Tristan smiled at her, but addressed the hostess. "Holmes, ma'am, Sherlock Holmes and my partner, Watson," he said, taking off his hat.

The hostess smiled at him. "Of course, sir. I assume you have an alias as well?"

"Why, yes ma'am. That would be Visconti, Tristan Visconti."

She smiled again and crossed his name off the list. "Welcome to the party, Mr. Holmes, Mr. Watson. Enjoy your evening."

The men walked toward Kate, and Tristan took her hand to kiss it. "You look amazing. Are you a phoenix, Miss van Dyk?" he whispered into her ear.

Kate shivered. "Why, yes I am, Mr. Holmes. And may I just say you two look quite dashing." She took a step back and held out a hand to Tristan's friend. "Mr. Watson, a pleasure to meet you." And indeed it was, for she'd been fearing Tristan would bring a woman as his plus one.

"Call me Roy, and the pleasure is all mine, ma'am. Thanks for extending the invitation," he said with a smile as he shook her hand.

"Kate," she replied. "When you say ma'am, I start to look for my mother."

Roy gave her another smile. "Kate it is then."

She showed them inside and immediately felt several pairs of eyes on their party of three. Deborah would probably be jumping at the chance to be introduced, and indeed, her friend didn't disappoint her.

"Kate darling, John needs you in the kitchen. Is this our new neighbour?" She was all smiles toward Tristan, and Kate sighed inwardly.

"Tristan, may I introduce you to Deborah, my friend and business partner. Deb, this is Tristan and his friend, Roy."

"It's so nice to finally meet you, Tristan," Deb said, shaking his hand.

Kate knew enough about Deborah's body language to know she had her powers on full force. She took another inward sigh. Deborah would always be protective of her.

"And you, Deborah. I trust you approve of what you feel and see?" Tristan asked with a smile.

Deborah seemed a bit put out, but made a quick recovery. "Well, yes, but then I would have to give you the benefit of the doubt and assume you're playing fair, Mr. Visconti," she replied with half-closed eyes.

Oh, my god, she is actually flirting with him, Kate thought with a smile. Not that Deborah would be sexually interested in any man who'd caught the eye of one of her friends. She did test them, though, to see if they were the faithful kind. With curves in all the right places, Deborah was a sight to be seen, especially this evening. Her Elektra costume left little to the imagination.

Tristan didn't take the bait, however, and said he could make the same remark about her, as they were obviously both empaths.

Flattered by Tristan's response, Deborah decided to come clean. "You're actually in the wrong, Mr. Visconti, I'm not an empath. I have empathic abilities and I have healing ones. I guess my genes are a mixture of my mum and dad. My father is a healer and my mother was indeed an empath. I have a kid brother who has the same abilities."

Tristan looked surprised. "Then they must be quite powerful abilities, as I felt you searching through my thoughts. And please call me Tristan."

Deborah shook hands with Roy as well and promised Kate to show the men around, and yes, she'd behave herself. Kate heard them continue their discussion about empathic abilities and decided she'd just have to trust Deborah.

When she found John, he almost snatched her behind the counter. "What took you so long? Now look over there, in the corner by the stairs, is that who I think it is?"

Kate strained her neck to see who caught his attention, and immediately understood who John looked at. "Why yes, John, I believe it is. Fitting costume as well," she said with a grin. "Perhaps I should go over and sit on his shoulder or arm," she added mischievously.

"Cat! Don't you dare! You could have told me you know him. You know we adore the man."

"Well, he's actually a friend of my mother's. They met at a theatre production, I believe. I can't remember which one, though. She was one of the sopranos, and he'd hurt his back during one of the performances. My mother recommended me, of course, so I massaged the pain out of his lower back. He's not a regular or anything, John. Stop drooling."

"You massaged the man himself, oh my."

Kate rolled her eyes. "Would you like me to introduce you?"

John looked positively terrified. "Would you? I'll die, but yes, please."

She took him by the arm and walked over to the stairs. "Hello, headmaster, so nice of you to drop by our annual party. May I introduce my good friend and caterer of tonight's party, John Williams?"

"Why, Kate, am I correct in assuming you resemble my trusty phoenix? You look smashing, I must say." Professor Dumbledore held out his hand to John. "A pleasure to meet you, sir. The food is exquisite. I dare say even our house elves couldn't produce such a banquet."

John mumbled something incomprehensible, which sounded like "thank you very much." "It is a great honour meeting you, sir," he said more coherently.

"Oh, none of that, my good man. Now, if you'd be so kind to explain this particular appetizer to me. It's mouth-watering, and I'll use my powers of persuasion to make you give me the recipe." John looked absolutely flabbergasted.

Kate was still grinning from ear to ear when she saw the headmaster guiding a *101 Dalmatian* toward a tray of food. The Bennett sisters attracted a lot of attention, not surprisingly. She looked around to see how everybody had dressed up. She noticed a remarkably good impression of Severus Snape, and had to look twice to see who it really was. Charlie's Angels were sipping some non-alcoholic cocktail. Kate had decided to serve nothing with alcohol in it, unless it was used in cooking for the appetizers, because it'd have vaporized. A lot of their clients were having problems with some kind of addiction, and this was supposed to be a party, not a test of inner strength.

A lot of Harry Potter characters roamed around. Apparently, JK Rowling's characters were still very popular. She also noticed several Captain Jack Sparrows and men in tuxedos, obviously pretending to be James Bond or something. Four of her regular clients had teamed up as well and walked around as the Fantastic Four. Meg and Harry were joined by a Legolas, an Aragorn, an Arwen, an Eowyn, and quite a few Gandalfs and Sarumans. Kate thought they looked beautiful yet surreal, standing there all together. Queen Elizabeth was present as well, as were the three musketeers. There was a man in an iron mask, whom Kate didn't recognise. A group of writers had decided to come as the original *Star Trek* crew, and as Kate looked at the client who resembled Uhura, she was pretty sure nobody had ever seen the woman in quite such an outfit.

That was what Kate loved about Halloween. People could pretend to be someone else, to really let their hair down, so to speak, and she was glad to see everybody had made such an effort. Last year they'd chosen a Charleston theme, which was also very nice, and the year before that they'd gone with the colour red, which had turned out to be rather shocking. It'd hurt her eyes after just one hour, and she hadn't been able to find anyone. So from then on she'd decided to forego colour themes.

She went to check upstairs on the rooftop and found Leah there in deep discussion with another famous writer. They were apparently discussing their agents, and she overheard the writer saying to Leah, "I'm telling you, nobody understands how much we suffer. The tedious things we have to put up with, honestly!" Her friend was obviously amused by his remark.

Kate gave her a wink in passing and took a few minutes to just enjoy the scenery. The sounds of Muse filled the air. "Follow Me," one of her favourites. For some reason, it reminded her of *The Never Ending Story*, even though the movie had been released ages before that song. Maybe it'd inspired the band, who knows. She often wondered where artists got their ideas from. It was what interested her most about a song, the underlying meaning. What it meant to them personally.

"Hello, Kate, this is some party, I must say." Roy came to stand next to her. Kate noticed Tristan was still in discussion with Deborah, poor man.

"I'm glad you like it, Roy. Have you and Tristan known each other for a long time?"

Roy nodded. "Well, for at least ten years, anyway. I joined the company when Tristan was already working there, but we've been partnered from the beginning, so we got to know each other pretty well. He's a great man." He looked at her as though he weighed his options. "He thinks very highly of you. I've never seen him quite so taken by a stranger so quickly. You must be very special, indeed."

Kate looked at him. "Well, if it's any comfort to you, I don't normally take to strangers myself. Tristan is the exception to that rule. He must be special as well."

Roy smiled. "Point taken, ma'am. And it's none of my business. I just don't want to see either of you get hurt. We're not exactly long-term relationship material in our line of work."

She gave him a penetrating glare. "Why is that, Mr. Watson?" She decided to see if she could glean any information from Roy and call his bluff. "Is it the travelling or is it the danger involved? Not for me, I mean, but for him. Is the company afraid I'll blow his cover to kingdom come?"

Roy stared at her. "How much has he told you exactly?"

She pushed her luck. "Well, as you said, I seem to be the exception to his normal rules, so you tell me."

Roy was about to answer when Deborah intervened. "Honey, this is one hell of a party! And you have my permission to like our new neighbour. He's cool." Deborah and Tristan joined them.

Tristan laughed at Deborah's remark and smiled at Kate. "See, I'm cool," he said.

Roy was all smiles as well, and seemed to have completely forgotten their conversation. Kate sighed in frustration. She was sure he'd been about to say something that would have given her another piece of the puzzle that was Tristan.

Tristan, who probably picked up on her frustration, cast her a slightly worried look.

She relaxed and gave him a kiss on his cheek. "Of course you're cool. You're Sherlock Holmes, for god's sake!" They all grinned.

Kate excused herself to go check the party downstairs, and Deborah decided to join her, leaving Tristan and Roy up on the rooftop terrace.

"He really is very nice, you know," Deborah said. "And he truly likes you. I can tell."

"Thanks, darling, I'm glad you've taken to him. I only wish I knew more about him."

Deborah looked surprised. "I'm sorry, but I disagree. I mean, I think you probably know more about him than most people, and you've only known each other for a couple days. Don't forget that."

Kate sighed. "I know. I'm being silly. I'm overreacting, and I'm an ungrateful bitch."

Her friend laughed. "You're not a bitch. Well, you can be, but not in this case. You just want to know everything about him. That's called 'being in love,' I think. Welcome to my world of pain."

Deborah had been in and out of love a couple times over the last few years, but it wasn't easy finding a soulmate, and Deborah wouldn't settle for anything less. Nor should she, Kate mused.

"Hmm, maybe you're right. I still get the feeling he's hiding something from me."

Deborah nodded. "He is, I felt it."

Kate looked at her, surprised. "And that doesn't bother you?" she asked.

"No. Normally, it would, I know, but I think he has a really good reason for it. He'll probably tell you when he thinks the time is right. I don't know. Just call it a gut feeling. He's one of the good guys, of that I'm absolutely sure."

Kate smiled and squeezed her hand. "Thanks, hon."

They got another drink before they mingled with the guests. Every now and then Kate saw Tristan again. He was never far away from her. Whenever she was upstairs on the rooftop, he'd follow her, and when she went downstairs, he did the same. She didn't find it annoying, though. It was oddly comforting and flattering to know he kept an eye on her. The party was just beginning to put the P in party when Deborah came over to her with a worried look.

"What's wrong?" Kate asked.

"The prime minister is making an important announcement at nine thirty. Didn't you get a notification on your iPhone?" Deborah asked.

Kate ran her hands over her body. "And where exactly would I hide an iPhone in this outfit, darling? I haven't got it on me. It's still in my bedroom." She looked around and saw lots of people checking their mobiles. Some were even talking on their phones. She frowned.

"Kate! Could you turn on the TV?" someone yelled from across the room.

"Sure!" she yelled back, and after a few seconds, the flat screen in the living room area sprang to life.

She went upstairs to the rooftop to turn the flat screen on there as well, and when she came back down again, she found Leah, Meg, Romy, and Sue standing near Deborah, talking rapidly.

She went to stand next to Leah and looked at her friend. "Is it serious?" she asked in a whisper.

"I'm not sure actually. I'm more concerned about Meg's reaction."

Kate looked at Meg, who was indeed acting a bit weird. She looked frantically at everybody in the room, changing her focus to someone else with just a few seconds interval.

"It's the grey mist again," Leah said. "She's seeing it everywhere now." Meg's husband stood just behind her, running his hand over her back, trying to calm her down.

"This can't be good," Kate softly said to Leah.

"No, I don't think it is. All I'm getting is that our prime minister has finally made her decision, but I have this dreadful feeling it's going to concern us all. Tristan and his friend are behaving quite weird as well. As if they're preparing for the worst."

Kate strained her neck to locate Tristan. Finally, she saw him standing near the bar in the kitchen where he was now talking to John and Chris, who pointed in her direction after a couple seconds.

Tristan turned his head and smiled at her. It was a smile that said don't worry, everything's going to be okay. Kate returned his smile and then focussed her attention on the other people in the room.

"I think because he's an empath, he's picking up on all the emotions in the room. There's probably a lot of anxiety running around right about now," Kate said.

"Yes, I thought of that as well, but it's more than that. As I said, they're bracing for impact. I'm sure of it. Oh well, we'll find out soon enough."

The TV screen flickered and the BBC news tune filled the room. "This is a special broadcast. We have a live connection with Downing Street where our prime minister will address the nation."

The screen showed the prime minister sitting behind her desk. She took a deep breath and rearranged the papers before her.

"Good evening, ladies and gentlemen. I sit before you with a troubled heart. I should state up front that after giving this speech, I will lay down my position as prime minister, as my declaration will mean a breach of security protocol. However, I feel very strongly that the people of Britain have a right to know what's going on. That they have a right to be with the people they love."

Everybody had gone deadly quiet.

"Some people at the news network have agreed to arrange this live feed at great personal expense, for which I'm very grateful. They will make sure I'm able to finish my speech before anyone can interfere." She took another deep breath and looked straight into the camera. "It's with great regret I have to inform you all that an asteroid is on a collision course with Earth. The point of impact will be England, near London, to be exact. Unfortunately, this is of little consequence, as the asteroid will eventually damage the entire planet. It's too big.

"Everything that is humanly possible has already been done, to no avail. The asteroid remains. We don't have the means to destroy it or change its course. Trust me in saying that we did all we can, globally. The common opinion was to avoid mass hysteria, and I'd agreed to that as long as there was hope, even a little. Hope has run out, however, and if I'm getting the opportunity to spend my last moments with the people I love the most, so should you.

"The asteroid will hit Earth this Saturday at precisely two minutes after eight p.m. Greenwich Mean Time. It's now Thursday night, which leaves us less than forty-eight hours to enjoy each other, to enjoy life. I appeal to you all to focus your efforts on contacting or being with your loved ones. I know I will. Turning against any form of authority will be completely pointless. Only the highest-ranking people have known about this. Your local police officer will be just as shocked hearing this news as you are. Please help each other in reaching your loved ones in any way you can. I also appeal to hospitals in the hope they will try everything in their power to leave the patients in good care. I understand hospital personnel will want to go home as well, and they should get that chance. I'm hoping, however, hospitals will either make room for their own family members to join, or leave their patients in the care of their loved ones. Please be careful going out into the streets, as people will be scared. There is no point in getting yourself killed in a car accident, trying to reach your loved ones. Take care of yourself and each other. I wish you all Godspeed and a peaceful ending."

The screen went black. It took a few moments before the room came back to life. People were just staring at each other, not believing what they'd just heard. Kate's mind was whirling. This couldn't be happening. Yet she knew within every inch of her body that it was true. Everything started to make sense now. The prime minister's strange behaviour, her lack of emotions, lack of hope. Meg's grey mist, Lee's visions of New Zealand on the other side of the world. Of course they'd hide heads of state, royalty, and other important people over there. If Earth stood any chance to survive, they'd want to make sure the human race could survive. She felt sick. People were leaving. She should probably say something, but nothing came out of her mouth. Someone held her hand. It was Leah. She had tears in her eyes.

"Of all the things I imagined, that wasn't anywhere near it," she whispered. Kate put her arms around her and squeezed her tight. "Some seer, huh?"

"Stop it," Kate said. "You knew something was wrong all along. The prime minister hadn't decided to tell us yet, for which I'm very grateful, by the way. You've been focussing so hard on her it left little room for other things, I think."

Leah gave her a feeble smile. "Thanks, love, you always know how to cheer me up, even when the world is coming to an end."

Kate pulled herself together and reached for a kitchen chair. She climbed onto it and raised her voice. "Could I have everybody's attention please? I notice some people are already leaving, which I perfectly understand, of course. I'm so sorry. This was obviously not how this was supposed to end, but a party seems very trivial now anyway, doesn't it?"

People were coming down from the rooftop terrace, and most of them stopped to listen to Kate.

"I know we've all had a very nasty shock. Well, that's the understatement of the century probably. I don't want to keep you any longer, but I do want to wish you all well, and most of all, wish you hope. I know it seems hopeless now, but our Earth has survived many things, so all may not be lost. In the meantime, take our prime minister's advice, spend as much time with your loved ones as you possibly can, and please, return home safely. You're all very dear to me and I'd hate to see anything bad happen to anyone before all hope is lost. So please be careful out there. We don't have any idea how people are going to respond to this. It might not be very safe outside. So again, please be careful. Thank you."

As she stepped down from the chair, people applauded. Some of them came over to say goodbye or give her a hug. A few of her more regular clients even gave her meaningful looks. She heard comments like, "If anyone can do it, you can, Kate." and "You're special for a reason. You know, this might be it." She shook hands, gave hugs and kisses for over half an hour, and then only a few guests remained. Not surprisingly, her own circle was still complete. Meg's husband was still there, as were Romy's partner and the twins' spouses. John and Chris were cleaning up in the kitchen as if nothing had happened at all.

Tristan said goodbye to his friend, who came over to shake Kate's hand. "I'm very sorry we had to meet like this," Roy said.

"As am I, Roy, as am I. You're welcome to stay."

He smiled. "Thank you, that's very kind of you, but I have things to attend to. It's probably weird to say I hope to see you again, but I do mean it."

She gave him a warm smile. "Take care, Watson. Get home safely." He saluted her and then left with a last meaningful look at Tristan.

Romy crashed onto the couch. "So, what's the plan? How are we going to save this bloody planet?" They stared at her.

Meg's husband walked around in an irritated fashion. "Please, Romy, don't be dramatic. I know you and your whole little group think you're special, and I'm not denying you people can do things, my wife included, but this is the fucking planet were talking about! Meg and I will go home and be with each other as much as we can, right, Meg?" He looked over at his wife, who'd come to stand next to Kate.

She looked sad. "Harry, you know I want to be with you more than anything. If there's any chance, any chance at all, we can do something to save the planet, I have to give it a go. I wouldn't be able to live with myself otherwise."

Romy's husband stood as well. "Oh, come on, Meg, that won't be a problem, will it, since we'll all be dead in two days, anyway. That's pretty much bullshit!"

Kate raised her hands. "People, please, let's keep it civil. No one's forcing anybody to stay. I certainly won't. Harry, Martin, I understand your feelings. Really, I do. Of course you want to be with your wives. We're all in shock now. This is probably not the time to be planning anything. I think you should all go home, have a good night's sleep and rethink this tomorrow."

"We're going to plan something though, right? Right?" Deb asked, looking around the room.

"I can't speak for anybody else, but I will, yes," Kate replied.

Leah re-entered the room. Kate hadn't even noticed she'd left. "I just talked to Ryan on the phone. The prime minister's news has spread like wildfire. I think half the world knows by now. Ryan says people are going crazy in New York already. There's a run on supermarkets to get people enough food to last them these two days." She shook her head.

"Well, at least that won't be a problem here," Kate said, looking around. "I could feed an army with what's left over from the party."

"You've got that right," John said from the kitchen.

Tristan took a seat on the couch. He oozed an air of calm, probably his empathic powers at work. "Look, if I may suggest something? There are people on the streets everywhere by now. It won't be the best time to return home. Also, I'm not sure how long the public transport lines will be open to the public. Who came by car?"

Meg, Romy, Sue, the twins, and John raised their hands.

"Good. Now it's probably best to wait a few more hours until after midnight. Then the streets will be less crowded, making if safer to travel. Anyone with a car can drop the others off. In the meantime, Catherine, if you're planning something, it couldn't hurt to discuss it. It'll give us something to do, and we'll spend our time together in a useful manner."

Everybody seemed to relax a bit. "Well, that makes sense," Martin said. "I suppose it'd be better to wait a bit. I hadn't thought about the madness outside."

They all agreed, and John and Chris selected a few plates with finger food, so they could nibble on something. They also brought back a couple bottles of sparkling water.

"Best to keep our heads clear, don't you think?" Chris asked. There was a mumble of agreement.

"Though getting completely pissed sounds like a pretty good idea as well right about now," Harry said with a sigh.

Meg smiled at him and patted his shoulder. "We'll get through this, sweetie, we always do." Harry squeezed her hand.

Kate looked at Tristan. She was grateful he'd calmed everybody down, but she had a lot of questions for him. Like, for example, why he wasn't anywhere near as shocked by this news as he should be. Which led her to believe he'd already known what was going to happen. Come to think of it, that was probably the reason he'd come to London in the first place. She hoped to get some alone time with him later this evening. She wasn't going to let him off the hook that easily. Right now, her group looked at her to hear what she had to say.

"Okay. We had a Samhuinn ritual planned this Saturday. I was going to use my elements to try to restore as much balance to the world as possible, using them full force. The original plan was to combine all our powers and use me as a vessel. It would multiply mine. I'm not sure this will work, though. It's something we never tried before. I was actually going to suggest a trial run for tomorrow, but all things considered, we'll have more important things to do. Everybody will want to be with family or say goodbye. Speaking for myself, I'll definitely want to see my mother and uncle if I can."

"Right," Leah said. "Let's look at this thing logically." A few of the girls looked at her with a smile. "Yes, well, as logically as possible," she said in a huff. "We have an asteroid. If it's going to destroy Earth, it must be pretty big. I'm sure some idiot pressed a red button to try to nuke the damn thing, but even if they were able to blast a piece off, it still remains large enough to annihilate our planet, but it's still an asteroid. It's made up out of the elements, right?"

"I guess," Sue replied before anybody could respond. "Yes, I think you should be able to connect to it, Kate."

"Okay, that's good," Deborah said, "but connecting to it won't destroy it, right? How do we go about that?"

They all looked at Kate, but she looked at Meg, who shook her head. "Oh, sweetie, I wish I could, but I'm no master of death. You know that. I can only see death. I can't control it," Meg said.

The twins looked at each other and frowned. "No. Not control it. How about summoning it?" one of them asked.

They stared at them. "What do you mean?" Meg asked the question that had to be in everybody's minds.

"Well, it's Samhuinn, which is ruled by the Cailleach, the goddess of life, death, and rebirth," Gezna, the eldest by a minute, said to the group. "She's not exactly cuddly, but could you summon her, Meg? Maybe if we're able to use Kate as a vessel, the Cailleach can take her over, which will enable Kate to not only connect to the asteroid but also destroy it. She'll have the power of death, so to speak," Rezna smiled at her twin sister.

"Oh, boy, I don't know Gezna. That's an awful lot of ifs," Kate said. "As you said, the Cailleach is perhaps the most unpredictable of goddesses I know. If I let her take over, there's no knowing what she'll decide is the right thing to do. She might think it's a great idea to destroy Earth."

"Maybe Deborah could gauge her intentions? And, Leah, you could try focussing on the Cailleach to see an outcome," Tristan suggested.

Leah looked at Tristan with a speculative gaze. "That's actually not bad. I could do that. Deb?"

"I could try meditating and focus on her, sure. Get a feel for her vibe. It changes every year."

"Joni, what about your powers? Do you think you can tap into the earth, make it stronger?" Kate asked.

Joni had a connection to the earth, but only the earth. Kate and Joni had combined forces on several occasions, especially when they'd first met a couple years ago when the earth's balance was off scale. After they'd learned about each other's powers, they'd put a lot of energy into restoring the planet's energy and balance until Kate couldn't hear it crying anymore.

Joni looked up at her with a serious expression. "Of course, Kate. Anything I can do to help. Consider it done."

John and Chris looked around the group. "Is there anything we can do to help?" Chris asked. "I mean, really, if there's anything we can do, just let us know."

John put an arm around him. "Well said, my love." He gave him a kiss.

"That's sweet of you guys, and I'm not saying no to that offer, but right now I can't think of anything. I mean, you're both special to me, you know that, but you don't have any special powers that could be of use right now. No offence," Kate said with a warm smile.

"None taken, sweetheart, but the offer stands. If you guys need extra locations or food or anything, let us know." John said.

Harry, Martin, and the twins' spouses looked at John and Chris. They didn't have any special powers either, and probably felt as if they should say something as well.

Kate noticed the look on their faces and stepped in. "Thanks again, guys. Look, I'm sure there are lots of things we're not seeing right now. It's fair to say we don't have any idea what we're going to wake up to tomorrow. It's going to be another world. We might need all sorts of things, and when it comes down to plain muscle power, it's always nice to have a few men around. Anyone who's willing to help out would be more than welcome."

All the men in the room made noises of agreement. "Sure, Kate." "Anything you need, you just give us a shout." "Of course we'll help."

Kate smiled, and quite a few of her circle sisters did as well. "Thank you, gentlemen. It's good to know we have some male backup power on hand."

Sheila came back from the hallway. "The whole entrance is full with presents, Kate. Do you need any help getting them in here? Some of them look quite big or heavy."

"Oh, that's right," Meg cut in. "I completely forgot with all the commotion. It probably seems silly now, anyway, but your friend left a painting for you, Kate. I thought it was rather impressive."

"Which friend?" Kate asked.

"Um, I don't know actually. He introduced himself as Saruman. Did you catch his name, honey?" She looked at Harry, who shook his head.

"No, I think none of us mentioned any names," her husband answered. "We were pretty much into the whole role0playing game."

Meg retrieved the painting from the hallway and then set it down gently in front of Kate, who unwrapped the other half of it. The second the whole thing was revealed, she and Leah both jumped up as if something had bit them.

"Fuck!" Kate cried out. Leah forcefully swung her away from the painting. The rest looked shocked.

"It's the painting from the museum, isn't it?" Deborah asked with a frightened look on her face. "It's Alan's painting."

Tristan examined the painting and then looked at Kate. "Is it, Kate? Is this the painting you were talking about?"

She just nodded. "I can't believe he was in here, in my apartment. Just like that. Why didn't he talk to me? I didn't even see him."

"Yes, you did," Meg said. "I saw you looking at us. You know, when we were all standing together. He was right there, next to Harry. God, I can't believe I'd just been standing there, talking to him. He was really nice to us and very nice about you, Kate."

"Yes, he was," Harry cut in. "He said more than once what a lovely lady you'd become."

"What else did he say?" Tristan asked quietly. He handed Kate a little white note. It read, *Soon you will see.* He looked at her. "It was stuck on the back of the painting. It's the original, by the way."

Harry and Meg glanced at each other. "Um … what else did we talk about?" asked Harry. "Nothing much really. We talked about *Lord of the Rings*, obviously, and about the Halloween party. He said this was the first one he could attend. That you were old friends, and that he'd been otherwise engaged before this party. Well, he wasn't lying about that, now was he?" he finished sarcastically.

"No, he certainly wasn't," Kate replied quietly. "Soon you will see. What do I have to see? The world coming to an end? He'll die with it. Why would that make him happy? No, that can't be it. What then?" She continued to mumble options under her breath.

"And you're still not seeing the big picture," Romy said, pulling Kate back to the conversation at hand.

"What?" she asked.

"From the dream. That's what he said, right?"

Kate was confused for a moment. "Yes. Yes, you're right. That's what he said to me. You think they're related?"

"I should think so, yes," Romy replied.

Her group agreed, and there was even a mumble of agreement from some of the men.

"Yes, that's all very nice, but if we don't know what it means, it's not going to do us any good," Leah cut in, always the practical one.

"Leah, can you see something beyond Saturday?" Tristan asked. They all looked at her.

Leah sighed. "I'm not sure, Tristan. I think I can, but it's hard to distinguish between real visions and wishful thinking right now."

He nodded. "I understand. You'll let us know when you do get something, anything you're convinced of that is real?"

"Of course, you have my word," she promised.

They talked over several possibilities and scenarios for another hour until Kate noticed people were starting to get really tired.

"Okay, enough is enough, people. It's way past midnight, and we've done as much as we can for tonight. Anybody who doesn't want to go home is more than welcome to crash here."

Tristan cut in. "That goes for me as well, if anyone needs a place to stay for tonight."

Kate smiled at him. "Thank you, Tristan. Everybody who does go home, will you please, please text me the minute you arrive? Otherwise I'll be up the rest of the night, worrying myself sick."

Tristan stood. "Listen, everyone, just one more thing. Tomorrow's going to be another world. Try to keep that in mind when you wake up and don't panic. The electricity might be down, the phone lines may be down, including the mobile network. I highly doubt public transportation will still be functioning, and you probably won't be able to get groceries. These are just some of the things we're going to have to deal with, just to give you a heads-up, so to speak."

Everybody got up. "Of course, Kate," Harry said with a warm smile, "we'll text you, and thanks, Tristan. You seem to know a lot about these sort of situations."

Tristan nodded. "Unfortunately, I do. Not on this scale, of course, but I have a pretty good inclination what we're going to face the next two days."

Meg and Sue divided everyone else into two groups, which left the twins, and John and Chris free to use their own cars, as they lived in different parts of London. Meg and Sue both had big vehicles. Deborah and Leah decided to stay at Kate's, for which she was secretly grateful. She did, however, want to talk to Tristan. So when he walked down with the others to see they at least left safely, she went down with him, leaving Deborah and Leah upstairs.

"So," Tristan began when the cars were out of sight and they walked back into the hallway, "you probably have a question or two."

She had to smile at his resignation, but she wasn't about to back down. "As a matter of fact, I do. For starters, how come you weren't surprised about a minor little thing like the world coming to an end?" Her voice dripped with sarcasm.

They slowly walked upstairs, and Tristan stopped on the third floor. "My place for a moment?" he asked.

"That would probably be best for now, yes," Kate said.

Tristan opened his door and then they sat on the couch next to each other. "To answer your first question, I was very much surprised, but not for the reason you just mentioned. Unfortunately, I've known that our world is coming to an end for quite some time, and as you've probably guessed by now, yes, that's the reason I'm here. The broadcast wasn't supposed to happen, however. Obviously, somebody at our company screwed up big time, because usually we keep tabs on what certain people are going to do. Our prime minister did an excellent job of hiding this until it was too late. She had a point, of course, but I know what this will do to our society, and it isn't going to be pretty. It's going to make your attempt a lot harder." He looked a bit sad.

"So, you lied to me?" He looked at her quizzically. "About the prime minister, I mean. You said she wasn't your client. Has Roy gone to check on her? Shouldn't you be with your client?" She let out a sigh and continued. "Look, I'm not mad. I figured your job involves a certain amount of secrecy, and I understand you can't tell me everything."

He laid his hand over hers. "Catherine, I never lied to you. One of many things my boss isn't too happy about. You're right about one thing. I should be with my client." She nodded and was about to stand again to let him leave when he softly said, "Which is why I'm still here. I thought you'd figured it out by now." She just looked at him. "You're my client,

Catherine. I was assigned to encourage and help you save the planet. I have to admit, I wasn't really looking forward to this assignment. As I said, we knew about the asteroid long before anyone else. To be frank, I had little hope we could do anything to make a difference. I thought this whole mission was a bit pointless and a waste of time." He looked at her. "Then I met you. And from the first moment I shook your hand, I was intrigued. I couldn't get a grip on your emotions, which was a first for me. I've met other elementals before, but it never was a problem. In hindsight, I think that's probably because I've never met someone who's a true elemental, so to speak. Meaning someone who has the ability to summon earth, air, fire, and water at will, all at the same time. As I've told you before, there isn't anyone on our planet, as far as we know, who can do that. And we know quite a lot."

He smiled. "When I found out what you could do, my hope returned. It was frustrating, you see. I'd been assigned to a hopeless mission, in my eyes at least, and from the moment we'd met, I really liked you. Which made it even more hopeless, because I wanted to get to know you better, and I felt as if that wouldn't be possible. By then I'd met Leah, and I have to admit to having Roy check out some of your other friends. I knew you weren't alone with your powers. That night in the restaurant, which I enjoyed very much, by the way, you changed my life. From that moment on I knew what you could do, in theory, at least. I started to believe you could do this, and that I could help you believe in yourself." Kate stared at her hands. Tristan shifted on the couch. "Well, say something. How mad are you?"

She shook her head. "I'm not mad, Tristan. Confused, yes, and maybe a bit disappointed, but that's probably also directed at myself for not knowing the truth. I hate looking like a fool." She pushed a strand of hair away in an irritated manner. The feathers were starting to annoy her. "Actually, yeah, I am mad. Because you didn't trust me enough to tell me the truth. We could have made plans much sooner if you'd confided in me, instead of leaving it to the last moment. Come to think of it, that's only because everyone knows now. How the hell were you going to tell me we had to stop an oncoming asteroid?"

Tristan sighed. "I was going to tell you." Kate looked at him sceptically. "Really, Catherine, I was going to tell you. Tomorrow, in fact. I wanted to talk to you first, so we could come up with a plan to involve the rest of your group. They're very strong women, by the way. You have some amazing friends. There would have been no mass panic, only within your circle, and I could have helped to make you all focus, see clearly. Well, that's gone to the dogs now."

Kate sighed. She wanted to stay mad, but she also realised that was hardly productive, and she couldn't deny Tristan really did try to do the right thing. She was disappointed, however, because he hadn't trusted her enough to tell her sooner. She could have kept her mouth shut. Could she, though? She suddenly wondered if she would have told her mother, for example. She knew the answer was yes. If she felt that way, others in her circle would have told their family as well and so on, and so on. She sighed again. Ugh, she hated it when other people had a point.

"Okay," she said. "On a practical note, how much help are we getting from your company?"

He looked surprised. "Don't you want to talk about this? I mean, I completely understand that it's a lot to take in."

She shook her head. "I'd rather not. For one thing, it's counterproductive, because it'll only fuel my anger again. In my mind I know you were probably right to act as you did, but my heart still feels betrayed and disappointed, and unlike my elements, I can't shut that out on command."

There was sadness in his eyes, but he nodded. "Of course, anything you need."

She almost felt sorry for him. Dammit! It should be the other way around. She was the victim there, not him. "Look, it hurts, because I care, okay? It's not very often a man comes along whom I have feelings for. Let's leave it at that for now."

He gave her hand a soft squeeze. "Okay, but for the record, that goes for me as well. The having feelings part, I mean."

She smiled ironically. "I bet they're pleased with that at your company."

Tristan suddenly looked grim. "No, they're not, but that's not your concern." He got up from the couch. "You asked what kind of help you could expect from my company. I'll be here as long as you need me. So will Roy and Charles, who belong to the same division. Furthermore, location-wise we'll make sure nobody gets in your way. We've already cleared London Fields. It'd be good to know the exact location, however, and your approach route." Kate laughed. Tristan looked up. "What?" he asked.

"Nothing. It's just I feel as if I'm suddenly in *Mission: Impossible* or James Bond."

He smiled a bit sheepishly. "Sorry, occupational hazard I guess."

"Tristan? How bad is it going to be? On the streets, I mean. You sounded pretty worried about that."

He nodded. "I am. I've been in this situation before. As I said earlier, not on this scale, much smaller, but people don't respond very well to mass destruction. There are exceptions to the rule, of course, as with everything. On a whole, though, expect the worst. People won't be going to work anywhere. The prime minister may have addressed caretakers in her speech, but I doubt very much if they'll heed her advice. Traffic will be absolute madness. People will be trying to get away from England as far as possible, only to realise that airplanes aren't flying either. Well, maybe tomorrow they still will, to some degree, but it'll be quite costly. Most people won't be able to afford a ticket out of here. Boats, same story. People on the mainland will have a better chance of getting farther away from England. And they will try, believe me. You'd be amazed what people are capable of doing when faced with mortal danger."

Kate nodded. She didn't need a lot of imagination to believe that. "Where would you go, if you could, I mean?"

"I wouldn't go anywhere, because there's no need to. You'll stop it. I know you will."

She smiled. "Well, thanks for the vote of confidence. I think you have to work a bit harder to get me to feel the same, but that's not what I meant. If you were just another, um, civilian?" He smiled. "Where would you go?" she finished.

"I'm not sure. I'd like to see my parents, I guess."

Kate gave him a sad smile. "Of course. Italy is a bit hard to reach. I mean, what you just said, you probably wouldn't even make it to the mainland."

"That wouldn't be a problem. I do have some other skills, you know. The company didn't just hire me because I'm an empath. Well, actually, that was the main reason they hired me, but they expect a lot more than that from their employees. I can fly as well for example. I even loved it so much, I bought my own plane. Just a Cessna, nothing fancy, but I could, in theory, fly to see my parents."

Kate looked at him with one raised eyebrow. "Nothing fancy. You do realise you're talking about a plane, right?" She shook her head. "Look who I'm talking to. You own a Stradivari, for god's sake. A Cessna must be like buying a bicycle to you."

"In all fairness, I didn't buy the Stradivari, remember? My parents did. However, my job does have a nice 'high-risk' payment, so I make a pretty decent living."

High risk, I'll bet, Kate thought. She stood as well. "I think I should try to get some sleep. It's been a long night."

Tristan walked her to the door. "Catherine? Are we good? I mean—"

She gave him a soft kiss. "Sshh. I know why you did what you did, and I understand. It doesn't mean I have to like it, though. So are we good? Not exactly, not right now, at least, but we will be. I promise."

He smiled and kissed her. "Thank you, that's important to me. You're important to me. I hope you know that."

She nodded. "I do."

"Listen. I heard you say you wanted to visit your mother and uncle tomorrow. If you have any trouble reaching them or getting there, let me know. Charles will be happy to drive you anywhere, and we have means to get gas as well, should that become a problem."

"Thanks." She turned around. "Is Charles really your personal driver?"

Tristan smiled. "Yes, he is, but as you've probably guessed by now, he's much more than that."

"Hmm … yes," she said. "I like him."

"He'll be delighted to hear that. He encouraged me to listen to my heart. He knew I liked you before I did."

Kate held the door to the lift. "So, I'll see you tomorrow?" She looked at him, a bit worried.

"I'll be here, Catherine. Should you need me in the middle of the night, just call me. I mean that. Whenever, wherever, just call."

She smiled. "I'll do that. Goodnight, Tristan, I hope we'll be able to get some sleep."

Tristan frowned. "Do you need help with that? I could calm you."

She shook her head. "No, thanks, I'm good. Really, I'm doing remarkably well, considering what I've heard tonight. Hmm … I think Jane would be quite proud of me, actually."

He looked confused. "Jane?"

"Sorry, *Pride and Prejudice* reference. Never mind, not important. Sleep well, Tristan. I'll see you tomorrow." She blew him a kiss from the lift, and he caught it.

Well, she thought, *this one is definitely going down in the books as the most interesting Halloween cocktail party to date.* Tomorrow she'd drill Tristan on the asteroid. Anything he could tell her might come in handy to either her or one of her group. She doubted there would be a *How to Destroy an Asteroid for Dummies* book. Connecting to an asteroid. Well, at least it'd be an interesting Samhuinn, she mused. Boring was so last season. She could do with a bit of excitement.

"Well, I least I haven't lost my sense of sarcasm," she said before she exited the lift and then opened her front door to see her two best friends. Tomorrow would be another day. And they'd make sure there would be many more to come.

FRIDAY

KATE WALKED into her living room to find Deborah and Leah already at the breakfast table. "Morning," she said with a yawn. "Did either of you get any sleep?"

"Some." Deborah nodded. "I was up again rather early, though, and I took a walk around the neighbourhood to get a first feel on how London is coping."

"And?" Kate asked while grabbing a croissant from the table.

"It's not good from what I could tell. All the shops are closed around here. I didn't get as far as the City. I stuck to Shoreditch. I had to walk as well, because taking the Underground is out of the question. Completely deserted. I checked at each station."

Leah browsed through the morning paper. She held it up for them. "This one was still available."

"It was in my mailbox?" Kate asked with a tone of surprise.

Deborah shook her head. "No. I bought it on the street. They're selling it everywhere. I was lucky to get one."

It'd been a long and short night. They'd stayed up until everybody had texted their safe arrival. Falling asleep had turned out to be a challenge with all the noise on the streets. Cars honking, alarm systems going off, dogs barking. Kate was actually amazed the mobile phone service was still up. Tristan had predicted electricity would probably go down somewhere in the next twenty-four hours, probably sooner. Depending on how long people kept checking the turbines. Apparently, electricity was something that had to be checked several times a day to keep it working properly and safely. Something she'd never even considered. Stupid really. She wondered what else she hadn't thought about.

"So what does the paper say?" she asked.

Leah looked up. "Well, the headline says PRIME MINISTER: IS SHE MAD OR ARE WE ALL DEAD? Lovely, isn't it? It goes on about the possibilities of this being some sick hoax, but the general opinion around the world seems to be that we are, indeed, totally screwed. It has a lot of articles with advice on travelling, getting supplies, staying safe and so on. Well, you get the picture. Speaking of pictures, there are some nasty ones in here. People are obviously panicking."

Kate looked at her. "I'm glad you got to talk to Ryan."

"Me too. I spoke to my parents as well. I don't think they have any hope of us succeeding, but they wish us all the best, and they said they'd pray for us."

Deborah and Kate smiled. "We need all the prayers we can get I think, so that's really sweet of them," Deborah said. "Do you think they're going to be okay?"

Leah nodded. "I think they figure they've lived a good life. They won't be going anywhere, and my mother, ever the hamster, has more than enough supplies to last them for two days."

Kate looked at Deborah. "What about you, sweetie, did you get in touch with your family?"

"I spoke to my brother last night. It was rather emotional, because he thought it was just a joke. When I explained it wasn't, he totally freaked out, and it took me more than an hour to calm him down." She sighed. "My parents are actually on holiday in Australia. It's not New Zealand, but close enough. I spoke to them as well, and they're going to stay there. They wouldn't be able to get back, anyway, and their chances of survival are better over there, or so they figure. Not that they need chances of survival, my mother was kind enough to say." Deborah gave them a sad smile.

Kate had only briefly talked to her mother last night, telling her she'd drop by today, come hell or high water. She was glad to hear Simon had come over immediately, though, so her mother hadn't had to spend the night alone. She was just about to sit down when her doorbell rang. By the sound of it, it wasn't the one downstairs in the hallway. She opened her front door.

"Good morning, Catherine, can I come in?" Tristan looked as if he'd been up for hours, unlike Kate, who felt as if a train had waltzed over her.

"Don't you look chipper. Sure." She held the door for him.

He greeted Leah and Deborah, who offered him a croissant, which he took. "Morning, ladies. Thanks, Deborah. Did you girls get some sleep?"

Leah shrugged. "A bit. We were up rather late with phone calls and such. After all, we don't know how long we'll still have a connection."

Tristan nodded. "That's one of the reasons I came over. I took the liberty of adding all your numbers to ours. You'll have no problem reaching each other. Unfortunately, I can't do that for all your loved ones. That would be a bit hard to explain. As far as recharging goes, plug everything in as long as we still have power and turn off your 5G. It'll save batteries."

Leah looked surprised. "Wow, thanks, Tristan. Your company really has some pull. And, of course, we understand. It'll be very convenient to be able to reach each other."

Tristan gave her a small smile. "You're more than welcome, Leah. I also wanted to remind you that as of today you can't go in any lifts anymore. We don't know when the power will shut down, and you don't want to get stuck inside. Take the stairs, ladies, everywhere."

They all nodded. "Good thinking," Kate said. "Anything else that might come in handy?"

"Be careful when using a car. Not everyone in London has one, and I've had a lot of reports coming in about stolen vehicles. People are desperate to reach their families, and will do things they normally wouldn't. When you drive, try to never to do so alone, and maybe bring something to defend yourself, like a baseball bat or something."

Deborah stared at him. "And you're not even kidding. I can tell by the look on your face. Wow, I never thought I'd have to worry about things like that."

"Nor should you, Deborah, in a normal situation. These are extreme circumstances. And I have to say, it's going rather well, so far. Lots of people think it's some bad joke, and there are still others who haven't heard the news. Because of this, some companies are still up and running. Mind you, tomorrow will be worse, because it's the weekend and news has a funny way of spreading like wildfire. Eventually people will realise this isn't a joke and react differently, most likely panic. We saw the first wave of that last night, just after the news. Leah, I also put a tail on Ryan.

I'll give you updates on him whenever I can. New York is in a bad state. Roy told him the best thing he could do is stay put and go outside as little as possible. He said he wanted his kid sister to stay with him, and he'd try to get to her today, but he'd remain inside after that."

Leah's eyes watered. "Thank you, Tristan, I don't know what to say. That means a lot to me. Ryan told me yesterday on the phone he'd try to get to Cindy. She's handicapped, you see. They're twins. Ryan is the eldest by a couple minutes. There were complications at Cindy's birth, and he grew up feeling responsible for that. He loves her very much. I hope he can get to her."

Tristan looked at her. "Give me a minute." He took out his phone and walked into the hallway. Kate heard him talking about a possible escort. A few minutes later, he returned. "I can't make any promises, but they will try to give Ryan an escort to her home and make sure they arrive back safely. As long as there aren't any big disasters happening, they might be able to spare someone for a few minutes. It's the middle of the night now in New York, and it'll be easier to move around. They'll contact him and give it a go."

Leah nodded. "Again, thank you. I know you don't have to do this." Kate had filled them all in last night.

He shook his head. "No, I do, actually. It's my job to see to it you have everything you need to succeed. That doesn't stop at supplies and safety. Your chances of succeeding will improve if you're in a positive state of mind. Worrying about loved ones would be considered counterproductive, which is pretty much what I just told my boss, seeing as my cover's blown, anyway," he finished with a slightly arrogant smile. "He hates being lectured, but he did see my point. A lot is riding on this."

Kate sighed. "Don't remind us."

"I also came by to check when you wanted to visit your mother, Catherine. I'd feel a lot happier if I knew Charles drove you, if you don't mind."

Kate smiled at him and shook her head. "Not at all. To be honest, that would probably make my visit a lot easier. I was planning to go just after lunch, if that would be convenient for Charles."

Tristan nodded. "Not a problem. Let's say one thirty?"

"That would be perfect, yes," she confirmed. "On a more practical note, should we start defrosting our freezers and such?"

Tristan shook his head. "No, don't do that. Not yet, anyway. As I said, some companies are still up and running. People don't want to risk pissing off their bosses and losing their jobs over some sick joke, which is working in our favour at the moment. As long as the turbines are being checked, we'll have power. I did hear, however, that MI5 will confirm the prime minister's announcement later this morning, and from then on things will escalate. People will leave work, of this I'm sure, but we'll still have a few hours before safety protocol automatically shuts down the plants. Your fridge can go a good six hours without causing a minor flood. So if you possibly can, try to postpone it until morning or late this night."

Deborah looked at Tristan. "Will travelling be safer tonight or early tomorrow morning?"

"Probably early in the morning, but if either you or Leah want to check your homes, I'll make sure you get there. Just give me a call."

"Thanks," she said. "Now if you'll excuse me, I have to get a feel for a certain goddess, and I need some peace and quiet for that. Kate, can I keep using your guest bedroom?"

"Of course, sweetie. Be careful," she added.

"Always," Deborah replied with a smile.

"Well, I'll go into the other room and try to do my homework as well then. See if I can get anything useful for a change," Leah said with a wink at Kate.

"Good luck, hon. I'll drill Tristan on the asteroid."

Leah smiled. "You do that, and make sure Joni receives all the information she needs as well."

Kate nodded. "Absolutely."

After Leah and Deborah had closed the doors behind them, Tristan came over to give her a kiss. "I didn't say good morning properly when I came in," he said with that boyish grin of his. "Good morning, Catherine."

She slowly let go of him. "Good morning, Tristan," she replied. "I could get used to such a greeting."

He smiled. "I'm glad to hear it. I wasn't sure how you'd feel about me after all the things that happened last night, but so could I. I believe I heard you say something about drilling me?" He pretended to look scared.

Kate laughed. "Yes, company man. For your sake I hope you've come prepared. And you're not getting rid of me that easily."

Tristan opened the suitcase he'd brought. It even had a DVD screen inside. "I'm glad to hear it. And I have everything here you might want to know. We've made a little film about the asteroid's course. You can see what to expect. I'll make sure Joni sees it as well. Anyone else?"

"Meg," Kate immediately replied. "She may not be a master of death, but she knows more about it than anyone I know." She hesitated. "Well, that's not exactly true, of course, but Alan isn't really an option, now is he?"

Tristan sat next to her, putting the suitcase on the side table in front of them. "He would be, if we could find him."

She looked at him. "You're trying to find him?"

"Of course we are. I'm certainly not a fan, but even I have to admit his powers could come in handy. So far, we have nothing."

She looked at him, smiling sadly. "You're forgetting he's also an empath, which doesn't make him a seer, but his powers are very strong. Whenever he feels anxious, he'll move. I don't think you'll find him unless he wants to be found. He was able to walk around here for more than two hours without being found out. And that's with a bunch of specially gifted people present. I think that says enough."

"Any more insights on the 'soon you will see' card?"

"None." Kate sighed. "Alan always liked riddles and puzzles. I never had the patience. Funny thing is, I thought I'd be more scared, knowing he's out there, fully restored, but I'm not. I don't know why exactly. Maybe I'm just being naive, but I'm actually kind of glad I didn't destroy his soul, after all. It always bothered me that my powers could do something like that." She gave Tristan a soft smile.

"I understand the sentiment, and I'm glad you're not worried. I hope you'll forgive me if I worry for you, though."

Kate smiled. "Hmm, I think I can live with that. Now, show me what you have, and we'll see what we can do about this thing."

"Yes, ma'am," he said before hitting the play button.

* * *

"Thanks for letting me sit in the front, Charles. It'd feel a bit weird to sit in the back just by myself."

Charles smiled. "No problem, Miss Catherine. I'm glad to be of service. How are you holding up?"

As promised, Tristan's driver had shown up at precisely one thirty, and they were now on their way to Kate's mother. Her uncle would meet them there.

"Absolutely terrified, but pretty good, all things considered. It's not every day you have a chance to save the entire world." She smiled.

"I knew you were special the first moment I saw you, Miss Catherine. You have that unique ability over you."

"My powers, you mean?"

"No, miss, I mean your faith in mankind. Not many people can hold on to that when faced with a crisis. You believe in yourself and in your friends, even now. Maybe even especially now. That's why I think you'll succeed." He gave her a warm smile. "He thinks so too, you know." He looked at her. "I've never seen him so happy with someone."

Kate felt herself blush and looked out the window. "Have you known him long, Charles?"

"For over ten years, ma'am. And I'll look out for him as long as he'll have me."

"He doesn't really have a bat cave, right?" Kate asked jokingly, but her voice held a touch of serious doubt as well.

Charles laughed. "No, miss, I can honestly say he does not, and believe me, I would know. The company doesn't employ many empaths as strong as Mr. Visconti, and they take care of their more, let's say, special agents. Which is where I come in."

"So you're sort of like a bodyguard as well?" Kate looked at Charles. He seemed very fit for his age, but he was at least in his fifties. Not exactly the epitome of strength and power. She wondered if Charles had powers of his own.

"I'm many things, miss. I'm sorry I can't tell you more, but working for the company, someone's always listening." He gave her a wink.

Kate smiled. "Don't worry, Charles, I won't make you spill the beans. I think I got Tristan in enough trouble as it is. Did he break many rules? In confessing to me that I'm his client, I mean."

"About every rule there is, ma'am. And he doesn't see you as a client. Which is where his problems and rule-breaking began, of course.

Don't you worry. Mr. Visconti can hold his own. And obviously, he thinks you're worth it. I happen to agree with him on that account."

Kate felt herself blush again. "Oh. Thank you, Charles. I like him very much." She looked out the window, suddenly sad. "He probably won't be staying in London once this is over, will he?"

Charles hesitated. "Probably not, ma'am. I will say this. He'll find a way. You hold on to that faith of yours." He gave her a warm smile.

They were almost at her mother's house. Kate was shocked to see the street almost entirely deserted on a Friday afternoon. It was usually full of children playing on the front lawns, but now it was eerily quiet. Mr. And Mrs. Hadley's house looked empty and their car was gone. Probably gone to see their children.

"Take as long as you like, miss. I'll wait here for you," Charles said.

"You're welcome to join me inside, Charles. I feel kind of bad leaving you here in the car all by yourself."

"Don't you worry, miss. I have plenty of things to sort out and check up on for Mr. Visconti. This car comes with a lot of extras." He gave her another wink.

Kate decided it was pointless to give it another go. She opened the door and said goodbye to him. As she approached the house, her mother opened the front door.

"Oh, I'm so glad you're here, darling. I have to admit I was a tad worried. People are starting to behave rather unpredictably." She gave Kate a hug.

"Tristan's personal driver, Charles, drove me, Mom. He'll be driving me back as well and will wait for me here."

Her mother looked surprised. "Well, I'm glad to hear it, but you could have invited the poor man in. What happened to your manners, Catherine?"

Kate sighed. "I did invite him in, Mom, but Charles is more than just a driver. He said he had a lot to do in the meantime. Things he had to check for Tristan, for example, so I didn't push." She gave Charles a wave, and he waved back, nodding at Kate's mother.

"Well, you'd better come inside then." Her mother closed the door, and Kate hung up her coat.

Simon was already in the hallway to greet her. "Catherine, so good to see you," he said with a warm smile.

Kate hugged him. "Likewise, Simon. I'm so glad you could be here for Mom." He gave her shoulder a soft squeeze. Her mother looked at her, and Kate sighed. "Yes, Mom?"

Her mother quit staring and looked in Kate's eyes. "Sorry, my dear. Your aura is a bit weird. The colours are immensely bright for starters, but there's also a black circle hovering above your third eye. I've never seen it before. I'm sorry to say it, darling, but it gives me the creeps."

Kate tried to appear unconcerned. "That's probably related to the whole grey mist thing Meg's seeing. I'll tell you all about it. Where's Uncle Ben?"

"Right here, gorgeous!" A tall and slender man got up from the couch in the living room and came over to lift her into the air and give her a bear hug. Kate smiled as he let her down again.

"It's great to see you, uncle, though I wish it'd be under better circumstances. I'm glad you could make it."

"Any excuse to see my niece. Besides, someone has to put your mother's findings in perspective." He winked at Kate, who tried to hide a grin.

"Really, Benjamin!" her mother huffed. "I'm just trying to be honest here. It won't do her any good beating around the bush, now won't it? Besides, it might mean something to her and, therefore, maybe help her as well, right, darling?"

Kate looked at her mother. "Right, Mom," she said, smiling. She rolled her eyes at her uncle. Simon and Ben did their best not to laugh.

As her mother left for the kitchen, probably to make some tea, she said, "I saw that, Miss Catherine."

Kate tried to look guilty, which was kind of difficult as both Simon and her uncle were still laughing.

After her mother came back with tea, scones, and cookies, Kate asked if she was still good on food supplies.

"Sweet of you to ask, but yes. Simon brought some things over from his place as well. We shouldn't have any trouble for the next three to four days. Hopefully by then everything will be up and running again. Or am I wrong in assuming that?"

Kate looked doubtful. "I actually have no idea. I mean, I think that once we prevail, it'll be business as usual, but that's only an assumption, of course. Someone with authority will surely make an official announcement as soon as they find out the threat is indeed over. Globally, I presume. After that, I think things will pick up pretty quickly, don't you think so?"

Her uncle nodded. "I think you're right, honey. I still can't believe you're actually going to do this. I mean, don't get me wrong, I have complete faith in you and your friends, but it's still rather scary. You haven't done anything like this before, after all. Has Tristan said anything about your chances of succeeding?"

"He's actually surer of our success than we are. I'm still freaked out, to be completely honest with you." Her mother handed her a cup of herbal tea and a chocolate chip cookie. Kate took a bite and then continued. "I trust my powers, and we sort of had a plan for Samhuinn, anyway, to combine all our powers and use me as a vessel, but still …"

Her mother nodded. She'd heard this already from Kate. "To restore the balance of the earth," she explained to Simon and Ben.

"Yes," Kate said. "In a way we're still doing that. We'll use me as a vessel. Only instead of directing our energy into the earth, we'll direct it to the asteroid. There's only one hiccup, and I still think it's kind of a big one." She sighed.

"You can connect to it, but you don't know how to destroy it," Simon said.

She looked up, completely surprised. "How did you know?"

"I didn't, but we'd been going over this before you arrived, and your mother knows you pretty well. She figured you could connect to it quite easily, as you're an elemental, but that still leaves the question, how do you get rid of it?"

"Well, yes," Kate said, looking at her mother with a bit of a sad smile. "I can't get rid of it, but maybe the Cailleach can."

Simon and Ben appeared confused. Kate looked at her mother, who now had a worried expression.

"That's a pretty big leap of faith, honey. You're going to let her take you over, you mean?"

"It's the only way. She has the power of death. I do not. It's that simple, really. I have to take a chance. It's not as if I haven't done it before, Mom. Letting her take over, I mean."

"Well yes, Catherine, but in a regular Samhuinn ritual, honouring the dead and letting the participants honour her. This is a bit different, you have to agree."

"I do, but it's the best we could come up with." Kate hesitated. "There might be another way, but it's a long shot at best, and Tristan's not a fan of that particular plan." She looked at her mother again. "Alan's back."

Her mother's eyes hardened instantly. "I beg your pardon?"

"He woke up from hospital, his health fully restored, a little over a month ago. I found out myself when I called them."

"Why on Earth would you call them?" her mother cried out.

"Because he appeared in one of my dreams, well, more like a nightmare, really, and that became a little too real the next day. I don't want to go into details, but Lee thought it wise to check up on him, so that's when I found out. He was also at my cocktail party for over two hours without anyone noticing. Peachy, huh?"

"No, not at all, Catherine. I don't like this, I don't like this one bit. Ben, what do you think?"

Kate looked at her uncle as well.

"I think Alan's one crazy fuck, that's what I think, but that's hardly the point, is it? He hasn't done anything to hurt you, Kate?"

Kate shook her head. "No, but he's left me these little clues. Like 'you're still not seeing the big picture' and 'soon you will see.' I have no idea what they mean."

"Um," Simon cut in, "who's Alan?"

Kate's mother sighed. "Catherine's ex. Alan was one of her teachers back in Holland. They started dating after she graduated. Alan's an empath and a master of death, which means he can't only control your emotions, he can also kill you or make you kill someone else. Eventually his powers went to his head, and he chose the dark side. Catherine stopped him, at great personal risk, and his own powers backfired on him, leaving him in quite a mental state. He didn't recognise her or himself. He'd been in a mental hospital in Amsterdam ever since. Well, that's the short version, anyway."

"Sounds like a lovely chap," Simon said. "And you're sure he doesn't mean you any harm?" He looked at Kate.

"Well, I'm not sure, sure, but yeah, pretty much. I can't really explain it, but I'm not scared or anything, at least, not of Alan. There's a different vibe around his astral form. If I had to put a name to it, I'd say he feels peaceful to me, if anything. I know that sounds weird, but I really don't think Alan poses a threat. Not to me, anyway. Lee focussed as well, of course, and she's not getting anything threatening either, only visions of his quotes, and that's just more frustrating than anything else."

Her mother didn't look happy, but she said, "I trust your judgement in this, Catherine, so let's leave it at that. God knows you have enough to worry about as it is."

Kate explained what was actually going to happen Saturday night. She tried to remember everything Tristan had told and shown her. She explained about the "window of opportunity" as he'd called it, which meant they'd only have ten seconds or less to connect to the asteroid and destroy it. They wouldn't be able to see it until it hit the atmosphere. Simon remarked that was cutting it pretty close. She agreed, but they'd have to make do. Somehow she didn't think the asteroid would slow down just because she asked it to. They had to laugh when she shared that with them. They also talked about what to expect in the next two days, so her uncle, her mother, and Simon could prepare for a possible power shortage.

When Kate looked up to check the time, it was almost four o'clock, and even though he'd said he had plenty of things to do, she didn't want to leave Charles alone any longer. Saying goodbye was harder than she thought it would be.

"Don't be silly, darling, we'll see you on Sunday," her mother said. "I'll bake us some scones, and you can brag about saving the planet," Her eyes, however, were awfully shiny, and Kate hugged her longer than she normally would.

"I love you, Mom," she said, her throat tight.

Her mother gave her a kiss. "And I you, sweetie."

She hugged Simon as well and whispered into his ear, "I think my father would have approved, Simon. You take care of her now, okay?"

He looked touched. "Thank you, Catherine. I will, don't you worry about that." He gave her a hug as well.

Kate turned to her uncle. "I'm sorry I didn't get to see the rest of the family, Uncle Ben. You'll give them a big hug from me, won't you?"

"Of course I will. Besides, you'll see them this Christmas, remember?" He smiled, trying to keep it light, and gave her a big hug.

"Of course, looking forward to that. I'll even bring the big harp this time. I have a hard case for it now. I completely forgot to tell you, Mom," she said, looking over her uncle's shoulder. Her mother smiled.

"Excellent!" her uncle said. "Another private concerto. Your aunt will be thrilled." He helped her in her coat. "You take care now, Kate. Give our love to the girls, and go knock 'em dead. Well, the asteroid, that is. Ugh, you know what I mean," he said when Kate and Simon looked at him with one raised eyebrow. Her mother laughed.

Kate walked to the car, and with one last wave, she opened the door and then got in. "Drive, Charles, just drive," she said, her eyes glistening.

After she arrived home, Charles had managed to cheer her up a bit, and she felt her usual self again. She thanked him for that and for driving her.

"Happy to be of service, Miss Catherine. If there's anything I can do tonight or tomorrow to help you out, just ask Mr. Visconti. You take care now, and make sure you get a good night's sleep. You'll need your strength tomorrow."

"I will, Charles, and again, thank you."

He got out and then opened the door for her. Kate smiled and gave him a hug. He looked surprised but pleased.

"You're a good man, Charles. Tristan is lucky to have someone like you at his side."

"Thank you, ma'am, but I consider myself the lucky one. I'll wait until you're inside. Be sure to take the stairs."

"Oh, right, thanks for the reminder. Bye, Charles. I hope to see you again soon."

She let herself in and then waved to Charles before she turned the corner to climb the stairs. Damn, living on the top floor had never been a problem. Stupid electricity. Then again, it wasn't worth getting stuck in a lift over such a silly thing like taking a few flights of stairs. It'd be good for her. Once she finally reached the top floor, however, she had some other sentiments.

Leah, Deborah, and Tristan were all there, Leah looking rather exhausted.

"Hi, sweetie," Kate said to her, "everything okay?"

Leah sighed. "Just very tired. Tristan's been breathing down my neck to get anything, so I've been focussing like crazy. I never thought I'd say this of someone else, but I think he's more of a workaholic than me." By the sound of it, it was a dubious title to receive. "Deb almost hit him over the head when he wanted to postpone lunch because she was getting a feel for the Cailleach." Leah smiled at the memory, and Kate had to laugh. She could well imagine Deborah's response.

"I presume lunch prevailed?" she asked with a grin. They'd been pretty slow that morning, so breakfast had been served rather late.

"After some debate, yes. I think Tristan's learned not to argue with either of us when it comes to food. He's pretty quick on the uptake. How was your afternoon?"

"Good. And emotional, of course, but not overly so. I stuffed myself with scones and chocolate chip cookies. I have a bit of a sugar rush. Not that it helped in climbing those damned stairs. I never realised how many there were. I have to do something about that. I thought I was in pretty good condition. I mean, I run and go to the gym two times a week."

Leah nodded. "I know what you mean. I guess it's just a different movement. You look fine to me," she said with a smile.

Kate waved her hand. "Oh, it's no big deal. I'm fine. I was just a bit disappointed I wasn't exactly taking two stairs at a time."

She'd seen Tristan do that this morning when he went up again after he'd escorted her downstairs to meet Charles. He was on the phone right now, probably with someone from the company.

"Hey, sweetheart, how did it go with your family?" Tristan asked after he gave her a kiss. Leah and Deborah exchanged smiles.

"It went fine. A bit emotional, of course, but I'm glad I saw them. Not that I won't see them again, but … Well, you know what I mean."

"I do," he said. "I just got off the phone with Meg. Leah said you might need a place to practise or come together, and Meg's store seems the most suitable location. You can gather there tomorrow afternoon as well before the ritual. Roy will make sure you have a clear route from her house to London Fields."

"Oh, excellent. Thanks. Meg was fine with it?" she asked.

Leah and Tristan nodded. "Yes, she was happy to help out. The Cailleach feels 'soft' to her, if that means anything to you? And Deborah, you said you got the same vibe, right?" Tristan looked at Deborah.

Deborah nodded. "Yes, she does feel soft, almost gentle, so I think we won't have any trouble on that account, Kate."

Kate felt relieved. "Well, that's one less thing to worry about. Lee, anything?"

Leah looked at her. "Yes, actually. It's good news for now, though maybe not in general. I saw the ball drop. In New York, I mean."

Kate looked excited. "That's good, right? That's like way after tomorrow!"

Leah frowned. "Yes, darling, but if you let me finish, it dropped rather fast. I'm not sure if that is something to be happy about."

"Oh." Kate's excitement ebbed away. "No, that's not good. I mean, it's good for now, right?"

"For now, we'll go with good," Tristan said, looking at Leah with a slightly accusing glare.

When he talked to Deborah in the living room, Kate walked into the kitchen and touched Leah's arm.

"What was that all about?" she asked.

Leah rolled her eyes. "Dear Tristan doesn't want to worry you about things that aren't of any concern. Well, not for now, at least."

Kate laughed. "Does he now? Oh, boy, he still has a lot to learn about us, doesn't he?"

"He does," Leah replied. "In all honesty, the whole protective vibe is kind of cute. He just has to learn not to do it when we've been working hard and are, therefore, hungry."

She nodded understandingly. "Um … Lee? Would you mind if I spend the night at Tristan's?"

Leah looked at her. "No, of course not, honey, but forgive me for saying this, I'm a bit worried. Now that we know, well, we still don't know anything really. Anyway, what I was going to say rather more coherently than this is that you don't know if he'll stick around. Company men don't sound like the lasting kind, and you're falling pretty hard for him."

Kate put her hands over Leah's on the kitchen counter, and said, "Thanks for caring, but believe it or not, I wasn't actually planning on having sex with him." Leah looked sceptical. "Well, okay, that might come afterward, and before you go on, yes, I know what I'm getting myself into. It's actually something he told me. Tristan's very close to his parents, and they must be scared senseless, knowing their son is doing 'something dangerous.' I doubt even they know much about this so-called company. Tristan confided in me that he has a small private airplane. He could fly out to be with them tomorrow."

Leah looked even more sceptical now. "Honey, I think destroying the asteroid will be easier than convincing Tristan to leave you at a time like this."

"Perhaps, but he's here to do everything he can to make me feel happy and successful, right?"

Leah raised an eyebrow. "You're going for emotional blackmail? Wow, rather you than me. Why is this so important to you? Don't you want him near?"

Kate looked frustrated. "Yes, I do. Of course I do, but Tristan still has both his parents. He has a mother who loves him and a father. A father who must be worried sick about his son. He should be with them. It's important to have the people you love near you when you think things can't get any worse."

Leah looked sad. "Is this about your father, Kate? He was well aware of the risks his job involved, and from what I could see, always loved his job. He loved you both very much, and would never, ever hold it against you or your mother that you weren't there."

"I know that. Still, if given the chance, is there anything you wouldn't do for your family and friends? Tristan has that chance. He can be with his parents. They'll probably never admit it, but I'm sure they want him there by their sides. It's worth a try, I think."

"Well, good luck then. Are you staying here for dinner, though?"

She nodded. "That would be the most practical, I think. We can empty the freezer, and eat some of the remaining appetizers."

Deborah entered the kitchen. "Shall we see if there's anything edible in the freezer?"

Leah and Kate smiled. "Our thoughts exactly," Kate said.

*   *   *

Tristan had been somewhat surprised when Kate had asked him to go down to his apartment, but he had complied nonetheless.

"Why are you trying to ground and centre me?" he asked, handing Kate a glass of wine.

Kate looked up. "Excuse me?" she asked.

"I can feel earth all over the place. You're obviously trying to ground or calm me for something."

Kate felt annoyed. So much for that plan. She explained carefully why she thought it was a good idea for Tristan to visit his parents.

"No. Absolutely not. Out of the question!" He stood again after just sitting down. "Is that why you wanted to talk down here?"

She just looked at him. "Will you let me explain?"

She wasn't playing completely fair, but she let all her emotions surface. The pain of losing her father, the worry about her mother, the rest of her family and her friends. She told him how she'd felt not being there when her father had died. How she wanted Tristan to be there for his parents, that it was the right thing to do. And they'd still be able to stay in touch. Roy and Charles would still be there.

"If you can honestly say I won't be safe here without you, I'll leave it alone."

He looked like a caged animal. "Ah, Catherine, that's just not fair. Don't get me wrong, of course, I'd like to see my parents, but I'd be worried sick about you."

"That's nonsense. You said yourself we'll be able to reach each other by phone, or do you honestly think Roy and the rest of your division can't handle this?"

"What? No, of course not. I trust them with my life."

"Well, apparently not with my life. Tristan, look, this would really make me happy."

He sighed and ran his hands through his hair. "Emotional blackmail, just great. An empath beaten by means of emotional blackmail by an elemental. That will go down well on my file."

She smiled. "So you'll go?"

He came over to her and cupped her face. "It's as if you want to leave, Catherine."

She looked at him and let fire take her over. "I don't want to leave. I want to stay." She looked straight into his eyes, leaving him no room to mistake her meaning.

He pulled her even closer. "Then stay."

SATURDAY

KATE DIDN'T WANT to wake up. She was afraid to open her eyes and find that Tristan was already gone. When she moved, she felt his body next to hers, and she relaxed. She moved closer, and when he put an arm around her in his sleep, she snuggled up to him. An hour later, she woke again, sensing she was being watched.

"Good morning, beautiful," Tristan said, gently kissing the top of her head.

"Good morning," she said, a bit self-conscious. Last night had been rather intense, and she didn't really know how to behave right now. "Do you mind if I take a shower here?"

"Not at all, though I wouldn't say no to sharing one, either."

She smiled, feeling better. "I have little confidence in your powers of self-control, Mr. Visconti, and you do have a plane to catch, so to speak."

Tristan looked at her with puppy dog eyes. "I promise to be good."

"Well, that wasn't really my concern," she said, feeling herself blush slightly.

Tristan grinned, and she felt her face getting warmer. Bugger, she hated when that happened. Last night had been, well, pure magic, to put it mildly. She had never had sex like that, if she could even call it that. Kate was no expert on tantric sex, mind melting and all that stuff, but she thought they had pretty much invented a new book last night. It was as if her whole body had been attuned to his, sensing his needs as he'd sensed hers. He wasn't afraid of her elements, either. He'd embraced them, as if they had embraced him in return.

She tried to locate her clothes and found a trail through the entire apartment. What the hell had they been doing? She could remember ending up in his bed, holding on to him as though her life depended on it, feeling fire inside her and around them as she came close to her climax, pulling her over the edge when Tristan breathed her name in a hoarse whisper. After that things were kind of blurry.

Tristan obviously decided to give her some time, because he said, "Oh, go on then. I'll fix us breakfast in the meantime and see if there's any news we should be aware of."

She gave him a grateful smile and then went into the shower. She didn't take long, just long enough to wash her hair and get cleaned up. She rubbed herself dry with one of Tristan's towels, wrapped it around her head, and stole one of his t-shirts. She went to the living room to see whether he'd made any progress.

"Hmm, that looks much better on you than on me," he said while getting some croissants and two *pains au chocolat* out of the oven.

"Ooh, that smells nice." Kate's mouth watered. "And thanks, I guess. Any news?" she asked, as she sat and then buttered a croissant.

"Power is down, as expected," he said. "A few more cars were stolen, some supermarkets have been robbed, and there was an incident at the docks. People were trying to get out by boat and there was a shooting. One man was fatally injured, two were wounded. Try to avoid public transport today. Don't go near the Underground. Nor the docks or any shopping malls. People will become more violent during the day. Maybe I should just stay here?"

Kate sighed. "Tristan, we've been over this. I'm not a child, and Roy and Charles will still be here if I need anything. London Fields is set up, and I wasn't exactly planning on anything else." She paused. "Hang on, if the power's out, how the hell did you make these?" She pointed at her croissant.

"I have my own generator. It's not rocket science, you know."

Kate rolled her eyes. "Oh, bla! Anyway, you're going. You'll be doing your parents a huge favour, and if the shit really hits the fan, you could even get back in time. Though I really think you shouldn't. You're the one saying I have nothing to worry about, so stop worrying. Not wanting to leave me here alone isn't exactly a vote of confidence."

He looked annoyed. "That's slightly unfair, don't you think?"

"Yes, but if it's working, I won't be taking it back." She gave him a kiss. "I thought we agreed on this."

He sighed. "We did. Okay, I'll leave instructions with Roy, and if there's anything, and I do mean anything, that you need, you give him a call. He'll notify me if he thinks I'm needed."

"I promise," Kate said, crossing her fingers behind her back.

She wouldn't be the reason he'd have to fly back, worried about something silly. He'd told her it'd be a four-hour flight just to get to his parents, and she wouldn't make him do that twice in one day. Not if she could help it.

They'd agreed Tristan would leave after breakfast, so he'd be in Italy well before dusk. He'd check in with her as soon as he arrived.

After breakfast, she went into the bedroom to get dressed. She braided her hair in one big braid, leaving it wet just this once. She very much doubted Tristan would have a hairdryer, and she thought it'd be a waste of the use of the generator, anyway.

"Do you want me to go upstairs with you?" he asked after she'd returned to the living room.

"No, I'll explain to the girls. Don't you worry about that. As long as you don't forget to text me once you're there, because this whole you flying a plane thing doesn't sit very well with me." She smiled.

"Yes, ma'am," he said as he gently pulled her braid. "You do realise I've flown that thing like a thousand times, right?"

"Even so, I hate things that are out of my control."

He looked at her. "That makes two of us."

Kate looked sympathetic. "I know." She stood on tiptoe to give him a kiss. He leaned forward and immediately deepened it. She sighed into his mouth.

"You should go now," she mumbled, "before I decide to keep you here." She felt him smile under her lips. He'd said something similar to her on one of their dates.

"I'll see you soon. Remember, don't try to control your powers, let them out full force, connect to the Cailleach and it'll work. You can do this. I know you can."

She laughed. "Yes, sir. Thanks for the pep talk. Now get out of here." She gently pushed him toward the stairs in the hallway. He closed his front door and then gave her one last kiss.

"You're not getting rid of me. I'm in love with you."

She sighed, pretending to be annoyed. "Now he tells me." She smiled. "I love you too, Tristan."

He let go of her hand and then walked down the stairs. Kate waited until he was around the corner. Time to fill in her best friends. She sighed and climbed the stairs to her own apartment.

Leah and Deborah had been somewhat surprised to learn that Kate had actually succeeded in persuading Tristan to visit his parents, but they were less surprised when they heard she'd pulled some major emotional blackmail.

"Don't you want him here, sweetie?" Deb asked.

"He's worried sick as it is, and I know his parents are very important to him. Those people may have some idea what it is their son's doing, professionally, I mean. Needless to say they'll be worried sick. He can't do any more than he's already done, and what still has to be done, Roy can do just as well. I really thought he should be with them. They deserve to have their son with them, don't you think?"

The girls agreed. "Absolutely. And as long as you're okay with it, we're okay with it," Leah said with a warm smile. "The power's out, by the way. Your fridge is still doing fine. I think it'll be another two hours before we need to clean it out."

Kate nodded. "Yes, Tristan told me so as well. He suspects electricity will be up and running early tomorrow morning or maybe even late this evening, depending on how fast authorities can confirm the threat is indeed over."

* * *

After they arrived at Meg's, escorted by Roy and Charles, Meg had cleaned out her entire work space. "I thought we might try the vessel thing," she said. "Just on low voltage, so to speak, but it might be wise to test if you can indeed act like a vessel."

The other girls were there already. Sue looked a bit grumpy. "What's up with the personal bodyguards? I could hardly get rid of mine," she whispered to Kate.

Kate gave her a sympathetic look. "I'm afraid that might be my fault, sweetie. I persuaded Tristan to go to his parents today. I think he might have gone overboard protection wise. Sorry."

"Hmpf, I guess we'll live," Sue grumbled, but she gave Kate a smile just the same.

They set up the circle and then asked Roy and Charles to stay clear of it as much as possible. Both men looked really interested.

"Can they be trusted with this kind of, um, information?" Sheila asked Kate, who stood next to her.

"Let's put it this way. I'm sure we'll go down in some file, but honestly, at the very first sign of anyone wanting to dissect us like a bunch of frogs, I will blow their asses to kingdom come." She didn't even try to lower her voice, knowing full well Roy and Charles could hear her. She even thought she could see a smile on Charles's face, but when she looked at him, it was gone.

"Well, okay then, I was just saying." Sheila grinned.

They called the quarters, Kate focussing on each element as they went around the circle, making them come alive. Sue created it, letting her powers shine through as well. Kate could see the golden healing ring around them as Sue passed each of them. They breathed in and out together until they breathed as one.

"Okay, Joni, I'd like to try with you first. As a trial run, so to speak," Kate said. "Can you focus your earth powers on me? Not full force, just a bit."

Joni seemed to focus, and immediately smiled. "It's working!" she cried. Kate heard it as well. It was like a humming, a heartbeat in the room.

"Wow, what is that?" Deborah asked in wonder.

Kate and Joni smiled. "It's Mother Earth like she's supposed to sound," Kate said. "This is what I hear when the earth is balanced, healed." Joni nodded.

Roy pretended there was something in his eye. Kate cut him some slack and looked the other way.

"It's beautiful," Deborah said. "Do you want to try the entire circle now, Kate?"

Kate nodded, and they focussed again. After they'd had another success and had tried some variations, she decided that was enough for now. They thanked the quarters and then closed the circle. After they were done, she wanted to try her elements one at a time with a bit more force.

Meg looked slightly scared. "Do try not to demolish the place, will you?"

Charles stepped forward. "Miss, if I may, I might be of assistance here."

Kate looked at Charles. "What do you mean, Charles?"

"Well, I'm what you call a blocker, which comes in quite handy when people insist on trying to shoot you, but I'm sure it'd work the same with your elements."

"That's a pretty nifty gift you have there, Charles," Kate told him. "Many things, indeed." She smiled. He smiled back.

They tried with Kate on one side and Charles on the other far end. The first time she threw fire at him, things went wrong right away. Leah cried out a second before Kate released her ball of fire, having already seen the outcome. It bounced off Charles without any problems, but it came back and exploded next to Kate against the wall.

"Kate, jump!" Leah yelled.

"Wow! *Godskolere*!" Kate cried, having just escaped her own fireball. "Sorry about that. Everyone okay?" They nodded.

"Kate, maybe we should leave fire alone for now, okay?" Meg asked. "Be a dear and try air."

Pretty soon they were all completely windswept, but Charles was still standing behind his block. "Full force, Charles?" Kate asked. Charles nodded.

The girls joined Kate on her side of the room, just to be safe. Kate released air and sent it off in one straight line. It collided with a smash, and Charles was thrown back.

"Charles! Charles, are you okay?" Kate came running over.

"I'm fine, ma'am. That's some power you have there. No one's ever been able to do that, and that's just one element. I think that asteroid's in a world of trouble." He got up and brushed off his jacket. Kate smiled.

"Kate, couldn't you try exploding the asteroid with fire from within or is that a silly question?" Samantha looked at her.

"It's not silly at all, and yes, we did think about that. Same with air. I could try to blow it off course. Unfortunately, I don't think I have that kind of power. All my elements combined might do the trick, but then we have the following scenario. Where would the debris go? It's too much of a risk. I don't know how much of it I'll hit. It shouldn't be here in the first place, and that's where the Cailleach comes in. She rules life and death. If it was never born, never created, it can't be here, right? Well, that's the theory, anyway. Not solid proof, I'll grant you, but it's the best we can do without damaging Earth."

Samantha looked satisfied.

"I think we've all had enough for one afternoon, don't you? Let's save some for the actual ritual," Kate said. Leah sniggered.

Meg had prepared some sandwiches and a big bowl of soup for everyone, and they sat on chakra and other meditation pillows to eat. Meg's husband came to join them. While Roy and Charles went over the route again, Kate kept touching her neck.

"Something wrong, sweetie?" Leah asked.

"My necklace, it's gone. I think I left it at Tristan's. Stupid."

Leah looked at her. She knew how important that necklace was to Kate. "Roy, do you have a key to Tristan's apartment?" she asked.

"Yeah, why? Do you need anything?"

"Kate thinks she left her necklace there. It's rather important to her."

Roy was already on his feet. "No problem. I'll get it. Kate, where do you think it is?"

Kate shook her head. "No, that's silly, Roy. I'll get it myself. Besides, it'll give me a chance to change into something else, because I'm rather sweaty."

He looked uneasy. "Um, Tristan specifically told me—"

"Yeah, yeah, yeah, don't lose her for one second, or something like it," she cut him off. "I'm a big girl, Roy. Besides, I'd rather you get my girls there safely. Start setting up the circle. I'll meet you at London Fields. Romy, can I borrow your car?"

"Sure, here are the keys." Romy threw them toward Kate.

"Thanks! I'll be back in no time."

Before anyone else could object, Kate was out of the room. She got into Romy's car and then drove to her apartment. The streets were almost completely deserted. Roy might have had a point, after all. They were eerily empty.

Climbing the steps at a fast pace—practice does make perfect—she went up to the third floor. In the apartment, she entered the bedroom and looked under the bed. Bingo. The ruby lay there, softly shining. She grabbed it and wasted no time. She locked up and then climbed more stairs to her own apartment. There, she quickly changed into some black stretch jeans and a black long-sleeved t-shirt. The elements would keep her warm, and that way people would less likely see her moving around the park.

She looked at her watch and realised she really had to leave now. The word ironic would gain new meaning if she missed this window of opportunity. Dreading the sensation in her stomach, that she was still missing something, that her powers weren't going to be enough, Kate closed her front door for perhaps the last time and then walked downstairs.

Just as she was about to close the door of Romy's car, someone yelled her name. "Catherine! Wait!"

She got out of the car and looked around. Tristan ran toward her. What the hell was he doing there?

"Goddammit, Tristan, you should be in Italy by now. I thought we agreed you'd go to your parents. What the fuck!" She felt anxious again.

"No, wait. Catherine. Look at me. Something happened. I don't have time to explain. I think I found the key to destroying this thing. Now we have precious little time, so just listen and hear me out, okay?" He tried to catch his breath, as he obviously had been running.

She gave him an almost imperceptible nod.

Tristan took a deep breath. "Okay. We've been going over this for the last thirty-six hours, and you still feel as if you're missing something, right? What if you *are* missing something? I need you to go back for me. To when you were facing Alan across the industrial building."

Kate looked confused, but remained silent.

"What if Alan wasn't trying to kill you that night? You said you felt death coming toward you. And it suddenly hit me. What happened to it? Where did it go? You unleashed your elemental power on Alan and that hit him full force, but where did his power go? The power of death?"

"What?" Kate shook her head. "It backfired, I guess. Why is that so important? Tristan, I haven't got time for riddles, and this isn't helping!"

"Hang on. I don't think it backfired at all. I think it went into you. I think Alan transferred his power of death to you, which would make you a master of death. Combined with the elements to connect to the asteroid, you'd have the power to destroy it. You won't have to rely on the Cailleach. You had it all along."

Kate started to point out that was just ridiculous when Tristan continued.

"Just think about it, Catherine. The dream. 'You're still not seeing the big picture,' he said. Then the painting with his message. 'Soon you will see.' What if those things weren't to scare you? What if Alan tried to make you understand you have his power? You said yourself you weren't even frightened of him anymore. I think that is why Meg sees a dark grey mist around you and just a bit on everybody else. Because you can control death. I really think that is the key." She felt every bit of truth Tristan had inside him wash over her.

Kate hesitated. She knew Tristan believed this to be true, but did she?

"Think, Catherine, think. How did it feel? Our lives may depend on it."

She closed her eyes, and in a flash she was back in Amsterdam, facing Alan. As she watched herself release the elements to charge him, she turned her focus away from her elements and focussed on the grey mist coming toward her instead. It swirled through the elements and came straight at her. Her eyes widened. That wasn't possible. She would have died. As she relived the moment, the mist had almost reached her. For a moment, it clung to her, as if getting to know her identity, and then it went inside her. Her eyes flew open. No, no, no, that was unbearable because it'd mean she'd made a terrible mistake, and the responsibilities of that came crashing down on her full force.

"But ... but then he never meant to kill me. Oh god. Oh god, I almost destroyed his soul, and he never meant to kill me! Why, Tristan? Why did he do that?" Her eyes were overflowing with tears as grief and guilt washed through her like a rat gnawing his way out from the inside.

Tristan sent love, peace, and quiet over Kate. "Breathe, darling, breathe. It's going to be okay. Alan's obviously fine. Remember, and he's here for a reason. So you can destroy this thing. If anything, he'd want you to focus on that. That's why he gave you all those cryptic messages, I think. He must have thought you'd figure it out. Now, look at me." He softly lifted her chin, and she looked him in the eyes. "You can do this. Give it all you've got and it'll be enough. I promise."

Kate gave him a feeble smile. "I know. I felt it inside me. I think maybe I knew all along. That's probably why I've been feeling so restless for the last couple months. With impending doom hanging over our heads, it must have activated death inside me. I just didn't recognise it, didn't accept it. That's probably why Meg couldn't get a grip on it either." She let out a long sigh. She'd have to deal with the implications of that later. She couldn't afford to lose focus now.

"Will you be here when I get back?" she asked.

Tristan smiled and laid his hand over her heart. "I'll always be here, my elemental," He leaned over and gave her a soft kiss on her forehead. "Now go."

Kate got into the car and then pulled out of the parking space. Out of habit, she turned on the radio. Placebo, how appropriate. "Scene of the Crime" was on.

The lyrics hit her like a ton of bricks as Brian sang to her. Her eyes prickled with tears. She blew Tristan a kiss in her rear-view mirror. As she turned a corner, he disappeared out of sight, and she pounded her hands on the steering wheel in frustration. Her eyes were full of tears now. She looked at her watch and realised this little intermission had cost her precious minutes.

Stupid, stupid, she thought as she sped up, turning the volume of the radio way beyond acceptable and pushing the car to its limits. The others would be worried sick by now. As the song continued and London flashed before her mind's eyes, running every red light she encountered on the completely deserted streets, images flowed before her eyes. Her father, smiling, holding the ladder for her when she'd wanted to reach the top shelf of their bookcase. Her grandmother, telling her she was special while Kate played with her ring, laughing as the ruby caught the sunlight. Her mother, singing while she played the harp for her. Her and Leah at their first Placebo concert, jumping up and down and screaming their lungs out to "Every You, Every Me." Lying on the floor in Leah's room in Amsterdam, listening to her friend reading. Buying Leah's apartment in London, hugging each other, because they'd now see more of each other. Deborah with her pink suitcase, telling her she'd follow her anywhere, and the look on Deborah's face when Kate handed her the documents, making her a full partner. Her group in a circle, hands together, as her dear friends would be doing right now. She saw Alan, looking at her with an expression of peace, and finally Tristan, playing his cello. She heard him whispering in her ear, *Tutto a suo tempo, miei elementi.*

She parked as close as she could get, Placebo still screaming through the car speakers. She jumped out and then slammed the door shut, not even bothering to lock it. For a second, Kate wondered if she'd ever hear the sound of her favourite band again.

As she ran at full speed, the sky already pitch-black, she reached for her elements and didn't even try to control her powers. She called upon the earth, and bits of grass and earth came loose from the ground, surrounding her as the earth itself trembled beneath her feet. She called upon air, giving her wings, making her run even faster, and the earth was now whirling around her, weaving in and out. She saw the group now in the distance. She could make it. She had to make it. Someone looked at her. It was Leah, looking utterly relieved to see her. She shouted something at the group. As Sheila and Sue opened their arms to create a gateway for Kate, she let water flow through her with all its emotions. As she stormed through the gate, Sue and Sheila closed it behind her, connecting their hands again. It resonated with a deafening bang. She abruptly came to a standstill, letting fire take her over. Almost at once fire was all around her, in and outside her body, charging her without hurting her.

Earth, air, fire, and water weaved in and out of her, taking over the circle, taking over the field. That couldn't last long, she felt it. The earth showed cracks beneath her feet already, and whirlwinds entered the circle. Fire and water formed a wall around the group, reaching up from the ground, a man-high wall surrounding them. Kate focussed her power toward the sky.

Any second now. As the women in the circle stretched their hands forward, Kate was almost thrown off her feet by the immense power surging through her. Her gifts had suddenly multiplied by twelve. There was a flash in the sky above her, and now she could see it. The asteroid. She was surprised to realise she thought it was rather beautiful. She focussed and let the black power of death manifest.

Looking up, she simply thought one thing. *You don't belong here.*

As the sky burst open, Kate squeezed her eyes shut to protect them from the blinding light. She flew through the air. After she opened her eyes, she found she was still airborne. She saw the stars surrounded by blackness.

We did it! she thought before she smashed into a tree and everything went black.

EPILOGUE

TWO MEN STARED at a satellite feed. It showed a rooftop somewhere in the middle of the city. "You do realise this is highly illegal, right?" the dark blond one said to the other. "If the boss finds out we're using the satellite for personal matters, it's my ass as well."

Tristan turned his gaze away from the screen for just a second to look at his friend and colleague. He raised an eyebrow.

"Okay, okay, I know you've covered my back lots of times. I'm just saying. And why is this so bloody important, anyway? I've already told you, she's just fine. They released her from hospital after just two days. Apparently, her ribs and lung made a remarkable recovery, no doubt due to the involvement of one of her more colourful friends. So why do we still care? You know you can't get involved. Standard procedure and all that. It's better to just let her go."

Roy looked at Tristan with a worried expression, and Tristan felt his concern. He'd never been so obsessed over someone. And obsessions were bad news, especially in their line of work. Obsessions could get you killed, or someone else.

Tristan still focussed on the big screen in front of them. Six women sat on the rooftop terrace, obviously having a good time. Well, they had every reason to be happy. It was a goddamn miracle they were all still alive and well. He'd been halfway to Italy when the company had called him, informing him they'd found Alan, or rather, Alan had found them and wanted to talk to Tristan. Catherine's life might depend on it. So he'd turned back, meeting Alan at an abandoned site in downtown London. Alan had told Tristan what had really happened that day many years ago. That Catherine was a master of death. That she'd been for years now, but he wondered if she knew that. Quite simply put, he didn't want to die, and he didn't want Kate to die either.

Tristan had asked how he'd managed to recover, and Alan had just looked at him, and said, "You of all people should know that. Or maybe you don't have the proper clearance for that information?" He'd smirked.

"Why didn't you tell her yourself?" Tristan had asked.

Alan had laughed. "Oh, please, as if she'd believe me. She'll believe you, the righteous empath." His black eyes had been cold like stone. "So run, little empath. Go save our world. I didn't wake up for nothing, you know. Oh, and, Tristan, just so you know, I haven't given up on her."

Tristan still had shivers down his spine when he thought about that particular conversation.

He spotted Catherine easily. She was quite an expressive person and leaned over a lot, which gave him a better view from above. He wished she'd look up at the sky so he could see her face just once. He waited for something else as well, though. He perfectly understood the dangers of getting involved with a "civilian," let alone someone like Catherine. The company was already expressing a more-than-average interest in her, and his recent actions weren't exactly helpful in lessening their interest. He did find that mildly worrying. The boss had never expressed an interest, other than professional, in their clients. He sighed. He wouldn't be able to visit her anytime soon. It'd draw a lot of unwanted attention from the inside as well as from outside sources. He certainly wouldn't be responsible for endangering her life any more than he'd already done. She had to know, she had to know he hadn't just left her, that he cared, would always care.

A minivan pulled up in the street and stopped in front of the building. Two men got out and then moved to the back of the van. They hoisted a large package onto a trolley before they walked to the apartment building. Tristan smiled.

"Have we seen enough now? Come on, man!" Roy said, anxiously looking around.

"Almost," Tristan said. "Almost."

* * *

They were just about to toast when Kate heard her doorbell ring. "Bugger!" she said. "Hang on with that toast, ladies. I'll be back in a minute."

She got up and then went downstairs. Her ribs still hurt a bit when she made sudden movements, but frankly, Sue had done one hell of a job. Kate simply hated hospitals, and she was very grateful she'd only had to stay for two days. The first day, she'd been completely out of it. The blast had thrown her quite forcefully into a tree, or so she'd learned from Leah, although the official story ran that she was thrown into the brick wall of her apartment building where Meg had brought her by car. As Sue and Deb had been completely drained from the ritual, they hadn't been able to heal her. After several precious minutes of trying again and again, Leah had overruled them, stating she'd take Kate to hospital. She'd called ahead to see if anyone was still there. She'd been pleasantly surprised when the person answering the phone had told her that doctors and nurses were coming back in at that very moment.

So they'd taken Kate to the hospital where she'd remained until Sue had been able to heal her properly. Romy had pulled a major glamour to convince the doctor it'd just been a minor injury, and he'd duly released Kate from his care.

Things were starting to get back to normal. People were returning to work. Stores, restaurants and pubs were opening again, everywhere. Slowly the world was recovering. It still dazzled Kate to see what just two days of complete and utter panic could do to their economy.

Kate looked at her cam and saw two FedEx men standing in front of her building. She pressed the speaker button. "Hello?"

"Hello, Miss Van Dyk? We have a delivery for you. You'll need to sign for it. Could we please come up?"

"Sure, I'll buzz you in. Top floor, gentlemen." She pressed the buzzer, opened the front door, and waited for the lift doors to open.

After a minute, they arrived at her apartment. One of the men rolled the trolley inside to gently put it down in her living room. The other one came over to her with some paperwork and showed her where to sign.

"Wow, that's pretty big," she said.

He smiled. "Yes, ma'am, but it's not that heavy." He looked at his watch to confirm the time of delivery. Then both men wished her a good day and left, closing the front door behind them.

Kate was a bit bedazzled. Who on Earth would send her something so soon after "the day the earth didn't explode," as her friends called it now. She took out a pair of scissors from the kitchen drawer and then cut the top of the package open. Once the cardboard was uncovered, a hard case was revealed. Her breath hitched. She recognised it. Carefully opening the case, she peeked inside. Yes, it was Tristan's cello.

"Okay, stay calm," she told herself.

After her return from the hospital, she'd immediately called at Tristan's, but nobody had answered the door. She'd tried again later that evening, and again the following morning. She'd called his mobile phone, but the number had turned out to be disconnected. She'd tried for four days until she'd realised he wasn't there anymore. Deb had called the real estate agency, and they'd confirmed the apartment was up for sale again.

Kate wanted to cry, but somehow she couldn't. She just didn't believe he'd leave her alone, not like that. She wiped the tears from her eyes and tried to focus. There had to be a note somewhere. Charles's voice came back to her, saying, *He will find a way, miss. You hold on to that faith of yours.*

She opened the case again, but noticed nothing out of the ordinary. She closed it gently and then went to the back of the package. There. A little plastic window for a home address. There was a blank piece of paper in it. She carefully removed it and turned it over. Smiling, she looked at her watch. Two more minutes. Knowing Tristan, he'd probably planned it to the second. Feeling immensely better, Kate took the stairs two at a time until she reached the rooftop.

The girls were still waiting for her to toast. "Well, what was it?" Deb asked.

Kate was almost radiant. She handed the piece of paper to Deb, signalling she should keep the text hidden from view. Deb read it, smiled, and then passed it on, discreetly covering it with her hand. When it finally reached Leah, she looked at the piece of paper in her hand. It just said, *Tutto a suo tempo, miei elementi, tutto a suo tempo.* There was one word underneath it with a time. "Smile. 14:00 p.m."

Leah looked at Kate. She was luminous. The clouds were all gone, replaced by the sun. She grabbed her glass from the table, and said, "To Kate, who taught us that death is only the beginning." The girls smiled, and repeated, "To Kate!"

Kate checked her watch and put her glass on the table. Suddenly, she raised her hands in the air and smiled at the sky. The other girls put down their glasses and copied her movement in a little circle.

* * *

"They are a weird bunch of girls, aren't they?" Roy asked Tristan. They were looking at six smiling women on the big screen, forming a circle. "Do you think it's some sort of closure for their rituals?"

Tristan grinned. "Yes, that's probably it. Kinda nice, don't you think?"

Roy just huffed. "Can we please turn it off now?"

As Tristan put his friend's mind at ease by disconnecting the satellite feed, the radio came back to life. The two o'clock news was just about to end. "As the economy is getting back on its feet, the reinstated prime minister urges people to return to work as soon as possible," the newsreader said. "While some people have been injured by the blast radius in London, no fatalities have been reported. And now on to the weather. John, do you have any news for us?"

"Well, Gary, I don't know if it's the impact of the asteroid, but the weather has certainly changed quite rapidly. Reports are coming in from all over Europe. If you take a look outside, you'll see the sun has suddenly come back out again, and it looks as if it's here to stay. We've just hit twenty degrees, and it's November, people! So enjoy the sunshine, folks, enjoy the sunshine."

Somewhere in central London, Tristan smiled and said to himself, *Good for you, Catherine. Good for you.*

Turn the page for an excerpt of

The Empath,

Book 2 of the Fire trilogy

THE EMPATH -
PART TWO OF THE FIRE TRILOGY

"IF YOU COULD SAVE OUR PLANET BY
GIVING YOUR LIFE, WOULD YOU?"

PROLOGUE

IT WAS DEADLY QUIET in the corridors of the mental hospital. A woman walked purposefully toward her destination: room 612. Sixth floor, sixth door on her left. Two men walked behind her, keeping a respectful distance. She knew the schematics of the building by heart. The company had been planning this to the detail, and she was ready.

"There will be trouble," her boss had said. "You'll have to immediately block him out once he's revived."

For that was her main gift. She was the company's top reviver. They rarely used her main gift, though. So when she got this assignment, she'd been very excited. She couldn't care less that she was going to revive a dangerous man. That wasn't her problem. The company would deal with him accordingly. She smiled to herself. They hadn't hired her for her warm and caring personality. *Hence, the distance between herself and her "bodyguards,"* she thought with a slight smirk. They feared her. And rightfully so.

She stopped in front of 612. Showtime. She turned to look at the two men behind her. They gave her an almost imperceptible nod. She was good to go. Slowly, she opened the door, stepped into the room, and closed it softly behind her. Near the window a man with long, white hair lay on a typical hospital bed. He wasn't strapped down or anything, probably because he wasn't in any condition to go anywhere. His eyes were open, but they were empty. Fascinating. Whoever had done this to him must have had great power, indeed.

She walked over to his side and stared into his face. Nothing. No blink, no dilation of his pupils, not a single response to her presence. Hmm, this could turn out to be more difficult than she'd anticipated. The excitement inside her grew. She loved a good challenge.

Looking at his face one more time, she leaned over and whispered into his ear, "This is going to hurt you more than me."

*   *   *

Tristan Visconti wasn't in a good mood. He'd just been assigned to what he considered a suicide mission. He'd even quarrelled with his boss about it, which was a first, but apparently there was no room for argument there.

"Listen, Tristan, this comes from upstairs, way above even my clearance, and they want you. They must really think we still have a shot," his boss had said. "In other words, don't even think about screwing this one up. Too much is at stake here, and we have less than a month to get you in position, okay? Stop sulking and get your act together."

It was the first time Tristan had received a reprimand from his boss. And that didn't sit very well with him. So he'd apologised and asked if he could at least pick his own team members.

"Sure, no problem. As long as you include Charles and Roy. You're going to need a blocker and a planner to pull this off," his boss had replied.

Tristan had assured him he was going to include them, anyway, and then they'd said their goodbyes to one another.

He ordered another coffee and sighed when the waiter passed his table. He might as well get started and learn all there was to know about his new client. Opening his case file, the first page showed a large photo of a woman in her mid-thirties with long, blonde hair. The caption read, Client: Catherine van Dyk – Elemental.

ABOUT THE AUTHOR

Lisa is the author of the poetry collections *Nothing is Forgotten* and *When Words Start to Sing,* and *The Elemental,* part I of The Fire Trilogy. She also wrote a short story for teenagers, *The Bridge Between Yesterday and Tomorrow,* which will be released late 2015. She has a background in social services and music, but writing has always been a part of her daily life. One night she dreamed the outlines of *The Elemental* and took it as a sign from the Universe to pursue a career in writing.

She grew up in a small town in the Netherlands where her parents always taught her to think outside the box. She has a degree in social studies and joined the Order of Bards, Ovates & Druids as an adult.

Lisa loves London—according to her, "the city where magic dwells"—and can often be found there. She still resides in the Netherlands, however, with her partner and their dog, Miss Ginger

Rogers, and if you're lucky, you may find her in her favourite coffeehouse, Barista cafe.

Lisa is also an editor for Folk Harp Folks, a magazine published by The Dutch Folk Harp society.

www.the-elemental.co.uk

www.ingramcontent.com/pod-product-compliance
Lightning Source LLC
Chambersburg PA
CBHW060051260626
47160CB00005B/1647